He scanned her unfinished, familiar bu... ... ... everything he had done to her, or would do, was his right. She wouldn't go with him, not for a million dollars.

Carlos nodded with a satisfied grin at Jace. "This settles our account." His gaze returned to her. "Little Princess, you don't even have to pack a bag. I'll buy you everything you need, anything you want."

It was there, in his anxious smile, vacant eyes, and impatient fingers. Sooner or later he would kill her and use his hands.

"I won't go with you."

Jace winced and sidled next to Carlos. "Give her a few days. She's just tired."

Carlos shook his head. "Jace, that's not like you. Do you let your whores run things? She's part of our deal. A deal I set up and can still cancel with one phone call."

"We can work this out. I'll talk to her alone. Give me a half hour."

She shook her head. "It won't matter."

Carlos narrowed his eyes, sneering. "Soledad Shoshone Montoya, such an exotic name for a little 'rican slut. I'll have you another time." He raised his right hand with his thumb and index finger an inch apart. "I came this close to finding you in San Juan. You're easy to follow. Men can't help but notice you, women, too. Just come with me now, and I'll forgive you."

She shook her head again. "I'll take my chances."

Carlos cocked his head and grinned. "I know where your family lives."

Praise for Keith Fisher and this book...

"*A SPOONFUL OF SOLEDAD* is a fast-paced and suspenseful novel. Soledad is an intriguing character, both good and bad, with a mission to complete."

~*Matthew Gianni, author*

~*~

"Soledad is like no other character: hard to explain but fun to experience."

~*Michel Lee King, author*

A Spoonful of Soledad

by

Keith Fisher

A Spoonful of Soledad

COPYRIGHT © 2019 by Millard Keith Fisher

Cover Art by *Kim Mendoza*

The Wild Rose Press, Inc.
PO Box 708
Adams Basin, NY 14410-0708
Visit us at www.thewildrosepress.com

Publishing History
First Mainstream Thriller Edition, 2019
Print ISBN 978-1-5092-2783-9
Digital ISBN 978-1-5092-2784-6

Published in the United States of America

Dedication

To the femme fatales who inspired me:
Tina Montoya (Vanesa Ferlito),
Kathie Moffit (Jane Greer),
and Kitty Collins (Ava Gardner).

Chapter One

Wednesday, 8:30 pm

Soledad spun to the beep of the monitor high on the kitchen wall. She had never seen the classic-looking, shiny red car turning onto their tree-lined, private drive. Unexpected visitors never brought anything good. Usually they wanted something, sometimes her.

Jace had promised time to recover from that last client, downplaying her near death experience as hysterical exaggeration, but the bruises on her neck said differently. Finger-shaped bruises, very similar to the ones in the Miami Police photos on the body of her friend, Shantelle.

After allowing her a long weekend off in Puerto Rico, after the bruises faded, Jace probably thought business would continue as usual. But it wouldn't. People who didn't know Jace well found him charming. In his early forties, tall, blond, and good looking with soft blue eyes and perfect teeth. He liked to sail, which kept him tanned and in shape. He used smooth words and a handshake to make deals, then delivered as promised.

She ran into the hall and almost collided with Jace rushing from the bar toward the foyer.

He scowled and pointed. "Go to your room and

stay there."

She slapped his hand away. "Who is it, Jace?"

"I don't know."

She raised her five-foot, ninety-four-pound body onto her toes and clamped her hands on her hips. "It's him, isn't it? That last client."

"I said, I don't know."

She stared up with lips pressed together. "I know that look." She saw a lie better than Jace told one. "You're lying, and you're afraid of him. Who is he?"

"Someone important. Go to your room. We'll talk about this later."

She shook her head. "What will you do? And don't say no to him now, then promise something later."

"I'll meet him at the gate. Now get out of sight and stay there." He pushed by and continued down the hall.

She marched to her room, slammed and locked the door, then slid the chain into place. Jace worked that way. He was big on customer service. A smooth talker and a good salesman who knew how to market her services. Clients weren't supposed to come here. Until Shantelle's death she'd felt relatively safe living at Jace's house. Accompanying him when he wanted a beautiful woman on his arm, which often served as an advanced viewing to a prospective client. Previews took place at Miami's best nightclubs and most expensive restaurants. Services were arranged at private homes or the finest hotels.

For the past four years, she only saw two classes of clients. First, Jace's wealthy repeat clients, intelligent, successful men who paid very well for her small size and innocent look. Most wanted her long, black hair flowing over bare shoulders. For an even younger look, a few requested she wear a ponytail that stretched to the middle of her back. All loved her light brown skin, large dark eyes, and full lips that created the exotic princess they imagined. Jace marketed her as a rare quality, a unique experience, a luxury to be enjoyed and appreciated for an evening or a weekend. Her price was not negotiable.

The second and most important class was Jace's business associates. Jace did more than furnish high-class call girls. He laundered large amounts of other people's money. Her role was either as a sweetener for a prospective deal or a thank you for a completed one. More of his customer service. These men often saw her services as a payment, and they wanted full value. That last client was one of those men. Their session had ended prematurely in more ways than one, and he probably felt a balance was due.

She crawled across the bed to the window and peeked between the blinds. Jace stood behind the closed metal gate. The car slowed to a stop, and its tinted window lowered. The driver leaned his face through the opening.

It was him, that brutal little pig. Her heartbeat quickened. Breaths came short and fast. Jace didn't point back down the drive, or argue, or even talk. He just listened, nodded, then pushed a button and let the gate swing open. *Jace, you son of a bitch, you didn't even try.*

That man had gripped her neck from behind, squeezed, then jammed her face into the pillow until she passed out. If Cal hadn't knocked in time, she'd have ended up dead, just like Shantelle. Whoever he was, Jace wouldn't stand up to him. They'd go to the bar, drink and negotiate, and make a deal. Jace would sell her out either tonight or later. Couldn't—wouldn't—let that happen.

She clenched her teeth and tensed every muscle. Breathe, long and slow. Ease the muscles, quell the fear. Think, focus, stay in control, because this evening had just begun.

She knelt by the bed, slid her hands beneath the mattress, and pulled out two Beretta .25s. The first, a gift from a repeat, weekend client. Ed Ellis was a cautious man, concerned with security, and had a private indoor shooting range, where he'd taught her to shoot. Sometimes they spent an afternoon on his yacht and practiced on his beer bottles and her Coke cans. A kind man, divorced twice, and didn't trust women, but they liked and understood each other. He worried about her, maybe afraid their weekends would end, but his concern seemed genuine. Sometimes clients forgot her time with them was strictly business. The best tips came from letting those men believe they were different.

Slide that Beretta back into place. Unregistered and untraceable, it would be her backup weapon. The other gun, Shantelle had given to her. No one knew she had it. She had never fired it or touched the clip or any of the rounds. If that cruel little man had to be shot, this gun couldn't be traced to her, but maybe to Jace. If Jace caught a girl with a gun, he confiscated it. A dead girl was an inconvenience, but a dead client was very bad for business. Shantelle would smile to know her gun might save her friend.

She pushed the barrel release lever. The top half of the barrel popped up on its hinge, revealing a round. She pushed the button near the bottom of the grip. A full clip slid out. She shoved the clip back into place, closed the hinge, then slid the Beretta deep into her sweatpants pocket.

She turned to the rattling of her doorknob. "Go away, Jace."

"Open the door. I only want to talk."

"We have nothing to talk about."

"He's sorry about what happened before. He came to apologize."

"Tell him to go service himself. His little hand is just the right size." She plunged her hand deep into her pocket and gripped the Berretta.

"Open the door. He'll give you a thousand just to hear his apology."

She turned the lock and cracked the door open but kept the chain in place. "Who is he, Jace? I know he's not one of your corporate clients looking for a fantasy weekend."

Jace wedged his face into the opening. "No. No, he isn't. It's Carlos Molina, Arturo Molina's son. You don't say no to a Molina."

Her shoulder braced the door. "I said no, and I meant it. That little pig almost killed me."

"You're exaggerating again, and this isn't a request. Now open the goddamn door! If I have to, I'll break it down."

"I'll still say no."

"Then you'll say it to him." Jace's voice softened. "Just come out, talk to him. He might make an offer you can't refuse. Anyway, I have no choice, so neither do you. Now open the goddamn door."

One way or another, it would happen. If Jace dragged her out, she would have no control.

She slid the chain and opened the door. Jace slipped in and leaned his back against the door. He wore his client-pleasing, salesman smile, looking at the ceiling, searching for the right words.

Jace's shoulders lifted, then sank as he exhaled an exaggerated sigh. "What happened last time won't happen again. He's as sorry as a man in love. He'll do anything to make up for what happened last time. He had problems that just burst out. He thinks he's in love."

"I doubt that."

"I don't. Men fall in love with you real easy."

"What if I say no?" But Jace was right. You didn't say no to a Molina. Maybe Shantelle said no, or maybe she didn't. Either way, the outcome was the same.

Jace's face tensed. "He has power, and he'll use it. But you're the best that's ever worked for me. That's why you live here. Why you get the best money. Just come out and talk to him. Take advantage of it. This could be the first of several nice paydays for both of us."

She closed her eyes and nodded. "I need a few minutes to calm down. I'll come out. I promise."

"You better." Jace stepped through the doorway and turned. "Five minutes. If you don't get your little ass out here, then we'll both come get you."

"I said I promise."

She closed the door, faced the full-length mirror, and hooked her hair behind her ears. The bruises in the mirror pointed back like a dark premonition. She closed her eyes and saw Shantelle's bruises pointing the same way. No doubt about it, Carlos had killed Shantelle, and Jace probably dumped her body. Sooner or later that little pig would kill her, and Jace would dump her body, too. Nothing or no one, not money or his best girl, was so important to Jace that he'd risk his own life. He was a smart businessman and would take a loss that hurt in order to avoid one that hurt more. Whatever Jace had going must be big enough to risk losing her. Big money and fear of a Molina were Jace's strongest motivations.

She dangled her arms. The cuffs of her baggy University of Miami sweatshirt slid over her hands and hid the gun in her right hand. She crossed her arms against her chest, trapping the barrel of the sleeve-covered gun in her armpit. It was well hidden and could come out quickly.

Fast, firm steps grew louder on the hardwood floor. She opened the door with her free hand, then recrossed her arms, careful to keep the gun hidden. She stepped into the hall. "I'm coming."

Jace nodded. "He's waiting at the bar."

She followed Jace down the hall until it opened into the living room and bar. Carlos drained his glass and strutted toward her. He stretched from the waist, lifting his shoulders to add an inch of height that didn't matter. If she didn't hate him so much, she could almost find him comical.

He stopped about eight feet from her. "First, I want to apologize." He stared, nodding with a wide smile. "And I promise, anything that happened before was a mistake and will never happen again."

She ignored his smile and studied his small, black, empty eyes. Usually clients stared with lustful appreciation, but Carlos couldn't hide the hate behind his eyes. His arms hung loose at his side, but his curled fingers scratched at his palms. He scanned her like a man eager to complete unfinished, familiar business. As if everything he had done to her, or would do, was his right. She wouldn't go with him, not for a million dollars.

Carlos nodded with a satisfied grin at Jace. "This settles our account." His gaze returned to her. "Little Princess, you don't even have to pack a bag. I'll buy you everything you need, anything you want."

It was there, in his anxious smile, vacant eyes, and impatient fingers. Sooner or later he would kill her and use his hands.

"I won't go with you."

Jace winced and sidled next to Carlos. "Give her a few days. She's just tired."

Carlos shook his head. "Jace, that's not like you. Do you let your whores run things? She's part of our deal. A deal I set up and can still cancel with one phone call."

"We can work this out. I'll talk to her alone. Give me a half hour."

She shook her head. "It won't matter."

Carlos narrowed his eyes, sneering. "Soledad Shoshone Montoya, such an exotic name for a little 'rican slut. I'll have you another time." He raised his right hand with his thumb and index finger an inch apart. "I came this close to finding you in San Juan. You're easy to follow. Men can't help but notice you, women, too. Just come with me now, and I'll forgive you."

She shook her head again. "I'll take my chances."

Carlos cocked his head and grinned. "I know where your family lives."

Her eyes widened, and her lips parted.

His grin grew. "Ohhh, I see that registered."

She loosened her arm on the trapped Beretta. This little pig just crossed a line and would never step back. She switched off the safety.

He winked. "You have two fine-looking sisters, and your mama's not bad for her age. Never done a cougar, but I might make an exception for her. But I'll leave it up to you. Come with me now, and I'll treat you like a princess. Come with me now, and I'll never bother your family. It's up to you."

And it was and might never be again. This man would always be a lethal threat to her and her family. And he'd carry it out. She took a deep breath. Her finger slid inside the trigger guard. Remember, both eyes open, aim at his solar plexus, squeeze.

She slowly shook her head.

Carlos's grin faded. "No? That's too bad. Then I guess I'll find you later, or maybe a sister. Yeah, the short one. She looks a lot like you." He turned and took two steps toward the door.

Jace rushed after him. "Wait, Carlos, don't go. I have a new girl, only nineteen, fresh to the business. You'll like her look. Has an ass like Soledad's."

Carlos flicked his hand and kept walking. "Not interested tonight. Maybe another time."

"I still have my deal, don't I?"

Carlos halted and slowly turned. He scanned her up and down, then aimed his gaze between her legs. "Only if she's included."

She clenched her teeth, swallowed, and widened her stance. Couldn't take a chance with the family. *God forgive me. Please understand.*

She uncrossed her arms and slid the Beretta from

her sleeve. Carlos's eyes bulged as he fumbled an automatic from beneath his coat.

Her left hand joined her right as her knees flexed.

Carlos jerked his gun up.

She squeezed the trigger twice. Two firecracker pops. Two shell casings hopped over her shoulder. Carlos's body twitched. His eyes bulged, and his mouth gaped. She squeezed the trigger again. He wobbled as the automatic slipped from his hand and clattered on the floor. His chin drooped. Surprised eyes fixed on the small, bleeding holes in his chest. His legs folded, and his body sank, collapsing on his back. His head bounced on the floor. Blank eyes jiggled, then became still, staring at the ceiling.

Jace stooped and grabbed Carlos's automatic.

She swiveled her aim. "Don't, Jace! Put it down."

He looked up but didn't drop or raise the gun.

"Jace, I just killed a man, because I had to. If I have to, I'll kill you, then call the police and tell them Carlos pulled his gun, and I shot him. Then you picked up his gun, and I shot you. I'll get off. Even if I don't, you'll still be dead."

Jace eased the gun to the floor, slowly rose upright, and held his open hands in front of his chest. "Whoa now, let's calm down. No one else needs to get shot. But you don't know what you've done. You stupid little—"

"Shut up, Jace. I know what I've done." She motioned with the Beretta. "Kick his gun over here."

Jace tapped his toe to the automatic and pushed. It glided across the floor.

"Just for the goddamn record, why the hell did you kill him? He was leaving. This could fuck up everything."

She knelt and picked up the automatic. "He threatened my family and would've followed through. Now he can't, and now we need to figure things out."

Jace shook his head. "Not we—you. You just killed Arturo Molina's son. You're already dead. You just don't know it."

"Think, Jace. We're in this together, because no matter what you say to the police, or the Molinas, they'll question me, too. And I lie better than you tell the truth. But that won't matter. The Molinas will kill us both, just to make sure."

Jace punched his fist into his palm. "Goddamn it all to hell!" He took another teeth-clenching breath, glaring down and shaking his head. "That little shit could fuck up a wet dream. I knew someone would kill him sooner or later, but the time and place couldn't be worse." He rubbed his forehead. "But the situation is what it is. We need to have a long, serious talk, but first things first. We have to get rid of the body and everything connected to it. I've done this before on short notice. I have a place."

"Where you dumped Shantelle's body?"

Jace eyed her. "You think too much. Shantelle was moonlighting. You never know who you get." He knelt and transferred items from Carlos's pockets into his, then stood holding a set of keys. "I'll put his vehicle in the garage, bag him, and stuff him in his trunk. Get some rags and bleach. You have a floor to clean. I'll have to get rid of the rags, too."

Jace walked down the hall and stopped with his hand on the doorknob. "You're right. We're in this together, and when I come back, I want both guns. I have to get rid of everything, so you better decide if you're going to kill me or cooperate."

He continued out and closed the door.

She stooped, picked up the shell casings, and approached Carlos's body. Blood trickled from three small wounds in his chest. She sucked in a measured breath. Her shoulders rose, then slumped, and a tight-throated sigh escaped. There was no turning back, only getting out, and for that, Jace was needed. She backed away two tentative steps, spun, and marched to her room.

Think carefully. A misstep now would be hard to explain later. Jace in possession of the murder weapon was a misstep. He might hold on to it and somehow use it against her. She shoved Shantelle's gun beneath the mattress and gripped the other Beretta. Give him this one, untraceable and had nothing to do with anything.

Look at the whole problem, not just the immediate one of Carlos's body. Jace thought the solution was to keep the Molinas from discovering who killed Carlos and where. But dumping Carlos was only the first step. After his body was found, the determining sequence of events would start, so find a way out.

Chapter Two

Wednesday, 9:55 pm

Soledad entered the living room carrying Carlos's automatic and a small red utility bucket containing bloodstained rags smelling of bleach. Jace sat at the middle of the bar, leaning over, inspecting the items from Carlos's pockets. A smoldering, half-smoked cigarette rested in the ashtray. He didn't turn or even look up. She had no choice but to cooperate, and Jace knew it.

She slid onto the last stool and set the bucket and automatic on the curved end of the bar. A large, unzipped travel bag sat on the stool between them.

Jace eyed the automatic. "What's it gonna be? You gonna work with me or kill me? And don't worry, I won't kill you. One body a night is enough to get rid of."

She pulled the Beretta from her pocket, wiped both guns with a bleach rag, then pushed the guns toward him. Now that Jace had the guns, he'd feel more in control. Let him think that. Nag, whine, and reason to keep some control, but don't challenge him.

Jace hefted the Beretta. "Where'd you get this little piece of shit?"

"From Mister Ellis. He worries about me. Thinks I need protection."

"He doesn't know you like I do." Jace dropped the rags and guns into the travel bag. "After we get out of this, I think it's time I send him a different girl. But for now." His attention shifted to the items on the bar. Spread out before him lay two phones, a wallet, a pack of Marlboro reds, and a gold Zippo lighter with an engraved Cuban flag with a diamond for the star.

Jace examined the pack of Marlboros. "Only one gone. Hopefully he didn't buy them nearby. That could be a problem." He separated the sides of the travel bag. "He has clothes, toilet articles, and a bottle of Viagra, which doesn't tell us much, but his phones and wallet do. A fake ID with a credit card under the name Luis Osuna. All his receipts are for that name. Plus, he was using a throwaway phone. His real one hasn't been used in five days."

Jace lifted his cigarette with his thumb and forefinger and took a drag. "Looks like he didn't want anyone to know he followed you to Puerto Rico, or that he was back. I know he came straight from the airport, so we may have caught a break. Maybe no one knows he came here. But if someone knew he was looking for you, you're a connection."

"And you're a connection, if someone knew he was looking for you."

Jace leaned back, tapping his ring finger on the bar. "What are you getting at?"

"The deal Carlos set up for you. The one he was going to cancel, but now he can't."

Jace leaned forward. "Like I said, you think too much. That deal is none of your business. In fact, from now on, nothing is any of your business. I don't see our options improving if we wait. Something we don't know about might bring the police here. I'll get rid of everything tonight."

"Then what?"

"We'll carry on with business as usual. Keep necessary appointments and listen without asking. When they find the body, and they will eventually, the police will look at the Molina Family's enemies. And Carlos had extra of his own. The police and the Molinas aren't shy. If either looks in our direction, we'll know."

"Tomorrow, I had some shopping planned. Friday, I have a doctor's appointment and a nail appointment."

Jace shook his head. "Those aren't necessary, they can wait."

"No, they can't. I need them. Especially the shopping. I don't drink, smoke, or do drugs. Shopping is how I relieve stress."

Jace leaned back and crushed his cigarette in the ashtray. "You don't look stressed to me."

"I internalize it. And if I don't find a release, it'll burst out. Ask Carlos."

Jace's eyes widened as his ring tapped faster, then slowed. He nodded. "Okay. There's something you can pick up for me at L'Voyage. Two special order marine bags due in on Friday. Waterproof, can float holding fifty pounds. They're for the boat. If bad comes to worse, we may have to leave that way."

"We? What if I don't want to go?"

"I can't leave you behind. You might think you can lie yourself all the way out and lie me all the way in. But you can't. On your own, the Molinas will find you and kill you." He leaned forward and stared. "Besides, your family could end up as collateral damage."

That was a not-so-veiled threat. "Okay, Jace."

He nodded. "It's good and necessary that you understand. We probably won't have to leave, but if it comes to that, I'm well prepared. Now, back to the shopping. No taxis. I'll assign you a driver. Fowler will do. I don't want you on your own for a second, and he won't leave your side."

She winced. "He's a gross, fat cockroach, always leering at my butt. You can't trust him. He'll wonder too much, and he doesn't work for just you. Cal is used to driving me. It won't look odd, and he does exactly what you tell him."

Jace leaned back with his thumb and forefinger rubbing his chin. "You're right about Fowler. He looks stupid, but he's not." He nodded. "Okay, Cal will drive you. I'll arrange it."

He glanced at the clock behind the bar. "Time for me to take care of business. Go to your room and stay there. I'm putting the house on lockdown. All the sensors, cameras, and alarms will be on. If you take one step outside your room, I'll know."

She slid off her stool and walked toward the hallway.

"Soledad."

She stopped but didn't turn.

"Don't get any ideas. Sometimes girls think they can go home, but they can't. Remember, you came to me—and stayed. No one forced you."

She spun, clenching her teeth. "For my family." Jace never understood family and never would.

Jace shook his head. "Every girl comes with a story and a reason, then stays for the money. You're here because it's easier and pays better than getting a real job." He leaned forward with a small sneer. "Would your family rather have you out of the business and waiting tables, or in the business, sucking cock and spreading your legs for money?"

She looked down and clenched her teeth harder. That hurt to the core. Jace liked to demean and define his girls in the basest monetary and sexual terms. Making them feel unworthy for anyone except him and his clients. His best means of control.

His sneer transitioned to a grin. "You could have left and found a decent job. In sales, high-end clothes, especially lingerie. Whatever a male customer bought, he'd buy it half for you. And imagine fucking you."

"I know what I am."

"Good. I'll admit you're different in one way. You're smarter and maybe still cling to a plan. I know you own a house in Puerto Rico and probably think you can retire and have a new life there. Forget that now. You killed a Molina. So get practical." Jace shrugged and tried to smile sympathetically, but his eyes said *you're mine, body and soul.* "Besides, you'll still have the clubs, restaurants, and shopping to enjoy. You can still help your family. Nothing will change. Just let go of your plan and embrace who you are. I've put you on a pinnacle. I oughta give you to Fowler for a night, then you'd know exactly how lucky you are."

She tightened her throat to cut off a gag. "You made your point. Okay, Jace. I'll do what you say." She turned, continued to her room, and locked the door.

She closed her eyes and shook her head. *Oh, Shantelle, I need you so much right now.* She should have listened to Shantelle instead of seeing money, but fanning hundred-dollar bills made beautiful music, and empty pockets didn't make a sound. Once she decided to work for Jace, Shantelle had become a big sister, always worrying, always giving advice. Separate the job from the person. Don't let the profession define you. People who love you don't feel the need to forgive. Most important, don't let Jace take your soul. He can only take it if you let him.

Jace's words hurt and maybe had some truth. Growing up poor, working minimum wage jobs to help the family, there had been little left for herself. Who did she want to help the most? Best to face that later. That was then. This is now. The long-term plan would never change, but the immediate plan had to.

The deal Carlos set up for Jace must be big. Jace would concentrate on that while worrying about Carlos's body and car. His eye on her wouldn't be as close. That's where Cal could be useful.

Cal still drove as an emergency fill-in but now managed some of Jace's special girls. He took care of them, made sure they kept doctor appointments, filled prescriptions, and didn't use drugs or carry a gun. He transitioned in new girls by holding their hands and giving them his shoulder. Things Jace tried in the early years, but it didn't come off as real. The girls liked and trusted Cal. Jace saw that and used it. He had less trouble with Cal's girls, which saved him money. Jace was a good businessman.

Cal was good looking, especially when he smiled. About six-two with dark shaggy hair, deep green eyes, and according to Shantelle, he had a good sense of humor. Shantelle said Cal was different, but she had looked at him through different eyes. She had loved him.

He was the closest thing Jace had to a friend, which

had risks, but a man's loyalty usually shrank as his penis grew. Jace thought Cal didn't break rules, but he did. He'd slept with Shantelle for over a year until her murder. The last time they talked, Shantelle was sure she was in love with Cal, which was surprising, but if anyone could fall in love after a dozen years in the business, it was Shantelle. She said Cal treated her with genuine concern and respect and liked spending the entire night. He even made his special eggs and coffee in the morning. He always made her laugh, which fit so well with Shantelle, because she loved to laugh. But what Shantelle liked best was her alone time with Cal. She always felt safe. He would never hurt her. He wanted to protect her. And just as important, Cal made her feel good about herself.

Feeling safe and feeling good wasn't love, but the next best thing, and love couldn't grow without them. She had envied Shantelle for that. A few times she'd even fantasized being with Cal, kind of finding love vicariously through her best friend.

Tomorrow, find out more about Cal. Get him talking. Most men liked to talk about themselves, especially to an attractive woman, as though they felt required to make themselves worthy. But Cal was different, more of a listener than a talker. He listened to Jace's girls, so he'd heard all the stories and all the lies, but he'd never heard them from her.

Good lies needed truth weaved in so tightly they became one sheer fabric. The best lies were the ones people wanted to believe. Give them details, because details sell a story. The right lies, to the right people, at the right time, was the way out. But she needed help from inside and outside.

She picked up her phone from the nightstand. Better use it now before Jace took it away. By this time, Mama should be in bed, and Cheyenne always had some kind of schoolwork keeping her up late.

It rang three times.

"Little Sis. Yeah, it's me. Sit down and stay calm." She took a breath and smiled out the exhale. "I want to come home for good." Silence. Cheyenne had begged and pushed and waited for this through two years of high school and nearly six years of college.

Then came crying mixed with thanking God, followed by a string of questions starting and ending with when, when, when? Emotional Cheyenne was ready to do whatever, whenever.

"Calm down. And don't tell Mama. I need your help tomorrow and probably Sunday. It could be dangerous."

"Make it dangerous for me, not you. Now, give me every detail."

Focused Cheyenne took over, and no one planned and carried out like Little Sis. By the time their call ended, everything was set. Tomorrow, get Cal's help. Give him a story with enough truth to hide the lies. If he'd loved Shantelle, he carried guilt about her death. That was his weak point, so use it, because nothing felt better than guilt redeemed.

Chapter Three

Thursday, 11:45 am

Cal Lee turned his five-year-old Chevy Impala onto Biscayne Boulevard and ended his second unusual call from Jace. The first had come at about six in the morning while he lay in bed with Ynez. Should have left her place right then, but mornings with Ynez made him forget how stupid he was. Less than four hours of sleep for two nights in a row. Too smart and too old for that kind of shit. Sometimes a mistake seemed so right going in, so wrong sneaking away, then right again when getting away with it.

Jace rarely called that early in the morning and only assigned him to drive Soledad on the last Sunday of each month to drop her off and pick her up from church. After church, before Shantelle was killed, he'd take her straight to Marny's Café to visit with Shantelle over coffee and pecan pie. Those two always took the corner booth while he sat at the counter. They were fun to watch, whispering and giggling like schoolgirls.

After Shantelle's murder, Soledad had him take her to Marny's only once. She slumped in the same seat in the same corner booth, sipped her coffee, and picked at her pie, sometimes looking across the table at Shantelle's empty seat, smiling, frowning, closing her eyes, and bowing her head. She'd never asked to go to

Marny's again.

Maybe Soledad blamed him for not taking care of her best friend. Maybe she thought he was just another Jace. Whatever the reason, she rarely said anything, except to give instructions. According to his girls, Soledad didn't like drivers, occasionally drove herself, but hated parking so much she usually took taxis.

The gate was open with Jace's dark green BMW parked in front of the house and John Fowler's gray Cadillac parked outside the garage. Fowler was an asshole and as crooked as they came. Jace had bought him as a cop over ten years ago. After Fowler got kicked off the force, Jace still contracted him as a bodyguard and sometimes to find a missing girl.

He parked beside the Cadillac and walked toward the house. Fowler stepped out the front door. They were about the same height, but Fowler carried fifty extra pounds. His hairy wrists and powerful hands stuck out from his cheap, too small, light blue sports jacket. Every time they met, Fowler's gut seemed to have added ten more pounds, but his clothes never caught up.

Fowler smiled and nodded recognition. In his late forties with a hairline receding to the middle of his large, round, sunburned head, Fowler's wide smile made him look like a jack-o-lantern in a nightmare.

"Cal Lee, haven't seen you for a while. How are your girls getting along without me?"

"Just fine. What're you doing here?"

"Same as you, business. Maybe I'll see you around." Fowler grinned and continued to his Cadillac.

Jace stood at the front door and yawned a tired smile. "Sorry for the early call. Let's go to the bar." Jace led the way with a slight trudge to his walk and sat heavily on the center stool. "Sit down, I want to talk to you about Soledad."

They both turned to the click of heels. A ponytailed Soledad, wearing an impatient frown, and sunglasses on top of her head, stopped at the entrance to the living room. She planted one hand on her hip while the other rested on a purse hanging from her shoulder. She wore blue jeans, a short-sleeved white blouse with an upturned collar, and a fluffy blue scarf around her neck. Kind of a fifties look from an Audrey Hepburn movie.

She folded her arms and tapped her foot. "Come on, Cal. I have lots to do, and it's almost noon."

Jace stared. "I'm talking to him. *In private*."

"Fine. I'll be in the car." She spun and marched away.

Jace smiled and offered a cigarette. They both lit up.

"Do you mind driving Soledad?"

"No, it's part of the job. I'm used to it on Sundays."

"Good, I want you to free up your afternoons for the next few days. You'll be her driver. She wants to do some clothes shopping and has some appointments. I'll have another manager cover your duties."

"If it's only for a few days, use Brandi. She helps me, knows the scheduling, and the girls listen to her."

Jace nodded. "Good idea. Now back to Soledad." Jace leaned forward and laid a hand on his shoulder. "Don't drop her off and leave her. Stay with her. Is that clear?"

"You mean go into the stores with her?"

"That's right. Go everywhere with her. Don't let her out of your sight, and when she has to pee, I want you right outside the door." Jace leaned back and took a long drag. "Can you do that?"

"Sure, but I don't think she likes me. When I drive her to church, she barely talks except to give directions."

"That'll work fine. Keep it that way. She knows you'll be watching her, so she'll probably treat you like shit. Just ignore her."

"I can do that."

Jace sat back and smiled. "Now, tell me about the new girl, Ynez. What's her potential?"

"I'm not sure. I'm still getting her settled in. This is her first time in the business, so I'll screen her clients extra close."

"Good idea. Have you looked at her closely? She's taller, but straighten her hair, have her lose a few pounds, and who does she remind you of?"

He shrugged. "I don't know. Next time I see her, I'll check her out more closely."

"You do that. She could be a star. I've only seen her on video. Next week, schedule her for an afternoon around the pool. I want to see her in a bikini, do an audition."

"I'll set that up." Audition meant Jace would sample her in bed.

Jace patted his shoulder and sighed. "Well, better not keep the princess waiting."

He started to rise, but Jace gripped his shoulder and leaned closer. "Soledad can be a handful when she's pissed, and right now she's pissed. She's smart and bossy. She thinks and acts quickly, and can take over a situation, so don't let her tell you what to do. If there's any problem, any question at all, call me right away. If you need to, just turn around and bring her back. I'll handle her. Is that clear?"

"Sure, Jace."

Jace's grip tightened and his face hardened. "Completely clear?"

"Yes, sir. Don't let her out of my sight. Don't listen to her. Call if there's any question or problem."

Jace nodded. "Good. Don't forget. Better get going."

He stepped outside, blinked, and dropped his eyes from the high sun. Damn, he hated being stupid, and sleeping with Ynez was really stupid, which was obvious now. But there was something about Ynez that he hadn't felt about anyone since Shantelle. A decision about her was needed soon, before she became Jace's new star. But this afternoon with Soledad was definitely much more on Jace's mind. As though she had a boyfriend on the sly, and Jace wanted a watchdog.

He took a last, deep drag, dropped and crushed his cigarette, and looked up at Soledad scrambling over the console and sliding into the passenger seat of Jace's BMW.

"Get in, Cal. I don't feel like sitting in the back seat. Do you have a problem with that?"

"No, that's fine." He slid behind the steering wheel and closed the door. "Where to?"

"Just get me out of here."

She stared straight ahead with her hands folded in her lap. Her purse and a Nordstrom's shopping bag sat on the floor between her feet.

He drove to the end of Jace's private drive. "Which way?"

"Left. I don't know, just drive. I wish I drank, so

you could take me to a bar. That might help."

"Kind of early for that. I'm supposed to take you shopping."

"You're supposed to watch me. Just drive."

Just like Jace warned, the shit treatment had begun. This would be a long afternoon.

He kept his eyes on the road except when they darted to her. She sat with her head bowed, staring at her lap, as though they had paused in the middle of an argument and she waited for an apology. He reached for the radio, but her hand clasped his and squeezed.

"Cal, I need someone to talk to."

"You should probably talk to Jace."

"How about you? You talk with your girls all the time. I know, because they talk to me."

"Yeah, but they aren't you. And you're Jace's…"

Her eyes narrowed, and her jaw tightened. "Jace's what?"

"Jace's responsibility."

She released his hand and slumped back. "That's a safe answer. But today, I'm your responsibility."

"Whatever." He reached for the radio.

Her hand shot forward and slapped his away. "You either listen to me or listen to silence."

He gritted his teeth. This had the beginnings of a really long afternoon. Coffee and a cigarette were required. "Once again, where to?"

"You don't like babysitting me, do you?"

"You said it, not me. How about Dadeland Mall?"

"I want to talk about Shantelle. We were best friends, like sisters. We talked. I know things about you two."

His jaw clenched. "You don't know shit." Easy,

calm down. Shouldn't have said that.

"Shantelle was in love with you. And you were supposed to take care of her, but you didn't."

He squeezed the steering wheel. Didn't need this crap. "Let's change the subject."

"I have an idea who killed her."

His eyes darted to hers. The tires hit the center lane road bumps. He corrected his steering. "If the police don't know, how do you?"

"That's what I want to talk about." She leaned closer. "Cal, something happened to me last Friday that makes me think I know who killed her."

"Then let Jace take care of it."

"Someone important killed Shantelle, and Jace cleaned up for him."

He side-glanced. Didn't she realize what she was saying? And who to?

She edged closer until her shoulder grazed his arm. "Don't you want to hear how I know?"

This was a dangerous information area. "Leave it alone. Some things are safer not to know."

She slammed back in a huff. "I guess Shantelle didn't mean that much to you. Just another whore taking her chances."

"Just shut up." His fingers flexed around the steering wheel. "This conversation is over."

She crossed her arms and let slip a long, soft sigh. "She loved you, Cal. She's worth a talk, isn't she?"

There was no sarcasm or contempt in her voice. Not an order or a plea, just a soft request for something owed. This was the point where he should call Jace, or turn around and drive back and say he couldn't handle her. People in this business weren't supposed to feel guilt, but she'd found the right button to push and knew just how to push it. He eased in a measured breath and nodded. "We can have a short talk."

"Thank you, Cal, but not in a car. I don't like them. Too many times they take me places I don't want to go. Take the next exit. Your place is only a few minutes away."

He held a side look.

She grinned. "Don't be surprised. I know where you live, that you like jazz, old movies, chorizo in your scrambled eggs, and a little cardamom in your coffee. Why your first name is Caleb. It's from a character in a Steinbeck novel, and your middle name, Dean, is from James Dean who played the character in the movie, *East of Eden*. Maybe that's where we are. Shantelle talked a lot about the man she loved." Her head flicked to the side. "Better get in the right lane."

"You're putting me in a difficult position."

"I promise, Jace will never know. This is just between you and me, and Shantelle."

He steered into the right lane. "We'll be there in a few minutes."

"Thank you again, Cal. I know what this means. Keep your eyes on the road and slow down. A few extra minutes won't matter."

Soledad slid her sunglasses on and sat with her hands in her lap. She didn't talk for the next ten minutes. Something said this entire interaction wasn't spontaneous, but she'd found his weak spot in Shantelle. Just take it one more step and see where she was going.

He opened the door to his ground floor, two-bedroom apartment and motioned Soledad to the couch.

She shook her head and continued to the small kitchen and dining area. "I like talking across a kitchen table. It's the best place to start a long day or end a long night. And this is both. Can you make coffee?"

"Sure." Needed sleep more, but coffee and a cigarette were the next best thing.

She sat silently at his small, round table. He measured grounds and water, gathered mugs and spoons, and waited for her to say something, but she didn't. Every clink of a cup or spoon magnified the silence. He set the sugar and milk between them.

"Black is fine." She wrapped her hands around the mug and looked up. "Don't worry, Shantelle only told her mother and me about you, and I won't tell. Not for you, for Shantelle, because she wouldn't want anyone to hurt you." She frowned and shook her head. "You're relieved, aren't you? Relieved your secret is safe from Jace. And maybe a little guilty for feeling relief instead of feeling for Shantelle."

"Don't play the guilt card. If you know something, tell me."

She sat back and sipped her coffee. "Do you know who Carlos Molina is?"

"Yeah, I know."

"I think he killed Shantelle."

He blinked, sipped his coffee, and peered over his cup. Maybe his eyes showed it, maybe not, but this was some serious shit. "If that's true, and that's a big if. It's very dangerous to know."

She nodded. "Yes, it is. Do you want to hear more?"

He shoved his chair back, took three quick steps, and opened his sliding glass door. "I need a cigarette for this." He leaned his back against the doorframe with one foot in the kitchen and the other on the small concrete patio.

He pulled out his last Camel. Jace said she was smart, bossy, takes control, and don't let her tell you what to do. Jace was right. They were here. Soledad had an agenda, and Shantelle was either the reason or a means. "Tell me what you know, not what you speculate."

She planted her elbows on the table and folded her hands. "Last night, Carlos Molina came to the house. I thought he was coming for me. I ran to my room and locked myself in. But I don't trust Jace, and I had to know. I cracked my door and heard them talking. I couldn't make out the words, so I sneaked to the end of the hall. They were at the bar, discussing. Carlos had another body for Jace to get rid of. And I quote. 'Dump her the same place as last time. It's been a year.'" She paused and stared. "And it's been a year since Shantelle was killed." Her eyes grew larger. "Don't you see? Carlos killed Shantelle, and Jace took care of her body."

"That's speculation and a real reach. Leave it alone." He tasted filter and flicked the butt into the courtyard.

"Cal, please come back to the table. I have something to show you."

He took time refilling his cup, then returned to his chair.

She leaned forward. "When the police questioned you, I know they showed you photographs of Shantelle's body."

She flipped her collar down, unfastened the top two

buttons of her blouse, and separated the collar. He glanced to her cleavage, then popped his eyes back to hers. She had to notice, but only stared back. She untied her fluffy blue scarf and slid it from her neck. She turned her head right and showed a single, thumb-shaped bruise. She paused, turned left, and revealed a larger dark shape, like the shadow of fingers pointing at him.

"Look familiar?"

He sipped his coffee and nodded. Pretty clear, Soledad had been grabbed from behind just like Shantelle, and probably by the same hand.

"Carlos Molina did this to me last Friday night. If I hadn't been lucky, I'd be dead. You arrived that night just before Fowler. Remember?"

"Yeah, I remember." Jace had made an urgent call but never said who the client was. "You went right to my back seat and didn't say a word the whole drive. Which didn't seem unusual for you."

"I was in shock. He almost killed me." She retied the scarf around her neck. "What kind of man are you?"

"Not a stupid one. I admit, this all sounds within the realm of possibility."

"There's more. After Carlos and Jace talked last night, Carlos left in his car and Jace left right after him. Jace didn't get back until about four this morning. They got rid of another girl. I just know it."

Jace had definitely looked like he needed sleep, but that was Jace's business. "Leave it alone. There's nothing we can do about it. And you're not the easiest person to believe."

"Uh huh. I see." She nodded, then glared. "Fine, then don't believe me. I thought you'd want to help.

The next girl could be one of yours. Carlos likes a certain kind. And if there's enough money involved, it doesn't matter if she's a star. We're all replaceable, including you." Her mouth tightened into a disgusted frown. "Thinking of the girls or yourself?"

He shoved out his open hand. "Hold on a second." He snatched his phone and pressed the screen. "Brandi. Yeah, this is Cal. Did all the girls check in okay? Are you positive? Good. Double check. I'll make it up to you. I'll keep in touch." He switched off the call.

Soledad stared with a disgusted frown. "A little late. What were you doing this morning?"

"I had some personal business, but all my girls are fine."

"I'm glad, but I know what I heard and saw. You don't believe me now, but if what I say is true, you can't go to Jace. Obviously, he doesn't want you to know. So what are you going to do?"

"Nothing." His fingers rattled inside his empty pack. "There's nothing I can do. You said you wanted to talk, and we've talked."

Soledad looked down, slowly shaking her head. "I don't know if you loved Shantelle, but you were supposed to take care of her. Now she's dead. So I guess that's where your responsibility ended." She sighed as if resigned to take no for an answer, then looked up with her lips pressed together. "That leaves it to me, and I want justice for her." She shook her head. "No, that's not all. I want revenge."

"Revenge is unwise at best. Leave it alone. There's nothing we can do." But she wasn't listening, and her steely-eyed stare had conviction behind it. This was not a woman to mess with.

"Fine, then, but you're my driver for the next few days. If you do nothing, and say nothing, maybe that's enough."

This had gotten way out of hand. "Let's leave it right here. I'm not going any further with it." He stood and pulled out his keys. "We have shopping to do. That's a detail Jace won't overlook."

"I have that covered." She sipped and peered over her cup. "Sit down, please. Let me explain."

"What the hell's going on?"

"My sister is on her way here to pick up my ID and credit card." She pulled out her phone and checked the time. "Cheyenne should be here in ten to fifteen minutes."

He stared and hefted his keys. This was preplanned and well timed. "What's going on?"

"Cal, sit down. Please. A few more minutes won't make any difference. I've been awake all night. I'm frightened, angry, and very tired. I need some rest. And you look like you could use some, too. Jace will never know. Do you really want to spend the day walking around women's clothing stores? And it'll be a long stretch between cigarettes."

He slumped into his chair and again fingered the inside of his empty pack. "Damn it."

"I can help there." She scrolled her phone screen and pressed. "Little Sis, you need to make a stop for cigarettes." She extended her phone across the table. "Tell Cheyenne what brand."

"Ahh, Camel Filters."

She drew the phone back. "Did you hear that? Good, make it two packs." She dropped the phone into her purse. "Add another five minutes for the stop. She's wound kind of tight, but I'll handle her." She popped up. "I need to pee. Where's your bathroom?"

He pointed down the hall. "First door on the left."

She walked away, and his gaze locked on her butt. He shouldn't do that and shouldn't let a beautiful body become a distraction. What hid inside her head was what counted. So, who was this woman? Steely-eyed and bordering on grim when things weren't going her way. She probed, then used guilt, bribery, and fast-talked to turn things around. She didn't have to use her sexuality. Men did that to themselves. She became almost bubbly with her plan in motion, whatever that was. But it included him being her driver. What the hell had he agreed to? And had he actually agreed? She got him with the promise of cigarettes and the threat of the mall. He shook his head. No, that was a weak, easy excuse. Dig deep and she was right. He owed Shantelle. Soledad just drew it out.

A soft knock on the front door grew louder. Soledad rushed from the bathroom to the door. She bolted the chain, raised on her toes, and peeked through the peephole. She cracked open the door. "You're a little early. Give me the cigarettes."

A small hand holding two packs of Camels poked through the opening. Soledad snatched the cigarettes and slapped two cards into the empty hand.

"Soledad, let me in. I have to pee."

"Pee at the mall." She handed her sunglasses through the opening. "And wear these while you shop." Soledad shoved the door shut with her shoulder and locked it. She tossed the cigarettes to him one pack at a time. "Cheyenne didn't really have to pee. She just wanted to get a look at you. Don't worry, she won't get in. You two will never meet."

"That's one thing we can agree on."

While he smoked, she cleared the table, rinsed the cups, and arranged them in the dishwasher. He flicked the cigarette butt into the courtyard as Soledad stepped beside him.

"We have four uninterrupted hours. Where's your bedroom?"

His heart jumped, and his mind leaped forward. Probably not a good idea. He pointed. "Second door on the left after the bathroom."

She took his hand. "Come on. We'll nap together. I want you with me. And don't worry, I won't run out on you or call anyone."

"Well, the bedroom's kind of a mess, and I haven't changed the sheets in a few weeks."

"We'll be on top the bed, not in it. Napping together, not sleeping together. I just want you with me." She cocked her head and smiled. "Please."

He nodded. That was a relief and a disappointment, and he was not sure which was most.

She grabbed his hand, led him down the hall, then cut into the bedroom. She crawled to the far side of the bed and patted the middle of the mattress.

"Come on, lie down." She yawned a smile. "It's all right. You know you want to."

She yawned again, which made him yawn. This might not be smart, but he wanted to. He laid his keys and phone on the nightstand. His knee sank into the mattress as he rolled his shoulder and flopped on his back. His head hit the pillow, and a deep breath escaped.

She lay down on her side with her head at the

bottom edge of the pillow near his shoulder. She patted his chest. "I want to know where you are." Her hand stayed there. "I set my alarm for five o'clock. Relax and think about Shantelle."

That was contradictory. "I'll try." He closed his eyes.

"Cal?"

"What?" He opened an eye and peeked at her face by his shoulder.

She wrinkled her nose. "You smoke too much."

"I'll try to cut down around you."

"Thank you." Her face relaxed as her breasts and shoulders rose, then sank. She sighed with the hint of a smile.

He opened his other eye. Her honey brown skin couldn't disguise a slight puffy darkness beneath her eyes. She had a small, rounded nose and full lips, which parted slightly as her breathing steadied and deepened. His gaze shifted down to between the two unfastened buttons of her blouse. She had smallish breasts, but lying on her side squeezed them together and forward, giving her more cleavage. Her breasts slowly rose and fell with each long, easy breath. He eased his thumb and forefinger around her wrist, lifted her hand a few inches above his chest, then lowered it back. She was out cold.

She curled and pressed her knees against his hip. His gaze shifted to her tiny feet, then slid up her thigh to her hip and waist. His neck stretched for a better view of her small bubble butt. Everything fit together perfectly. He flopped his head back and stared at the ceiling, urging his heartbeat to slow down.

She snuggled closer as her arm pressed on his

chest. He tucked his chin and looked down. The scarf had slipped and only partially hid the bruises. He loosened the scarf and eased it open. The bruises on the sides of her neck had faded least where the ends of fingers had dug in most. Just like the close-up photos Detective Trumbo had showed him of Shantelle.

As tired as he was, sleep wasn't coming. His gaze fixed on the dark finger shapes pointing back. Only the slow movement of Soledad's breasts pressing against his side told him she was breathing and that he wasn't beside a corpse. This was weird and creepy. Get out of this bed and smoke a cigarette.

He reached over his shoulders and pulled the pillow from beneath his head. The movement made her stir. Her arm squeezed his chest, then relaxed. Her forehead pushed against his shoulder, but her breathing remained deep and steady. He slid the pillow lengthwise beneath her arm, then shifted his body. He eased his legs away. She curled into a ball with her cheek pressed against the pillow and her arm stretched across it.

He crept from the bedroom to the patio and smoked two cigarettes, then sneaked back to the bedroom entrance.

Soledad hadn't moved except to curl into a smaller ball and hug the pillow tighter.

He walked back to the living room, slumped on his couch, and switched the TV to CNN on mute. News from the Middle East, the only place in the world where the situation was more confused than his, maybe. He rested his right eye, then his left, then went still as he read the breaking news headlines at the bottom of the screen.

Chapter Four

Thursday, 5:46 pm

Cal jerked his head, blinked, and tried to focus. What the hell was going on?

"Sit still." Soledad sat perched on her knees beside him on the couch, grinning while daubing a tissue to the corner of his mouth. "You sleep with your mouth open and drool out the side just like Bernardo did. But his tongue was bigger and hung out farther."

He snapped his head away, wiped his mouth with his sleeve, and took a deep breath, but the grogginess remained. "Who's Bernardo? What time is it?"

"It's almost six. Cheyenne has been here and gone. The boxes that aren't being delivered are in the BMW. I let you sleep as long as I could, but we should get back."

He nodded and rose, still blinking life into his eyes.

She held out his car keys and phone. "You left these in the bedroom."

"Thanks."

"Oh, and I used your toothbrush. Maybe you should, too. I'll be in the car."

He brushed his teeth, washed his face, and rinsed with cold splashes. He was hungry but rested and alert and needed his A-game. He'd done nothing but react to Soledad. Everything about her was quick and decisive.

The way she walked, talked, and thought. Always with quick questions and quick answers, leaving little time for thought. A good tactic on a person dazed and confused, but not anymore. With all the girls, the bigger the trouble the bigger the lie, and big lies needed small ones for support. Turn the tables. Get quick answers from quick questions. Maybe some truth would come out of it.

She waited in the car just like she had six hours ago at Jace's house, sitting with her hands in her lap and her purse and a bag between her feet. Same purse, different bag.

He started the car and headed for Biscayne Boulevard. "What's in the bag?"

"Takeout from Chili's. It's a detail that says we were at the mall. I had Cheyenne pick up a double order of ribs and fries. When Jace deals with a problem, he smokes a lot but doesn't drink or eat much. He'll be hungry. There's another bag in your fridge with green chili chicken enchiladas and black beans and rice. I thought you might be hungry, too."

"Where's the other bag?"

"What other bag?"

"The Nordstrom's bag you had this morning. You didn't have it when you talked to Jace and me. But it was in the car." He pointed between her feet. "Right there. And now it's gone."

"I gave it to Cheyenne. Every time I visit with her, I bring a present for Mama. She thinks they're from Cheyenne, but I know they're from me."

"What present? Don't think, just answer."

"Ahh, two Tito Puente CDs and a blue dress. Before Daddy died, Mama and Daddy loved to salsa dance. We're trying to get Mama more active. It's my idea."

He shook his head. "You didn't buy that gift today. Where'd it come from?"

"Cal? Why are you doing this?"

She looked hurt, like the questions were unfair, but don't let her take over. "Answer me."

"I always have a gift for Mama in advance. Check my room. There's two more bags. I always plan ahead. Why the third degree?"

"Your bruises. I want more details."

She folded her arms and hunched. "I don't want to talk about that."

"You did when it suited you. Now, how exactly did you get them?"

She side-glanced a glare, then looked down with closed eyes. "I hate doing this, but if it helps you believe me." She took a deep breath. "Carlos answered the door in a robe and made me turn around and keep my back to him. That's not too unusual. I got a look, but I didn't know who he was. He ordered me to undress and lie on the bed face down. A few times he said strongly, *don't look*. I got the feeling it wasn't just his face he didn't want me to see, which isn't unusual either. For almost ten minutes he did something in the bathroom. That's a little unusual, but sometimes a client has second thoughts or does coke or whatever to get himself ready. Next, he got on the bed and—is this necessary?"

"Keep going."

"I hate you."

"It goes with the job. Keep talking."

She forced out words through clenched teeth on

huffed breaths. "He lifted my hips. Then squeezed my neck from behind and shoved my face in the pillow. Do you have to hear the last details before I lost consciousness?"

"No. I get the picture. Pick up after that."

"I think I was out for only a few seconds, but things were hazy. The next thing I remember was a knock. I heard someone say, *leave*. It sounded far away. Must have been Carlos from the bathroom. Next, the whole door shook. That I remember clearly. I slipped my dress on and stuffed my bra and panties in my purse. I opened the door, and you know what happened next. I ducked past you and went straight to your back seat."

"That's all you remember?"

"Sometimes more, sometimes less. You have no idea what it was like. I know I wasn't penetrated, but there was saliva, sweat, and semen on me. Are those details you need or just spice for your imagination?" She glared through narrowed eyes. "And if you can't see that what happened to Shantelle and me was the same, then you're either blind or an uncaring creep. And I know you can see. Are we done with this?"

"One more thing. Your sister had to be on her way to my place before we even left Jace's. Explain."

She sighed and nodded. "I called her last night. I wasn't sure how it would work out, but—"

"But you played me."

"No, Cal. What I said, my bruises, and our nap. They're all real." She shrugged. "I had to find out how much you cared about Shantelle. I don't know if you loved her, but I think you cared deeply. Shantelle was sure of that. Might be the most you're capable of."

She was doing it. Slowing things down, turning them around, making it about him and Shantelle. *Don't let her go there.* "What does your sister know about today?"

"I told you before, she was covering the shopping for me."

"What reason did you give her?"

"I was vague, like there was something romantic between you and me, and we had problems to work out. She knows what I do. If she thinks I have a boyfriend, it gives her hope that I'm getting out." She let out a long sigh. "Please, Cal. I've had enough. Everything I've done today has been hard and real, and I hurt."

"Just one more question. Who's Bernardo? The person I drool like."

Hurt drained from her face. Her tight lips fought to suppress a smile, but the smile burst out on a giggle like a little girl with a joke she couldn't keep in.

"He was my dog when I was little. Daddy brought him home one day for me and Cheyenne. I was the oldest, so I got to name him. Daddy said he was a Saint Bernard, so I named him Bernardo."

"How original."

"I was only six. I loved Bernardo. He was so protective, and the best pillow I ever had. We'd curl up together on the floor and watch *Lady and the Tramp*. I pretended I was Lady, and Bernardo was Tramp. I haven't thought of him in years, until I saw you drooling."

She closed her eyes, her smile widened, and she was more beautiful than ever. But like a daydream disturbed, her eyes opened, and her smile faded.

"But not long after Daddy died, Bernardo got hit

by a car. Mama cleaned offices at night, so she was resting. I was supposed to watch Cheyenne, but I got busy with schoolwork. Somehow, Cheyenne slipped out and wandered into the street. Bernardo ran in front of a car to save her." Her face went blank, and her body froze. "Oh God, that part I wish I could forget. Everybody felt guilt. Mama tried to take it all so Cheyenne and I wouldn't feel any, but that didn't work. So we just don't talk about it."

She sat back and stared out the window.

They rode in silence. He turned the radio to NPR jazz. They turned onto Jace's private drive, and her head snapped to him. "Are you ready for Jace?"

He shrugged. "Jace has grilled me before. Then I told the truth. Now I have to keep lies straight. But I've been thinking. Maybe I should beg off for tomorrow and let someone else drive you."

Her eyes popped big. "Cal, you can't do that. This is Jace's solution, and he likes it. Tell me you'll drive tomorrow."

He stopped at the gate and punched in the code on the roof console.

"Cal. Say you'll drive me tomorrow. *Please*."

Another *please* out of her. She must really want him to drive. He didn't answer, and the gate seemed extra slow.

She cocked her head with a little grin. "Ynez called when you were asleep on the couch. She left a message. You're sleeping with her, aren't you?"

Damn it all to hell. Left the phone on the nightstand, and Soledad must've intercepted a call or listened to a message.

"Cal, the gate's open. Pull up to the garage, get out,

and drive home. I'll put the car in the garage and make your excuses to Jace. I know how to lie to him. I'll tell him you're rude, smoke too much, and I couldn't stand another minute with you. He'll call you, but you'll deal with him better on the phone. And you *will* drive me tomorrow."

He nodded and sighed surrender. Yeah, he'd drive her. He pulled to a stop in front of the garage and climbed out. In one smooth, quick motion, she slipped over the console and into the driver's seat. She pushed two buttons. The driver's seat slid forward, and the garage door opened.

He held the driver's door open. "Why didn't you tell me earlier about Ynez's call?"

"It wasn't any of my business, but I need you to drive me. Be here at ten thirty. We'll talk tomorrow about Ynez. Maybe I can help." She closed the car door, and the BMW disappeared into the garage.

By the time he reached the end of Jace's drive, a cigarette was lit, and Ynez's message checked. Told her never to do that. Why did she need to hear his voice? What was that about? She was too young.

For the rest of the drive home he went over everything, looking for a way out of tomorrow, but there wasn't one. Even if there was, that would be like sticking his head in the sand. Probably better to stay with her and see what she was up to.

He entered his dark apartment, went straight to the kitchen, flipped on the light, and opened the refrigerator. A bag with a takeout box from Chili's sat right in front. He lifted the container from the bag and flipped open the lid. They were beautiful, with sauce and black bean salsa. Even the smell of cold enchiladas made his mouth water.

Three sharp raps on the patio door cut through the silence. He flinched. The container slipped from his hands and squish-hit the floor. Rice bounced in all directions, but the rest stayed in the container and looked salvageable.

Another sharp rap. Probably Lenny Trumbo and his impeccably worst timing. Whatever he wanted, just stick to Soledad's story. Until it didn't work.

He opened the blinds, and there was that Audrey Hepburn look. What the hell was she doing here? He unlocked the door and slid it open. She ducked under his arm and slipped in with head down and hair swirling around her face.

"Soledad. How did you get here so fast?" He closed the door and pulled the blinds shut.

She spun and faced him. "I'm her sister, Cheyenne."

At first, he saw a twin. The hair, skin tone, height, and clothing said so. The same white blouse, upturned collar, and fluffy blue scarf. But her face was different. Very similar and very attractive, but younger, with slightly sharper features and narrower lips. Not only did she shop for Soledad, she was Soledad if anyone was watching.

"You shouldn't be here. Better go. *Now*."

She backed to the far side of the table, sat down, and gripped the sides of the table. "We need to talk."

He shook his head. "You're leaving right now." He strode to the table and grasped her wrist. "Come on."

She held the table with small fingers and white knuckles. Her feet hooked around the chair legs. "*I'll scream*."

"Please don't do that." He released her wrist and rubbed his forehead. "Wait." The open refrigerator door spotlighted his dinner. The enchiladas and black beans were salvageable, but most of the rice was scattered on the floor. He eased his fingers under the container and carefully lifted his dinner back into the fridge.

"Did I cause that? I'm sorry."

They sounded similar, too. "It doesn't matter. What matters is that you leave and never come back."

"I won't leave until you hear me out." If possible, her grip on the table tightened.

He should never have let her in. "I need a smoke for this."

He opened the blinds and door enough to stand with his back against the frame. He blew smoke into the night air. Cheyenne sat at his table, in her flipped-up collar and fluffy blue scarf, just like Soledad had six hours ago. Jesus Christ, this was déjà vu all over again.

"You have until the end of this cigarette to tell me why you're here. Then if I have to, the chair and table go out with you."

"I want to help Soledad."

"You can help best by staying out of it."

"I can't do that." Her chin dropped. Her head shook. "I'd trade places with her if I could."

"You kinda already did."

Her chin rose. Her jaw clenched. "I owe Soledad more than playing dress-up. A lot more."

Fear, determination, and confusion, all swirled around in large brown eyes. She wasn't hiding anything. This one could be believed. "Does Soledad know you're here?"

"Oh no. She has no idea."

"What did she tell you?" He flicked his cigarette butt into the courtyard and moved to the table. "You don't have to hold onto the furniture."

She squirmed in her chair, nodded, and placed her hands on top of the table. "Well, I took care of the shopping, so you two could work out your problems. Soledad was vague about that."

"Yeah, the shopping helped a lot, but start with last night."

"She called me and told me about you. I was glad to hear she has a boyfriend. I'm not so sure now."

"I hope she wasn't angry with me."

"No, no. She understands how difficult it is for you two to get together. She knows it's not your fault."

He smiled. "Thanks, I needed that. It's hard dealing with guilt. By the way, nice job on the clothes."

"Soledad's idea, she calls it a little edge. This is close to what she wore for her driver's license photo. I show her ID, and the cashier sees the clothes as much as the face."

"Smart." Not just for cashiers, but anyone watching. "Did she remember to give you the presents for your mother?"

"Oh yes. They're gift wrapped and ready for Saturday. Soledad never forgets Mama."

So that part of Soledad's story was true. "You have to admire that about her. With all that's on her mind, she doesn't miss a thing."

"I think it's because she's smart in math. She arranges a problem like a formula, then works out the solution."

"Math, huh?"

"Oh yes, she's really smart in math. She won't say

47

so, but she could have gone to college." She slouched and bowed her head. "Life cheated her."

He hunched to see her face. No fear or confusion, just pure, unconcealed guilt. "Well, things are changing for her."

She leaned forward with fidgeting hands and an uncertain smile. "Cal, can I call you Cal?"

"Sure." There was a hint of bourbon on her breath, but her eyes were clear, and not even close to slurring a word. Must have been a one-shot bracer.

"I know getting Soledad out of her situation isn't easy, and it might be dangerous for both of you, so let me help. I'll do anything, and I mean anything, at any time." She squirmed, unhooked her legs from the table, and stood. "But right now, I have to pee, real bad."

He pointed down the hall. "First door on the left."

Another thing she and Soledad had in common, a small bladder. There was no deception in this one. The best thing for her was to stay out of it, which she probably wouldn't do. So put her off. Make her think she's involved.

He stepped to the kitchen counter and grabbed his blank shopping list and a pen. This would probably work for a few days. He slid the pen and pad across the table as Cheyenne hurried into the kitchen.

"Give me your number. Don't call me or come here. If you do, you could foul up everything without knowing. Do you understand?"

She nodded and stared with big eyes.

"Completely understand?"

"Yes, Cal. Don't call or come over. You'll call me."

"For now, go home and keep your routine. I'll call

48

you when we need you." He stood and opened the sliding glass door. "I suppose you don't want Soledad to know anything about this."

"Oh no, she can't know. She'd stop me."

"You can count on me. Can I count on you?"

Her head bobbed. "I promise."

"You better go the same way you came."

She stopped at the door. "Cal, do you love Soledad?"

"That's between her and me."

"I know what I want to believe. She says you're a good man trapped in a bad business. Do you have moral absolutes?"

"What? Ahh, yeah, I suppose so."

"People who have them usually know." She looked up with the most pleading look he'd ever seen. "We have to succeed." Her voice cracked. "We just have to." She ducked her head and slipped out the door.

What the hell was that? Moral absolutes? Who asked a question like that? No one he knew, since college. He had moral absolutes. They just adapted to the situation. Never should have let her in. Everything about her said true believer on a mission. Soledad was right. She was wound tight, capable of something unpredictable and extreme, and with a martyr complex.

Chapter Five

Friday, 10:15 am

Soledad leaned close to the mirror and studied. A slight puffiness beneath her eyes, but the darkness was gone. Ten hours of sleep had helped. Couldn't afford to be that tired again, that was when mistakes happened. No telling what Cal thought yesterday. The way she'd rushed him into the bedroom, any normal man under normal circumstances would have thought he was being seduced. But she was just tired, and that nap felt so good, especially the falling asleep part. Shantelle had been right. Curled up with Cal felt good and safe.

She let her hair flow down the sides of her face and neck and over her shoulders, which combined with shadow to hide the bruises. She hooked her hair behind her ears. That revealed them. They weren't nearly as dark as yesterday but still visible. The bruises were her little edge with Cal. The only thing he believed, so she wouldn't hide them. He had to see them every time he looked at her.

She had three days, maybe four, to accomplish what was needed. Just one phone call was the only thing needed from Cal today. After that first big step, the police would find Carlos's body in the same area they'd found Shantelle's. Jace had close connections with Carlos and Shantelle. The police would see that and investigate him first and most thoroughly. Whether or not the police brought charges didn't matter. Jace only had to look guilty. Arturo Molina would take care of the rest.

She could go over it again and again, but a dead Jace accomplished so much it had to be right. She would be free of him and the Molinas, and Jace would die for killing the man who killed Shantelle. That brought a smile.

She flinched at the knock on the door.

"Soledad, hurry it up. I want to talk."

"In a minute." Whatever Jace wanted, she'd give him the Soledad he was used to. Be an irritation, even a pain in the ass, but not a problem.

Jace's knock became a pound. "Soledad, get your ass out here. *Now!*"

"All right all ready, I'm coming." She opened the door and almost tripped over the shopping bags. "Is this all the deliveries? Victoria's Secret said there might be a delay. Did they come?"

Jace shook his head. "I don't know. This better be all."

"Well, there's a few in the trunk. I'll get them."

"Then come to the bar. I want to talk." Jace rotated on his heel and marched away.

He was angry, and not just about the shopping. But what could—oh no. She pressed a palm against her forehead and squeezed her eyes shut. He'd found Shantelle's Beretta.

She raced down the hall, cut into the laundry room, and through the side door to the garage. She popped the trunk. Nothing looked disturbed. She removed the last two bags and lifted the spare tire cover. Her fingers wedged down and around the baggie-enclosed Beretta.

It was still there and should stay there. The trunk wasn't the best hiding place, but while Cal slept on his couch, there had been little time and few choices. She could have stashed it anywhere in Cal's apartment, and he wouldn't have known. No man or dog could drool like that and still be awake. Best to leave it right here for now, but it had to surface at the right time and in the right place. Just go back in with two bags and an attitude. Never let Jace see worry.

She returned to the bar and set the bags on the floor.

Jace looked up from his coffee. "Today is your doctor appointment, right?"

She nodded. "Yes, then I'll probably have a prescription to fill."

Jace leaned back, frowning.

She frowned back. "My doctor thinks I'm slightly anemic. It's a condition, not a disease. You don't have to contact any clients."

"Then what?"

"Lunch. A slow, relaxing lunch. For two days I've lived on fruit, cold cereal, and coffee. Then I have to pick up your bags and my boots, then get my nails done, including my toes. They give foot massages, too, and my feet still hurt from all that walking yesterday."

"I called Cal last night. He doesn't like driving you. I gave him an opportunity to beg out, but he didn't."

So that was what Jace had on his mind. "It's me he doesn't like, and that's his problem. He should be able to take care of one girl without her escaping—or getting killed."

Jace shook his head. "So that's what this is about. Stop blaming him for Shantelle's death. That wasn't his fault. No one felt worse. He even flew to New York for her funeral. So take it easy on him."

"You're more forgiving than me. I suppose I can just ignore him." She held out her open hand. "I need some money for the boots. There's nothing left on that card you gave me."

"What?" Jace stared, shaking his head. "You've only had it a month. It had a fifteen-thousand-dollar limit."

"I lost track. Shopping is great for stress. It's harmless, it's legal, and it's fun." She stared with a wide smile. "And all you need is money."

Jace's mouth hung open like something didn't compute. "It's not just the money. It's the spending. It might be seen as unusual." His ring tapped the side of his coffee cup. "It's a blip on the police radar. A small blip, but a blip."

"Well, I guess you should have given me a card with a smaller limit."

"I guess so." He took a deep breath. "It's probably okay, but it's my account. It could be seen as hush money."

"I never thought of that. What about my boots?"

"No card. Use cash."

She wiggled the fingers of her open hand. "Then I need some. Otherwise, I'll go to the bank for an unusual withdrawal."

Jace pulled out and opened his wallet. "How much do you need?"

She shot her hand forward and snatched the money. He stared at the empty wallet. "Damn, Soledad. Can you put it back as fast?"

She fanned out the bills. "Almost a thousand, this'll do."

"For a pair of boots?"

"Two pair, same boot, different colors."

Jace looked from his empty wallet to her.

"Jace, I know you have cash stashed around here. Just get some and replace it. Besides, my wardrobe benefits us both, but it's mine. Just write the clothes off on your taxes." Her attention shifted to movement on the monitor. "That's Cal. He's right on time. I feel good today. I'll be nice." She spun toward the hall.

"Wait. Don't forget my bags at L'Voyage. Luckily, they're paid for. Just pick them up. And on your way back, pick me up some more takeout."

"Anything in particular?"

"Surprise me."

She hurried out the front door. That went well. That was the Soledad Jace was used to.

She watched Cal park his Chevy, then back the BMW from the garage. He wouldn't be here if she hadn't intercepted Ynez's message and implied a threat. That message said a lot about how Ynez felt about him, but just like with Shantelle, there were truths he wouldn't share. That used to frustrate and hurt Shantelle. Cal didn't mind telling about his life, but serious things he passed over quickly in a matter-of-fact manner. The rest he told as funny stories.

The BMW stopped in front of the house. Cal reached back and opened the rear passenger door. She slammed it, then opened the front door and slid in.

"I hear you don't like driving me."

"It's not the driving. It's everything else." He

pressed in the code, and the gate opened. "Some ground rules. Under no circumstances do we go to my apartment. No unusual stops, and no sister meetings. And no naps."

"Sure, Cal, whatever you say."

"Jace said you have a doctor appointment. Let's take care of that first, then we need to talk."

"There's no appointment. I did a phone consult. First, we have to pick up some bags at L'Voyage for Jace, then I'll fill my prescription. Then how about lunch? You choose the place."

He nodded and turned the radio to a jazz station playing a song about a spoonful of something that people lie and die for. He didn't talk and that was just fine. Probably going over yesterday's events. Still figuring out his priorities.

They picked up Jace's bags and put them in the trunk. She filled her prescription while Cal waited in the car. He already smelled of stale smoke. When she returned from the pharmacy, he smelled of fresh smoke.

He opened the door for her. "If you're ready for lunch, I know a place about ten minutes away. It's bar food, but they have good burgers and fries. And it's a good place to talk."

"That's fine, Cal." She hadn't eaten a burger in a long time, but at the mention, she craved one.

They arrived at Jake's Tavern just as the *closed* sign flipped over to *open*. She took a step inside, pushed her sunglasses to the top of her head, and let her eyes adjust to the dim light. To the left ran a long bar with ten to twelve stools. The wall on the right, beyond the tables, held at least twenty trophies with golden metal men holding either a bat or a pool cue. Mounted

TVs hung above the bar with others evenly spaced high on the walls.

The bartender smiled and swung a towel over his shoulder. "Cal, you're early today. What can I get you?"

"Hey, Mike. How long before the kitchen opens?"

"Grill and fryers are heating up now. Want something to drink?"

Cal turned to her.

"A Diet Coke and a glass, no ice."

"A Sam Adams for me. We'll be in the pool room."

Cal led the way past the trophy wall into a recessed area with two pool tables. A four-foot-high, wood-paneled wall separated the pool room from the rest of the tavern. The top of the wall served as a shelf for bottles and glasses. He chose the farthest corner, out of view of the bar, then pulled out a chair and seated her.

She liked that. Shantelle said he was always a gentleman and always treated her like a lady. She sat back, smiling and nodding at the pool tables. "I know this place."

"You've been here before?"

"No, but Shantelle told me about it. You brought her here sometimes. Your safe place. She loved playing pool with you, even though she knew she made the game excruciatingly slow."

He smiled and a small laugh burst out. The kind that comes from the heart and mixes with memory. "I changed the rules for her. I'd cheat for her when she wasn't looking and give her a lot of do-overs. I never saw a person get so excited when she sank a ball. Didn't matter if it was hers or mine. She'd jump and squeal like she'd just won the lottery. I loved her laugh." He sighed, and his smile faded. "Maybe we shouldn't have come here."

"No, Cal, this is perfect."

"How much did Shantelle tell you about us?"

"Everything. We were best friends, like sisters. She had to talk about you. Always trying to figure you out, to know you. You tell stories, but you're not much for sharing your feelings, are you?"

Mike arrived with their drinks and menus. "Want to order now?"

"What are you getting, Cal?"

"A Big Jake's Cheeseburger, double bacon, and fries."

"Sounds good, but just a Small Jake's Burger for me, no cheese, no bacon. I'll share a few of Cal's fries." She grinned. "On second thought, I'll bet he's not the kind of man who shares his fries. A small order of fries for me."

Mike wrote on his pad. "Should be about twenty minutes." He turned and walked away.

She leaned back and crossed her arms. "Ya know, men who don't share their fries don't share their feelings. And men who share their fries share their feelings. They've done studies. It's a scientific fact. Have you ever shared your fries with anyone? And just taking some of theirs doesn't count."

"You get that from *Cosmo*?"

"Maybe. I know you didn't share many fries with Shantelle. What about with Ynez?"

Cal nodded and frowned. "I wondered when you'd bring her up."

She sipped her Diet Coke, then loosened her scarf,

and hooked her hair behind her ears. She leaned forward. "That message. Ynez said she cares a lot about you and hopes you care about her. She wanted to say *love*, but that's a word that would scare you away. I know from Shantelle you're not the kind who loves and tells. You brought me here because you've been thinking about Shantelle and Ynez."

He glanced at her neck. "I believe the bruises, so you can unhook your hair."

"Then you believe me?"

"I believe the same man who killed Shantelle did that to you. I don't know about the rest. And I don't think you know for sure either."

"I know it was Carlos Molina. Answer me this. Shantelle was killed a year ago. I still call Detective Trumbo every month, but nothing is being done. Why?"

"First of all, Lenny Trumbo won't tell you anything. But most likely, the police don't give a shit. Less likely, someone with influence doesn't want it investigated. But just because the police don't say anything, doesn't mean they don't know something."

She reached into her purse, pulled out a cell phone, and slid it to the middle of the table. "It's a throwaway. I always have a spare or two. Make an anonymous call to the police. Tell them there's a body in the same area Shantelle was found. If there is, you'll know soon enough. I already know." She laid a card on top of the phone. "Detective Trumbo's card. When I call him, he always says there're no new developments. There's one now."

Cal's gaze shifted from the phone to her. He pushed the phone back. "If it's such a good idea, you call."

She frowned. "I want it to be a man's voice."

"I'll bet you do."

"But Detective Trumbo knows my voice. I don't want the police to connect me."

"I'm sure you don't. How much are you willing to risk? Or do you just let others take risks for you?"

She stared and clenched her jaw. "Okay, Cal. I loved Shantelle, and I'll do what a sister would do." She picked up the phone and pressed the numbers. Cal cocked his head and stared with a skeptical, cynical, grinning smirk. He didn't believe she'd do it. And if she didn't, he might not believe or do anything else.

The call went through to Detective Trumbo's voice mail with instructions to leave a message after the beep. She talked in a forced whisper, using a thick Latina accent mixed with Spanish and Spanglish.

Cal's smirk faded as she switched off the phone. He leaned forward with his elbows on the table. "That was impressive."

She laid the phone and card on the table. "It's done. Do you know what it all means? What will happen next?"

"If you're right, and there's a body that's connected to Shantelle, the police will reinterview everyone, check alibis, and probably get search warrants. Jace won't like that."

"And what if Jace and Carlos Molina are connected?"

"All hell will break loose."

"Well, that's what's coming. So you better have a plan, because Jace and Carlos are involved in two murders. What if Jace ends up in jail? What if the Molinas decide that Jace knows too much? Have you thought about that?"

"Not as much as you."

"Cal, I don't want any harm to come to you or Ynez. How much do you care about her? Enough to get her out?"

He sighed and nodded. "Ynez won't survive. She doesn't belong in this business."

She frowned. "Unlike me, who was born for it."

"Don't put words in my mouth."

"Cal, do you remember the first time you drove me? Very early in my first year, only my second client."

"Yeah, I remember."

"You kept eyeing me in the rearview mirror and staring at me at each red light. Like you wanted to say something but kept swallowing your words. What did you want to say? What were you thinking?"

"I didn't know what to say. I thought you were underage and out of place."

"I was nineteen, almost twenty, but I was out of place. I made some bad choices, and so has Ynez. If someone had cared enough to help me, well, who knows? But you can help Ynez. Get her out."

"It's crossed my mind."

"Don't wait, do it now."

"You mean today?"

"I mean *right now*. Call her, tell her to pack. We'll take her to the airport."

Cal leaned back, looking nowhere in particular and shaking his head. "Slow down. These things take time."

"No, they don't. Do it before you change your mind. Before events take over and you can't. Before Detective Trumbo shows you pictures of Ynez's body with bruises on her neck."

He pushed his chair back and stood. "I need a smoke. I'm going to take a walk outside."

"Cal, wait. We know more than anyone else. If we're going to do anything, we have to do it now. Before others know what's going on. Before you care more about yourself than Ynez."

He frowned, clenching and unclenching his jaw, wrinkling and unwrinkling his forehead, as though arguing with himself and losing. He bowed his head, shook it slowly, then looked up with a chagrined smile. "I can't believe I'm gonna do this." He walked away, reaching for his phone with one hand and his cigarettes with the other.

Cal had a vested interest now. His immediate plans were intertwined with hers, but he probably didn't have a long-term plan. That would begin with his call to Ynez. The best thing now, keep him moving, and maybe distract him a little. Once Carlos's body was found, things would happen fast. They'd have to stay ahead of Jace, the police, and the Molinas.

Mike brought condiments and said their burgers would be ready in a few minutes. Cal returned, sat heavily in his chair, and slouched forward with a shrug. "Well, it's done."

"Will she go?"

He nodded. "It took some convincing, but she'll go."

She sipped her Diet Coke. "Did you have to promise to join her later?" She grinned. "And was it a lie?"

Cal leaned over the table and motioned her forward. She bent toward him, leveling her gaze to his, and she couldn't hide a small smirk.

Cal poked his face inches from hers. "*Hey, Princess.* Ya know, you can be a royal bitch. I'm trying to do the right thing, that *you* want me to do. And you give me smart-ass comments."

She blinked and swallowed. She didn't see this coming.

He sat back and crossed his arms. "What? Run out of clever, bitchy things to say? And I have shared my fries."

She bobbed her head and sat back. "I'm sorry, Cal. You're right. You are doing the right thing. I shouldn't be cynical. I guess something in me is hurt and angry that we didn't do this a year ago for Shantelle."

"Me, too. I hurt everyday because of what I didn't do. But I didn't think it was any of *your* business."

"Again, I'm sorry." Who was this man? He'd loved Shantelle, even if he'd never told her. What else hid inside?

"Well, anyway. Ynez is packing, and she'll be ready to go when we get there."

She nodded small and smiled large. "She'll need money." She reached into her purse. "Here's nearly a thousand from Jace, and I have another fifteen hundred. How much do you have?"

"Ahh, about a hundred and fifty on me."

"Well, that won't do. Think of this like a telethon, and you're making a matching donation."

His chagrined smile returned. "I can't believe I'm saying this." He eyed her like something bad was her fault. "I have emergency cash at my apartment. We'll have to go there." He leaned forward and wagged his finger. "But you wait in the car."

"Sure, Cal, whatever you say."

Mike arrived and set a plate in front of each of them. "If you need anything else, let me know."

The burger tasted great, the fries even better, as though her body were saying red meat and deep-fried potatoes were just what the doctor ordered. Cal must have been hungry, too, because he finished his burger and most of his fries before she was halfway through.

"Cal, it might not be necessary, but do you have an alibi for Wednesday night through Thursday morning?"

"Why would I need an alibi?"

"Like you said, all hell will break loose. That's when Jace will do anything to deflect suspicion. So, do you have an alibi?"

He shrugged. "I definitely have one, but it might complicate things."

It could be only one thing. "Ynez? All night?"

"Yeah. From about nine at night until nine in the morning."

"We'll deal with it." She leaned back and rubbed her stomach. "I haven't been this full in a long time. Makes me feel sleepy. I could use a nap."

Cal halted in mid-gulp and sputtered beer down his chin.

"I'm kidding. It's a joke." She couldn't suppress a giggle. "Well, Shantelle said you had a good sense of humor. I wanted to see it."

He set his mug down and wiped his mouth. "That wasn't funny."

"Yes, it was." She bit her lip to stop the giggle. "Cal, I know I've mostly just made you angry, but that was never my intent."

"I've never been exactly sure what your intent is."

"Well, we both want to help Ynez. We can agree on that."

Cal finished his last fry and drained his beer. "Then let's go."

"Wait. I should have done this before the food." She pulled out the white prescription bag from her purse and took out a plastic bottle.

"What's that?"

"Iron. I'm slightly anemic. That's one of the reasons I was so tired yesterday." She measured the prescribed amount into the supplied plastic cup. "The pharmacist said it doesn't taste good, but the pills were really big, and I even gag on aspirins." She closed her eyes, held the plastic cup in one hand, and her Diet Coke in the other. She threw the dark, heavy liquid to the back of her throat, followed by several gulps of Diet Coke. She shuddered, grimaced, and gagged down a swallow. "Mother of God, help me. That was horrible."

Cal grinned. "Now that was funny. We can leave now."

They used the drive to Cal's apartment to go over timing. They would drop off Ynez at the airport and trust her to follow through. That still gave enough time for the nail appointment, the stop at the boot store, and lastly, pick up some takeout for Jace.

They pulled in front his apartment.

Cal opened his car door. "Wait here."

"I suppose it wouldn't do any good to tell you I have to pee."

"Why didn't you go at the tavern?"

"Yuck. I don't pee in a restroom I can smell from the outside."

"Well, cross your legs. This will only take a few

minutes, and we're only fifteen minutes away from Ynez's apartment."

"Fine, just hurry."

Five minutes later Cal returned and dropped a manila envelope in her lap.

"Here's ten thousand more."

"Wow! How far are you sending her?"

"She'll need to get a place and a car and money to live on until she finds a job. She's talked about going back to school, too."

"Why, Cal, that sounds like a long-term plan developing."

"For her, not me. She's smart and wants to get into one of those medical assistant programs."

"How old is she?"

"Ahh, nineteen. Almost twenty."

"Kinda young for you."

"Yeah, I know." He turned on the radio.

She turned it down. "Who does she look like?"

Cal gave his head a slight shake. "I don't know what you mean."

"Yesterday morning, when you came to take me shopping. You and Jace talked at the bar. I said I'd wait in the car, but I didn't. I marched away, then slipped off my shoes and sneaked back and listened. Jace said she could be a star, and that she looked like someone. Who?"

He shrugged. "I have no idea where Jace got that."

"I guess I'll get a look for myself."

They rode in silence the rest of the way. Cal parked in the back by the dumpsters and led the way to a ground floor apartment. He tapped softly and waited. She stepped beside him and knocked loud and rapid.

"Crossing my legs doesn't work anymore. I'm about to leak."

The door swung open. Cal pointed as she rushed in. "Down the hall, first door on the left."

Her jeans and panties were around her ankles by the time her butt hit the seat. Thank God, Ynez hadn't packed the toilet paper. In fact, the entire bathroom looked unpacked. Towels hung on rods, two toothbrushes hung in a holder, and a razor sat on the edge of the tub. She stepped to the sink and washed her hands, then opened the medicine cabinet. It hadn't been emptied.

Footsteps ran past the bathroom, then a door slammed. More steps, knocking, followed by a door opening and closing. She cracked the bathroom door. Loud muffled voices came from the bedroom. That didn't sound promising.

Cal emerged, shaking his head. "She changed her mind. She won't go."

"Well, she has to. Let me talk to her."

"Be my guest. I can't get through to her."

She tapped on the bedroom door and eased it open. "Ynez, my name is Soledad. I'm Cal's friend. I want to help."

Ynez sat on the bed. Her shoulders slumped, her gaze blank. Even with her face smeared with makeup and tears, or maybe especially so, because Shantelle had cried over Cal, too. Her face was Shantelle's. Slightly darker skin, but the eyes, nose, and mouth were Shantelle's. But a young Shantelle, before she was a star.

Ynez swallowed and sniffed. Her eyes grew large and expectant like some magic solution was forthcoming. "I love Cal. I can't leave him."

The next thing she knew, she was sitting on the bed, hugging a crying Ynez, stroking her hair, telling her everything would be okay. Just like she had with Shantelle on more than one occasion. And for the same man. Ynez's sobs slowly subsided into a sniffling whimper.

She held Ynez by the shoulders. There was that face, forcing a pained smile. Those eyes, hoping, asking, wanting something. Hadn't figured on this. *Damn you, Cal.*

"So, you love him?"

Ynez nodded and squeezed out a few more tears.

Oh, my God. Where did that feeling come from? Sharp, fast, unexpected, but definitely there. Jealousy. That could complicate things, so just put it away and don't think about it. "Why do you love him? I have to know."

Ynez's pained smile softened. "I feel safe with Cal. When we sleep, I hold on to him and know he'll never hurt me." She shook her head in small jerks like trying to get rid of something that wouldn't leave. "Do you know what it's like to be in a place where you never feel safe? Where you never sleep safe, or wake up safe?"

She nodded. "Yes, I do."

"Where you believe what people say you are?"

She nodded again. "That, too." One of Jace's favorite tactics.

Ynez's smile spread to her eyes, making them clear and bright. "Cal makes me feel good about myself and goes out of his way to make sure of it."

"I know how important that is."

"With Cal, I come first." Ynez shook her head and smiled like something hard to believe was suddenly true. "I just know he'll fight for me, even if he knows he'll lose."

"Let's try to make sure it doesn't come to that. We'll keep you safe, but you can't stay here."

"He wants to send me to California." She clenched her jaw. "I won't go."

"Well, you have to go somewhere."

"I don't have any place, except with Cal."

"You can't stay with him. That would make things twice as dangerous for both of you. But what if you were still in Florida? My youngest sister, Josepha, goes to school in Gainesville. It's only a few hours away. You could stay with her until things settle down. Cal said you want to go to school. Gainesville has a university and a community college. You can check them out. Cal will call you every day. I'll make sure. And when it's safe, he'll come get you. I'll make sure of that, too."

"Promise?"

She crossed her chest. "I promise. Now, we don't have much time. You pack. I'll talk to Cal and tell him the new plan. And I have a few other things to tell him."

She left and closed the bedroom door. Cal stood in the middle of the living room. He glanced up from the TV.

"Thought I'd check out the local news. See if anything's developed. So, how'd you do? Will she go?"

She stomped across the room and slammed her fists into his chest. "*Damn you, Cal.*"

He staggered back. "What'd I do?"

"Why didn't you tell me she looks like Shantelle?"

"There might be a slight resemblance."

"*Slight* resemblance? She's almost a twin. If you don't see it, you're in denial or in some fantasy world." She shook her head and frowned. "Cal, I don't know what to think about you. I guess it's romantic, but it's kind of creepy, too."

"Does that mean you won't help?"

"Of course I'll help. How could I not? If anything happened to her, it'd be like losing Shantelle all over again. I couldn't live with that. But there's been a change of plans. We're sending her to Gainesville to stay with my sister."

"Cheyenne?"

"No, Josepha, the youngest. She's in prelaw at the University of Florida. Cheyenne is working on her masters at the U."

"A masters? She didn't look old enough."

She stepped back with her hands on her hips. "How do you know what Cheyenne looks like?"

"Well, ahh, she used your ID. I figure she looks like you, and you don't look old enough to be getting a master's."

"Uh huh." She narrowed her eyes. "There's something fishy here. I don't have time to get to the bottom of it now, but I will." She pointed to the bedroom door. "Go hurry her up. You'll put her on a bus to Gainesville. I'll use taxis to take care of everything else."

Chapter Six

Friday, 5:35 pm

"Cal, I'm paying for the takeout right now. Where are you?" Soledad shoved her receipt and debit card into her billfold. "Just stop in front. I'll be right out." She pushed through the door of the Tandoori Palace, carrying a white plastic bag containing four stacked Styrofoam containers. Cal reached across the front seat and opened the door. She slid in and set the takeout on the back seat. "We're right on schedule."

Cal checked the mirrors and eased into traffic. "Is everything set in Gainesville with your sister?"

"Josepha will meet Ynez at the bus station. She can stay as long as she needs. Any problems with Ynez?"

"Well, she was awfully clingy at the bus station."

She couldn't suppress a grin. "Cal, she's only nineteen. Think about it. You made a commitment to her. You're at least her protector—that she sleeps with."

"I know, I know. But I was thinking. Girls have left before. Ynez fits the profile. She's new and young and changed her mind. I can sell that to Jace. I'll wait a few weeks until Ynez is just another girl that didn't work out. Then, I'll arrange a different place for her that's safe and close by. What do you think?"

A better question, what on God's green earth was

he thinking? Oughta slap him upside the head and knock some sense into him. "That's stupid and you know it. You can't hide Ynez in Miami while working for Jace. But it won't matter. You don't seem to understand the situation." She leaned toward him. "Maybe not tonight or tomorrow, but very soon, a body *will* be found. Jace *will* be in trouble, and his entire operation *will* shut down."

"I'm not as sure of that as you." He studied the rearview mirror, then the side mirrors. "But ya know." A small smile rose as he gazed at the road ahead. "Nah, never mind."

"Cal, I saw something good on your face. What was it? Please, I want to know."

He shrugged and turned onto Biscayne Boulevard. "Ynez is out and safe, and no matter what happens, I'm glad I did it."

She grinned and nodded. Cal was looking out for a girl with nothing to gain for himself. "Why, Cal. That's a good thing. A very good thing."

"Well, maybe I do have a moral absolute."

Her ears perked. Only one person he got that from. "What did you say?"

"That I'm glad about what I did."

"After that."

"That I have a moral absolute."

He might, but he was also a liar, and not a very good one. "What's a moral absolute?"

"I'm not sure. I guess it's something inside that says what's right and wrong. Ya know, like a conscience."

She clenched her jaw and glared. "You have no idea what you're talking about. Pull over. *Right now*! I

71

don't want to hit you while you're driving."

He leaned away. "I think I'll keep driving."

"*Coward*."

Cal flicked his hand and rolled his eyes. "Whatever."

Dismissive? That would never do. "Don't you dare dismiss me."

"What put your panties in a bunch?"

"You talked to her, didn't you?"

"Who?"

That uh-oh look he tried to hide said it all. "Little miss moral absolute, that's who. Cheyenne. You talked to her. *When*? Don't lie to me, Cal."

"Whoa. Before your give yourself a wedgie, Cheyenne came to me. Last night, she was waiting on my patio when I came back from dropping you off. She wanted to help and asked me not to tell you. I sent her home and told her to stay out of it. That's the end of it."

She sat back and crossed her arms. "Oh, that little scamp. You just wait until I get a hold of her."

"What's her problem anyway? Moral absolutes? What the hell is that about?"

"I pay for her school. Cheyenne thinks if it wasn't for her, I wouldn't be in the business. She struggles with that."

Cal nodded. "She did seem in a hurry and carrying a lot of guilt."

"Drive slow, I need time to calm down. I'm not happy with either of you."

"I'm getting used to it."

Cal turned on the radio and glanced into the rearview mirror.

Getting used to it? Cal made her sound like a little

bitch that there was no hope for. She could be nice. He just hadn't given much reason. He should have told her right away about Cheyenne. If Cal ever had to tell a surprise lie, he wouldn't be convincing. He should leave that to those who knew how.

Cal slammed his hand on the steering wheel. "Damn it. The car's pulling to the right. We have a flat." He decelerated and pulled to the side of the road. "Feels like the rear passenger side." He stopped, turned on the emergency blinkers, and popped the trunk. "Call Triple-A. I'll check the spare."

"No. You call." She opened her door. "I'll check the spare."

"Stay in the car. I'll do it."

"Do as I say." She stepped out and rushed to the open trunk. She lifted the spare tire cover, stretched to the far side of the tire, grasping and pulling on the baggie enclosed Beretta. Her hand slipped from the gun. She shoved her fingers down, wedging them between the tire and the grip of the gun.

"What's the matter with you?" Cal approached the rear of the car with his phone to his ear while watching cars drive by.

She yanked the gun free and shoved it into her purse. Cal stepped beside her. She snapped her purse shut and pointed at the spare. "There it is."

"Gee, thanks. I couldn't have found it without you." Cal leaned into the trunk and pounded the spare with his fist. "Doesn't feel fully inflated. Triple-A will be here within an hour." He eyed a slowly passing gray Cadillac. "Ah, shit."

The Cadillac steered to the side of the road and stopped a couple of car lengths in front of the BMW.

"What's wrong? Who is that?"

Cal clenched his jaw. "It's Fowler. We were followed."

She clutched her purse. How could she have been so stupid? She should have seen this coming. Never underestimate Jace. "Cal, this won't be good for either of us, but he was following me, not you."

"Damn it!" He slammed the trunk shut. "I should've been more careful. Jace is going to know about Ynez."

"Trust me, Cal. Jace has a lot more on his mind than a runaway girl. She's replaceable. We all are when we become more trouble than we're worth. Tell Jace I talked you into sending Ynez home. It's all my fault. Give him every detail. Details sell a story. Blame everything on me."

"I won't do that."

"You have to. I'll make it work." She clutched his hand and squeezed. "Are you sorry you listened to me?"

He shook his head and sighed. "No, I did what I should. You just drew it out."

"Cal, listen carefully. Our stories have to match. Tell Jace you put Ynez on a bus to the airport. Under no circumstances can he know where she is. And Jace can't know about my phone call to Detective Trumbo. He would kill me for that. Tell the truth about everything else that happened today."

Fowler climbed out of the Cadillac, talking on his phone, nodding and smiling with big yellow teeth in the middle of his large, round, sunburned head. He pocketed his phone and walked toward them, grinning. His beefy fingers opened his collar, loosened his tie, and wiped away rapidly forming beads of sweat from his glistening forehead.

She squeezed his hand tighter. "You're a good man in a bad business. When it's safe, take Ynez far away and don't look back."

"What about you?"

"I have to finish what I started. Don't worry about me. I'll handle Jace. And no matter what, don't go to the police." She released his hand. "Let's see what he wants."

They moved to the side of the BMW.

Fowler pointed at Cal. "You're to wait with the car for Triple-A." He grinned at her. "Well, well, well. Soledad Montoya. So nice to see you again. You're to come with me. Your boss is waiting."

"Let me get Jace's takeout from the back seat." She opened the rear door, bent low into the car, and pulled the Beretta from her purse. She felt under the passenger front seat, but there was no place to wedge it.

Fowler stepped toward her. "Hurry it up."

She sucked in her stomach, slid the gun beneath her T-shirt and into the front of her jeans. She grabbed the takeout bag and held it in front of her stomach. "Got it."

Fowler grabbed and twisted her wrist. "Come on."

She winced and clenched her teeth but didn't make a sound.

Cal gripped Fowler's arm. "Let go of her."

Fowler nodded with a grin and released her wrist. "Sure, but she's coming with me."

She stepped between them, laying a hand on Cal's chest. "It's all right, Cal." She looked into his eyes. He was ready to fight for her, and they both knew Fowler could break him in two. "It's okay. I should go with him."

Fowler's grin widened. "Better listen to her. You're in enough trouble already."

Cal glared and released his grip on Fowler. "You were an asshole as a cop, and that hasn't changed."

She stepped toward the Cadillac. "Let's go. The takeout is getting cold."

Fowler winked at Cal. "I got a feeling we'll run into each other again when business and a girl won't save your ass."

She slipped into the back seat of the Cadillac and closed the door.

Fowler slammed his door, started the engine, and pulled into traffic. "You saved your boyfriend back there. I could have snapped his arm and left him writhing on the side of the road."

"He's not my boyfriend."

Fowler laughed. "For a moment he acted like one, but he came to his senses. You always have someone looking out for you and ready to fight. Lenny Trumbo in the old days, and now one of Jace's pimps. So what do you charge for an hour these days? Can you break a twenty?" He winked into the rearview mirror with his same old creepy smile and large stained teeth.

"Cal was right. You are an asshole."

"Oh, little sweet thing, you don't know the half of it. But one of these nights you might."

"Leave me alone." She slouched and slid to the side, out of sight of the rearview mirror. Jace would question her and Cal separately, looking for different answers for the same question, trying to separate truth from lies. Fowler only followed one of them from

Ynez's apartment, probably her, but it didn't matter. Tell Jace about Cal and Ynez. Keep his focus there. Tell him what he already knows, what he suspects, fill in details, give him the truth except where Ynez went. One lie woven into so much truth would be hard to notice.

Jace was a smart businessman who knew when to cut his losses. Bottom line, he wouldn't kill anyone over the loss of a girl, especially now. But if he suspected she was working to connect him to Carlos's body, he would kill her. Not today, but when he could plan better, when his big deal was completed.

She laid her purse against her T-shirt and felt the Beretta press against her stomach. Jace might search her. In the old days he often checked a girl's purse for drugs or a gun. Whatever else happened, he couldn't find the gun.

She set the takeout bag between her feet, bent over, and pulled out the Beretta.

Fowler adjusted the rearview mirror. "What're you up to?"

She opened the top container and glanced up. "Seeing if anything leaked."

"Sit up so I can see you."

She stuffed the gun between the double order of naan, snapped the container shut, and sat up. Get the takeout to the kitchen, hide the Beretta there. Sooner or later, the police will find Carlos's body, then they needed to find the gun.

The Cadillac turned onto Jace's private drive. In a few minutes, she had to convince Jace that everything she and Cal had done was about Ynez. Every word, every tone, every inflection, but most importantly, every emotion, must combine to sell that story.

The gate swung open. Jace stood in front of the house, feet apart and hands on his hips. Fowler's Cadillac slowed to a stop as the window glided down. He stuck his face through the opening.

"Cal Lee is waiting for Triple-A. Be glad to go back and wait with him."

Jace shook his head. "No, go to the girl's apartment. See what you can find out. I can have someone meet you with a key, might take an hour."

"Not necessary. I can get in, no problem."

She picked up the takeout bag, opened her door, and stepped out.

Jace grabbed her wrist. "Stay put." He turned back to Fowler. "How long will it take?"

"An hour to get there and search the place. How a place is left always tells you something."

Jace tapped his ring on the roof of the Cadillac. "Good. Call me as soon as you know anything."

Fowler nodded, shifted the Cadillac into gear, made a sharp U-turn, and drove away.

Jace faced her, clenching his jaw and tightening his grip on her wrist. "You have some explaining to do."

He took long strides, pulling her behind. She ran to keep from falling. He yanked her through the doorway, slung her around to face him, and slammed the door. Her heart raced. Control that. Stay calm, stay focused. Don't let a racing heart influence answers.

"Jace, I can explain about Ynez."

"I'll bet you can." He yanked her down the hall.

"I got your favorites." She pulled back and grabbed the kitchen doorframe. "Let me put the takeout in the kitchen. Then I'll explain about Ynez."

"Fuck the takeout!" Jace swung his free hand. She snapped her head away and ducked. The bag ripped from her grasp, opened, and hurtled into the kitchen. The containers smashed onto the tile floor and burst open amid squishing cracks and a muffled clank.

"It's in the kitchen now." Jace bent her left arm behind her back and rammed it up. Sharp pain shot through her shoulder. His other hand grabbed her ponytail by the roots and lifted. "Let's go." He pushed her in the back, forcing her to run on tiptoes to the bar.

"Stop! You're hurting me." Stay focused, and tell him what he suspects, what he'll know soon anyway.

"What're you and Cal up to?" He inched her arm farther up her back.

"I helped Cal send Ynez away."

"I don't care about a girl." He slowly pulled her ponytail back, forcing her to look up at him. "What did you tell Cal? What does he know?"

"Nothing about Carlos. I'm not stupid. No one can know but us."

"Empty your purse on the bar."

"I need both hands."

His hold on her hair tightened. He released her wrist and thumped the bar with his knuckles. "Dump it right there."

"Sure, Jace, sure." She slipped the purse off her shoulder and opened it several inches above the bar. First her prescription bottle and phone fell, then everything else dropped and bounced on the shiny hardwood.

She tensed, calculating the position of Jace's right shoe.

Jace reached around her shoulder, picked up her

phone, and slid it into his pocket. "I'll keep this."

She raised her right knee and grasped the top edge of the bar with both hands. Aim for his instep, but at least hit his toes.

She slammed her heel down and back.

Jace howled, his grip on her hair loosened. She swung her left elbow back, digging into his ribs. She jerked free and spun. Jace lurched, reaching for her, stumbling, grabbing the bar for support. "*You little bitch*!"

"Stop, Jace! Just stop and listen. We're in this together."

His chest heaved as he tested weight on his foot, winced, then eased onto a bar stool. "That fucking hurt." He untied his shoe and rubbed his instep.

"Be glad I'm not wearing heels. And it's your own fault. You don't have to hurt me. All you had to do was ask. I'll tell you everything."

Jace stared. "Sit down."

She slid onto a barstool, leaving one between them. "Cal's sleeping with Ynez." She softened her voice and slumped her shoulders. "He's in love with her. I helped him send her away. And it's all your fault."

Jace crossed his arms with an angry, then puzzled look. "Oh, I gotta hear this."

She leaned forward with a sad smile and folded her hands in her lap. This was it. Make everything about Cal and Ynez. Sell it now, sell it completely. She closed her eyes. A tingling sparked in her chest, spreading slowly, making each part of her body aware of all the other parts. Take a deep breath, will forth every hurt, every regret, every feeling of love for Shantelle. They were there and they were real, welling in her chest,

80

rising to her throat. Picture the photos of Shantelle's body, the bruises on her neck. See her helplessly struggling, her screams muffled, knowing she would die, then darkness.

Her eyes clenched, then slowly opened. Tears leaked from both corners of both eyes. She stared into the cold, calculating face that sent Shantelle to her death and dumped her body. Hate pounded inside, tightening her jaw, making her lower lip tremble. She bit the inside of her lip until she tasted blood.

"How could you do it, Jace? How could you hire a girl that looked so much like Shantelle? We were like sisters. It was like seeing her ghost." She held her stare, breathing hard and deep, swallowing, letting tears roll over her cheeks.

Jace leaned back and stroked his jaw with his thumb and forefinger.

She bowed her head. "I'm glad Ynez is gone, and I hope you never find her. I can't talk about this anymore. I need to think about something else." She slipped off the stool.

Jace's hand shot forward and gripped her upper arm. "Stop. Sit back down. We're not done yet."

She jerked free and returned to her stool. She sniffled, grabbed a Kleenex from the scattered contents of her purse, and daubed her eyes.

Jace swiveled to the bar. "Let's see what we have here." He picked up the white bag. "What's this?"

"My prescription, for my anemia. I got it at the pharmacy today."

"I know. Fowler kept me updated. But you didn't go to the doctor."

"They called, the blood tests came in. A visit

wasn't necessary, just the prescription."

He pulled out the bottle, read the directions, nodded, and set it in front of her. "You can keep it." He picked up her billfold and looked inside. "Not much money, but lots of receipts."

"They're receipts from the credit card yesterday and my debit card today. I gave Ynez most of my money, including what you gave me for the boots."

He set the billfold to the side. "That, I'll keep. You won't need it for a while. Now tell me everything. Let's start with Cal's phone call outside the tavern. What was that about?"

Fowler must have followed them right from the beginning. She sniffled again. "Cal was calling Ynez, telling her to pack, that we were coming to pick her up."

"Then outside Cal's apartment, what was in the envelope?"

"Ten thousand dollars for Ynez."

"Ten grand! Jesus Christ Almighty. He *must* be in love."

"He is. And don't say our Lord's name in vain. It's blasphemous."

Jace laughed. "You're a glorified hooker, and you're worrying about my blasphemy?"

"God forgives. You should start worrying about that."

He shook his head, still chuckling. "Too late, and I don't give a goddamn. Now, back to earthly matters. Where'd he take Ynez?"

"To the bus station. She was headed to the airport, and from there, I don't know. I didn't want to know, so I could never tell you. She's gone. You'll never get her back."

Jace cocked his head and studied, tapping his finger to his chin. "That's quite a story. I'm sure you and Cal got your stories straight, so they'll match."

"They'll match because it's true. Cal is different from us. He cares more about Ynez than himself. He'll risk everything to protect her. And when you love someone, you'll lie for them. You'll die for them."

"Or kill for them?"

She nodded. "Maybe that, too."

"Well, no one need die over a girl." He leaned forward with a sly grin. "You seem to have all the answers. So tell me, what should I do with Cal?"

She met his gaze. Quell everything inside. Jace was formulating, so use logic. "Nothing. At least nothing drastic. Remember, we're in something much bigger, and we're in it together."

"So you've told me. Although sometimes I think you're in separately, but continue."

She had to turn it around and have Jace answer questions. Make it about Fowler and Carlos, Cal and Ynez, anybody but herself. "We can't do anything to draw attention. You made a mistake bringing Fowler in. What did you tell him? That man would sell out his own mother, if he ever had one."

"I'm not stupid either. For him, it's all about a missing girl. Where she is and who helped her."

"Get rid of him, before he starts wondering. Someone is probably looking for Carlos. You had deals with him, and yes, I was one of those deals. That's a connection, and sooner or later the police and the Molinas will come to us."

Jace tapped his ring on the bar. "Yeah, I've thought

about that. Tell me, why shouldn't I gift wrap you and take you to the Molinas?"

"Because they'll kill you, too. And you already thought of that." Jace knew she was right. He'd give her to the Molinas only as a last resort, the last straw to grasp.

Jace stopped tapping his ring, made a fist, and punched his open hand. "What's that goddamn smell?"

"The spilled takeout. Roaches can smell through walls. I can practically hear them squeezing into the house and running across the floor." She shivered. "That makes my skin crawl." She slipped off the stool and stepped wide around Jace. "I have to clean it up right now."

"Wait, I have more to say." Jace eased off the stool and limped after her.

She raced down the hall, cut into the kitchen, scanned the floor, and snatched a roll of paper towels from the marble counter. There it was in front of the refrigerator. The Beretta had popped out of its baggie and lay covered in chicken vindaloo and rice. She reeled off several sheets, knelt, and reached toward the Beretta.

"Anything salvageable?" Jace stood on one foot with his hands braced high on the doorframe.

Stay calm, and don't draw attention to the spill. She looked over her shoulder while laying paper towels over the gun.

"No, it's all ruined." She reeled off more towels.

"Even the bread?" Jace limped forward. "Now I'm hungry."

She laid more paper towels over the spill. "You still have ribs leftover from last night." She stood and pointed to the far side of the small wooden breakfast table. "Go sit down, away from the spill. I'll microwave the ribs for you." She leaned over the spill and opened the refrigerator. Jace hobbled three steps, pulled out a chair, and sat with his injured foot stretched under the table. "Cold is fine, and grab a bottle of beer."

She grabbed the rib container and a beer and set them on the table. Jace popped open the container and dug in.

She returned to the spill, knelt with her back to Jace, and wrapped the soggy towels around the naan and Beretta. She scooped them up and glanced over her shoulder. Jace ripped off a rib and gnawed meat off the bone. She lowered the mess into the trashcan. So far so good, now continue with the distraction.

"What will you do to Cal?" She dropped the last of the towels and broken containers into the trashcan.

"That's none of your concern."

She gave her hands a quick rinse and returned to the table. "Shantelle was in love with Cal. You didn't know that, did you?"

Jace shook his head. "No, no, I didn't." He shrugged. "It happens. So what?"

"And they were lovers for over a year until she was killed."

Jace leaned back, wagging a rib at her. "You should have told me."

"Why? So you could stop something that made her so happy, and it wasn't doing anybody any harm. When you hired Ynez, you hired a young Shantelle, and that made something snap in Cal—and me."

"Stop!" He shoved his hand in front of her face. "You already told me that shit, and none of it matters now. I need to control the situation, which means controlling you. You'll stay at the house for a while. No phone, no computer, no outside contact."

"What about Cal?"

"I haven't decided anything, except that I can't trust him."

She slid into the chair opposite him. "Look at it this way. If Cal had come to you about Ynez, what would you have done?"

Jace stopped chewing. "I would have moved her to another manager and kept a close eye on both of them."

"And if they persisted?"

He cocked his head and stared into space. "If it looked like I'd lose them both, I'd put a price tag on her. No lump sum. Have Cal work at half salary for a year. He's been with me for ten years. He'd honor the deal and knows I would, too. Anyway, a lot can happen in a year. People change their minds."

"Then treat this that way. Don't make waves, especially now. Make a deal with Cal and keep things running as usual."

He bobbled his head. "I'll consider that, but I want to hear what Fowler finds." He leaned forward with his elbows on the table. "That doesn't change your situation. You stay."

"You've already made that clear." She rose from her chair, grabbed the broom, and swept scattered grains of rice.

"Good, because sometimes people see things and get ideas. *Don't*. You're mine until I let you go. Anyway, men don't want to save the Shantelles of the world. They want to save the Ynezes, the young and only slightly used. That's what Cal did. He and

Shantelle worked together for several years, but he waited to save the younger version. It's too late for you, too."

"I know what I am. I have no illusions."

Jace ate in silence while she mopped the spill area.

After all she'd done, maybe it was too late. Jace didn't take anything she hadn't given. More like sold. It always came back to money. She just needed to finish what had to be done. Maybe there was an answer at the end.

She finished mopping and returned to the table.

"Jace?"

He looked up with threads of meat stuck between his teeth and sauce at the corners of his mouth. "What now?"

"What about Sunday? I've gone to church every last Sunday of the month for over six years. It would look unusual if I didn't go. Cheyenne might come looking for me."

He wiped his mouth with the back of his hand. "We have a few days. We'll see how things go, then revisit that. But if you go, Cal won't drive you." He licked his fingers one at a time.

"If you're done." She picked up the container of cleanly picked bones. "I'll take out the garbage."

"Leave it." He pulled out his phone. "Did you pick up those bags at L'Voyage?"

She nodded. "They're in the trunk."

"At least you did one thing right. Go to your room. Locks and alarms are all set, so don't try anything stupid."

"Jace, if I was going to run, I would have already. But that would be stupid."

She turned and walked from the kitchen and down the hall. Her room wasn't a mess, but Jace had obviously searched. Probably looking for guns and phones. And probably sooner than later, the police would search, too, looking for the same things, plus clothes with gunshot residue. Nothing to find. The clothes she wore and the empty shell casings from shooting Carlos had been smuggled out in Mama's gift bag. Little Sis would permanently dispose of them.

She leaned her back against the door, sinking slowly to the floor. Jace seemed to buy that she was resigned to her circumstances. Hopefully that would make him less watchful, less suspicious. He came away unsure about everything that happened, but seemed to be looking to confirm her story, not disprove it. A big difference. He had a truth he could deal with and control. He'd check her story, and even if he didn't completely believe her, at least his attention was on Ynez and Cal. Fowler would confirm that Ynez was gone, and Cal would stick to their story about Ynez going to the airport. She sighed and smiled. Cal was a good man. He'd try to take the blame. When it came to his girls, and maybe her, too, he'd protect.

She took a deep breath and exhaled slowly. Maybe the garbage was as good a place as any for the gun. The maid and the garbage service came Monday. Things would be out of her control, and out of Jace's, too. Detective Trumbo needed to follow up on that call and find Carlos's body.

Chapter Seven

Saturday, 11:30 am

Cal jerked awake, lifted his head from the back of the couch, and wiped drool from the corner of his mouth. He blinked blankly at the muted television as breaking news headlines scrolled along the bottom of the screen. Must have fallen asleep watching the news, waiting to see if a body was found, hoping a girl hadn't been killed, that Soledad was wrong about what she'd heard, and everything was a mistake.

He uncrossed and lifted his legs from the coffee table, careful to miss a glass, a full ashtray, and an empty bourbon bottle. Thinking and drinking never accomplished anything and usually led back to the same questions without answers. A shower and shave would help, but first a couple aspirin and especially coffee.

He trudged to the kitchen and prepared the brewer. In a few minutes, the cure would begin. Things wouldn't seem as bad as they had yesterday. Everything that happened would become clear and explainable and make life a lot easier.

He lifted the cup, inhaled the steaming coffee aroma, and sipped that first slow soothing drink. His gaze settled on the empty chair where Soledad had told her story and revealed her bruises. He shook his head. No, life wasn't gonna get any easier.

Three aspirins rattled into his hand. He threw them to the back of his throat and took another sip of coffee. Big mistake. He shuddered. Three quick slurps washed down the bitter, melting aspirin.

Last night, Jace had grilled him pretty hard, asking every detail and getting the truth except where they sent Ynez. Soledad was right. The one lie blended unnoticed with everything else. She must have taken the blame for Ynez, because Jace seemed very understanding, nodding like he already knew the what and why of everything. Turning the incident, as he called it, into a business deal. Work for a year at reduced pay to cover his business loss. After six months, buy out the balance with a lump sum plus only ten percent. Essentially, buying Ynez at an employee discount. He'd left Jace feeling relieved that nothing worse had happened, not even asking about Soledad. Jace's last instructions—don't talk to anyone and don't go anywhere. Time for a cigarette.

He opened the sliding glass door and leaned his back against the doorjamb. Back came images of that son of a bitch Fowler's hairy, meaty hand grabbing Soledad. Her eyes telling him it was all right when they both knew it wasn't. Protecting him by leaving with a man that made her skin crawl. Why did it have to be Fowler? How could he walk away from that? Only a selfish son of a bitch, without even one moral absolute, would do that.

He lit a cigarette and inhaled deeply. The smoke felt good in his lungs but made his head a little cloudy. Getting fired would have been better, freeing him to take Ynez far away and not look back. That's what Soledad said to do. She had squeezed his hand and released him from any real or imagined obligation to her. But if he left, he'd always look back and always see Soledad. And not just her, he'd see Fowler taking her. Why in the hell did it have to be Fowler? Anybody but him.

He took a deep drag, then spoke to the sky as smoke puffed from his mouth. "How in the hell did I get into this?"

"Get into what?"

He snapped his head to the voice. The cup dropped from his hand and shattered on the patio. "Lenny! Jesus Christ, don't sneak up on a person like that."

Lenny pushed his narrow-brimmed hat back a few inches and shook his head. "I wasn't sneaking. So what the hell *did* you get into?"

"Ahh, nothing." He flicked his half-smoked cigarette into the grass. "It's personal."

"Maybe. But we need to talk."

Didn't need this. Lenny was a good cop. They went back to Lenny's days in vice, but not now. "This isn't a good time."

"I think it is. If we go downtown, it's Detective Trumbo. Here, it's Lenny."

"All right, come in." He scanned the courtyard but didn't see anyone.

Lenny stepped around the shattered cup and spilled coffee. "Kinda jumpy, aren't you?"

"Just tired."

Lenny looked like a cop. In his late forties, five-nine or ten, and about a hundred-sixty wiry pounds. He always wore a dark suit, narrow black tie, and that stupid Popeye Doyle hat that made him look like a detective from an old black-and-white movie. One of the good cops who was tough but fair. He closed the door and turned to Lenny. "Did anyone see you?"

"Not anyone that's looking. Is someone looking?"

"No, but I could have met you somewhere else. Someone might think I'm your snitch."

Lenny poked him in the chest. "Hey, asshole, I parked a block and a half away and came to the back. Would you rather I knocked on the front door?"

Lenny was right. "Sorry. Have a seat and tell me why you're here."

"How about some coffee. I could use some, and you didn't get to finish yours."

"Sure." He grabbed two mugs from the overhead cabinet. "Why are you here?" He set a steaming mug in front of Lenny.

"Good coffee, nice aroma." Lenny leaned forward with his elbows on the table. "Shantelle Williams. It's still an open case. And it's still mine."

"I told you all I knew during the investigation, and it was the truth."

"Maybe it wasn't everything. Probably no one wanted the killer caught more than you, except for maybe Soledad Montoya. Ya know, she still calls me at least once a month, wanting to know if there's anything new. Of course, I can't tell her anything, even when there is."

"Is there?"

Lenny pushed his chair back, stood, and stretched, then wandered to the living room entrance. "I see you're watching the news channel. Looking for something in particular?"

"What? No. It's just on. Again, is there something new?"

"Maybe. Yesterday, I got an anonymous call saying there's a body near where Shantelle was found. Know anything about that?"

He shook his head. "How should I? I didn't make the call."

"I know. When's the last time you saw Soledad?"

"Ahh, yesterday afternoon. I took her shopping, to the pharmacy. Ya know, errands."

"Kind of a demotion for you, isn't it?"

He shrugged. "There wasn't anyone else. Anyway, I take her to church once a month."

"Yeah, I know that, too. Saint Anthony's. It's near where her family lives. Back to the errands. Were you with her the whole time?"

"No. I dropped her off. She'd call when she was ready. Why are you asking me? Maybe you should talk to Soledad."

Lenny shook his head. "Not yet. Whoever made that call doesn't want to be identified. And a cop poking around, too close, too soon, might put that person in danger. That's why I came to you."

"Can't help you. So unless you're taking me downtown, I need a shower and a shave, and I haven't eaten yet." He opened the blinds and the patio door.

Lenny nodded and set his cup on the table. "Okay, I need to go over our old interviews. Might be something there that means more now." He pulled out a card and laid it next to his cup. "Call the cell number anytime." He stopped at the door and pushed his hat forward a few inches. "You seem a little nervous, slept in your clothes, and it's almost noon. Got something on your mind?"

"Whatever it is, it's my problem."

"Maybe it's someone else's, too. Soledad and I go back a long way. I don't want her getting hurt."

"Neither do I. She's fine. She can take care of herself."

"Not always." Lenny stopped at the open door. "Oh, one more thing. Carlos Molina is missing."

He froze for a fraction of a second, then sipped coffee and glanced over his cup. "So?"

Lenny held a stare. "You know who he is, don't you?"

"Yeah, Arturo Molina's son. How long has he been missing?"

"Not sure. Maybe a week. We're working on that. When's the last time you saw him?"

"It's been over a year. He was leaving Jace's as I was arriving. He drove away in a restored, cherry red, seventy-two Chevelle SS."

"Yeah, we're looking for that, too. Was he ever a client?"

"Not that I know of. People don't use their real names. Maybe Jace knows. Now if that's all?"

Lenny nodded. "Okay, Cal. That's all for now, but I'll keep in touch." He stepped toward the door, then stopped and turned. "There's a good possibility that the call and Carlos Molina gone missing are connected, so leads are followed up more vigorously, and lab tests go to the top of the list. So let me give you some advice. Keep the news on, be careful who you trust, and stop drinking."

"Yeah, yeah, I'll do that. I can take care of myself."

"Hey, asshole." Lenny poked him in the chest in the same spot as before. "It's not you I'm worried about. The only reason I never busted your ass is because whoever replaced you would be worse. But I might change my mind." He shook his head. "How the hell did you get into this business anyway?"

He shrugged. "Kind of an accident. I met Shantelle when I drove a cab. She had a great sense of humor, and we laughed a lot. Times when she didn't have a driver, she'd call me. Then an opening for a driver came up, and she set up an interview. Jace liked me."

"Yeah, you're likeable. But that only gets you so far. Why'd you stay?"

"I don't know. I just stayed and took what came along." He shrugged again. "I guess I took the path of least resistance."

"Well, you got resistance now, and you owe Shantelle. A man should pay his debts. That's how he stays a man."

That didn't sound like a cop talking, but Lenny was right. "I want Shantelle's killer found, and I don't care who or how powerful his boss is. When I can help, I will."

Lenny nodded and studied. "I know that. That's another reason I don't bust you. But don't wait too long." He stepped through the door, surveyed the courtyard, and walked away.

Whoa. That was some pretty heavy shit Lenny said at the end. Paying debts, being a man. Combine that with Cheyenne's moral absolutes, and there would be no following the path of least resistance. One thing was very clear. Lenny was looking out for Soledad and thought she was in danger. He was real serious about that. Sounded like he had an overdue debt of his own.

Lenny didn't give information for nothing. He

threw out baited lines, hoping for a nibble. He didn't come out and say it, but Lenny thought there was a good chance Carlos was the body in the call. Lenny had it wrong, though. Soledad said the body was another girl that Carlos killed and Jace helped dump. Something didn't add up. Carlos was missing and maybe dead. Not missing a week, because according to Soledad, Carlos was at Jace's house three days ago and left with Jace following him. Carlos hadn't been seen since. No wonder Jace was keeping a close eye on Soledad.

If Carlos was dead, that trumped everything. A dead girl brought a detective, but a dead Molina brought the full investigative powers of the Miami PD *and* the Molina family.

He could shake his head and doubt everything, but Soledad's bruises were real, and just like with Shantelle, caused by a small hand coming from behind. When they had napped together, he saw them up close and personal. Soledad may have been mistaken or lied about everything else, but not that. She said she had to finish what she started. Maybe his wisest move was to stay out, maybe even get out. Just empty his bank account, drive to Gainesville, pick up Soledad, and don't look back. Ahh hell, get it straight—pick up *Ynez*—and don't look back. He shook his head. Soledad was becoming that unscratchable itch.

Why the hell did it have to be that son of a bitch Fowler? Anybody but him. Because right now, Fowler taking Soledad trumped everything. It shouldn't, but it did, and that wouldn't change. Had to find out if Soledad was okay. Even if she was, how long would that last?

He moved to the same chair where Soledad had

showed her bruises, and Cheyenne had clutched the table. Ahhh, shit. He was gonna do it, knew it was stupid, but was gonna do it anyway.

There it was, beside two days of unopened mail, the pad with Cheyenne's number. Maybe somehow, she kept in touch with Soledad. Probably a long shot with risks. The one encounter with that intense, young woman had left him shaking his head and wondering about moral absolutes. But there was no question about her motives and loyalty. Everything was for Soledad. Another person with a debt to pay. He pressed the numbers.

"Who is this?"

A quick, tense voice. It was Cheyenne all right. "Cheyenne, this is Cal."

"Hold on." Silence, then the sound of a closing door. "I don't want Mama to overhear. I'm glad you called. I was just about to come to your place. I have—"

"Whoa, stop right there. Please don't ever do that. Have you heard from Soledad?"

"Not since Thursday night after the shopping. When I call her, it goes to voice mail. She should've called me about church tomorrow, but—"

"Leave this to me. Call me if she contacts you. I'll do the same for you."

"Cal, you didn't let me finish. I was coming to find you because Soledad and I have always had an emergency escape plan."

"Hold on. Slow down." This had to be headed off. Some half-baked escape plan would only make things worse. "Listen to me carefully. Don't do anything. Leave this to me."

"No, I won't. You listen to me. And stop interrupting."

Bossy must run in the family. "Okay. Let's hear it."

"First, don't judge me by our first encounter. I may have come across as a little intense that night, but I meant what I said. I'm focused now and have a clear goal. Soledad and I were supposed to talk Friday about escaping tomorrow. She was waiting for something to happen. She didn't say what. Did anything happen?"

Maybe Soledad was waiting for Carlos's body to be found or Ynez to escape. "Things haven't stopped happening."

"Well, I haven't heard from her, so I'm assuming she needs to escape. I thought your knowledge of her boss, procedure, and circumstances would help. Tomorrow, I *will* carry out that plan with or without your help. If you care about Soledad, meet me at Saint Anthony's in an hour."

Damn. Certainly a different sounding Cheyenne, and she didn't leave much room for argument. "Just answer me one question. How do you even know Soledad will be at church tomorrow? Jace won't let her out of the house."

"Cal, I grew up with Soledad. She gets people to do what she wants. She'll be there. Anyway, I have a plan. Do you?"

She might be right. For two days Soledad had gotten him to do things he never thought he'd do. People underestimated Soledad at their own risk. Good chance she'd be there. Anyway, he didn't have a plan. "Okay, I'll be there in an hour."

"Come to the back, to the clergy parking. No one

will bother us there. I'll show you our plan. You're an important part. Goodbye, Cal."

He slid his phone into his pocket. An important part of Cheyenne's plan. Why the hell not, he was part of everyone else's plan. Just keep them straight, and see how they fit together. One thing for sure, if Soledad came to church tomorrow, she'd have an escort the whole time, and it wouldn't be him. Any escape depended on separating Soledad from her escort, and his part would be as the separator. No doubt about it, the escort would be Fowler. Ahh, shit. Anybody but Fowler.

Chapter Eight

Saturday, 1:45 pm

Cal turned his Impala from a one-way street to the back entrance of Saint Anthony's. Fowler had tried to follow, but a tactic from a movie ended that. Just stopped at green light until the instant it turned red, then gunned through the intersection. Almost caused a few accidents, but it blocked the intersection long enough to lose Fowler.

The church, plus its school buildings, playgrounds, and parking lots, took up an entire block. He was familiar with the outside of the red brick and white mortar church from dropping off Soledad once a month for six years, but had never seen the inside.

He drove through the near empty school parking lot toward the back of the church. Cheyenne sat on concrete steps leading to a back door. She motioned him forward and pointed to a parking space with a sign that read, *Father Fernando Brady.*

He stepped out of his car. She wore blue jeans and a sweatshirt with her hair in a ponytail.

She patted the space beside her. "I'm glad you came. Soledad needs us."

He sat down and rested his forearms on his knees. "So what's your plan?"

She faced him as she tucked loose strands of hair

behind her ears. She wore no makeup, her jaw was set, and her eyes focused on his.

"Are you here to help or talk me out of it?"

"I'm here to help."

"Good." She grabbed his hand and popped up. "Come with me. It's better that I explain while I walk you through each step. Let's go to the starting point."

She took the stairs two at a time, tugging on his hand, up the concrete stairs and into a room with tables, chairs, and closets but empty of people.

"This is the usher room." She pulled him to a door on the opposite end and stopped short. She whispered, "We're about to enter the adoration chapel. Father Brady is in there, but we don't need to talk to him, so just follow me."

She led him into the chapel. At the opposite end a priest knelt before an altar. High on the wall above the altar, Jesus hung on a cross. On both sides were electric candles and statues of Mary and baby Jesus complete with halos.

Cheyenne pulled him with long strides across the back of the chapel, through another door, and into the center of the lobby. She pointed to the middle of five large wooden doors that led outside.

"That's where Soledad will enter."

"I know. That's where she always enters, but I guarantee you, this time she'll have an escort, and it won't be me."

"Soledad said that might be the case, and I've planned for it." She spun and led him through the middle of three doors to aisle seats of the back row of pews. She clasped her hands, bowed her head, and moved silent lips, then looked to the ceiling and crossed herself. "We need all the help we can get. Now, this is where Soledad and her escort will sit."

"How can you be sure? What if they don't sit here?"

"Cal, these seats *will* be empty. I've arranged it. Trust me on that. And men always want to sit in the back. Then ten minutes before the service is over, Soledad will decide to leave early."

"But what if her escort doesn't want to?"

She rolled her eyes. "Men never pass up an opportunity to leave church early. Soledad will make it happen."

She was right. Fowler wouldn't object to leaving early, and Soledad did make things happen. "Okay, then what?"

"I'll show you." She grabbed his hand. "We need to go back to the lobby." She led him back through the middle door, then turned and pointed to the door they had just come through. "Soledad will exit through that door. You'll be waiting out here. The lobby will be empty. I've arranged that, too." She faced him and took hold of both his hands. "Your job is to get Soledad away from her escort." She squeezed his hands. "Can you do that?"

He couldn't help but grin. Saw this coming, and the escort would be Fowler. But in the time it took Fowler to break him in two and leave him writhing on the floor, Soledad could get away. He shrugged. "Sure, no problem."

"Good. Once that happens, Soledad will go through the door to the adoration chapel. Father Brady will make sure that no one follows. I'll be dressed like Soledad and stay with Father Brady. Anyone watching will think I'm her. I'll stay while Soledad sneaks out through the usher's room. I'll have my car waiting for her. Let's go."

She led him back through the chapel, across the usher room, and out the back door. She pointed across the clergy parking lot to the school parking. "I'll have my car parked at the school, waiting for Soledad. Come on, I'll show you."

They walked through the parking lot and school grounds, past a few school buildings to a staff parking lot. She pointed to the intersection of the street Soledad would leave by and the cross street.

"They're both one-way. Even if someone figures she's getting away through the back, they have to go the long way around with two lights. It takes at least eight minutes to drive from the front of the church to here. I've tested it several times. We walked here quickly, and it only took three minutes. Running cuts that in half. I tested that, too. Everything is planned and timed. It'll work."

She talked a mile a minute, going back over the plan as they returned to the concrete steps. Other than his job of taking care of Fowler, the plan was short and simple. But everything depended on a priest guarding a door and making sure no one followed.

"How much have you told the priest? Does he know about me?"

She stared with a glare. "His *name* is Father Brady. I told him who you are and what your part is. He knows Soledad wants to get away from bad people, and he will help."

"You, wait here." Couldn't trust a man without asking some questions and sizing him up, even if he was a priest. "I want to speak with Father Brady."

She cocked her head. "What are you going to say?"

"I just want to be sure he knows what he's doing."

"Ahhh." She screwed her face up like bad news was coming. Like part of her plan might have a flaw. "Now, Cal, don't be alarmed by Father Brady's appearance. He's dying of cancer. He's been sick for months and has lost a lot of weight. But he'll do what he says. Father Brady baptized Soledad. She grew up as one of his flock. He feels he failed her and our family. He's heard Mama's, mine, and Soledad's confessions for years, waiting, hoping, trying to make things right. Father Brady has to be a part of this. We both do. He knows he's running out of time. He has strength that doesn't show on the outside. You can count on him."

"I still need to talk to him. You wait here." The Montoya sisters had a lot more faith in God and his representatives than he did.

He tapped on the chapel door and pushed it open. "Father Brady."

The priest turned from the altar and strode forward with straight, upright shoulders and an honest, friendly smile on a tired face. A tall man, his coat and shirt draped loosely on a skinny frame. He had a worn almost haggard look with sunken cheeks. Deep permanent wrinkles stretched across his forehead, but his dark, steady eyes had strength.

"Yes, Cal."

"Father, we need to talk. So I'll get right to the point. Do you know exactly what you're doing and why?"

Father Brady folded his hands against his chest. "God has given me faith. Not only in Him, but in my fellow man. Faith to follow my heart, and faith in the hearts of others. I will open a door so that Soledad can take a new path that leads back to God." He leaned closer with grim determination on his face and in his eyes. "And no one will follow."

This man believed what he said and would do what he said or die trying. He might not stop Fowler from following, but he'd at least delay him enough.

He nodded. "Okay, Father, I'll see you Sunday."

Cheyenne stood at the bottom of the concrete steps with feet apart and hands on hips. "Well?"

"He'll cover the door."

"I already knew that."

"How long have you had this plan?"

She thought for a few seconds. "Ahh, since high school, but the time was never right. Soledad always had things she wanted to accomplish first."

"What changed?"

She shrugged and smiled. "Maybe it's you, and I thank God for that. Or maybe because her friend Shantelle died. Soledad keeps secrets. Some she can't share. Others I wish she would share with me. The only thing that matters is that it's now. Do you have any suggestions?"

He had one for a focused Cheyenne, but not for a crazy Cheyenne. "There is something you can do, if you can pull it off."

"I'll do anything."

The second time she said that, and each time her dark brown eyes grew bigger and her teeth clenched harder. Like she wanted something that would make her suffer for Soledad.

He took a big breath. "I'm sure Jace has Soledad's

cell, so I can't call her. No telling what Jace will do if he thinks we're planning something. But you can call, so call her every few hours and leave messages. Get more impatient with each call. Threaten to come looking for her if she doesn't call back and come to church tomorrow. But it has to sound natural." He stared down with the most serious look he could muster. "Can you do that?"

She nodded a confident smile. "Yes, I can, and I know just how to do it. But if she doesn't call back, that doesn't mean she won't be here. You still have to come to church tomorrow."

"I'll be here. In the meantime, make those calls, and call me regularly. But right now, I need to get something to eat and do some serious preparation."

Chapter Nine

Saturday, 4:20 pm

Soledad sat on the edge of her bed, watching TV. Still no breaking news headline about the police finding a body, but they would soon. When they did, Jace might not know exactly what to do, but he'd keep her locked up. Maybe as a bargaining chip with the Molinas, but he could never explain away dumping the body. He would see his situation as bad and getting worse with his options becoming fewer and more immediate.

Fowler was another problem for Jace. He was that survivor cockroach who would do whatever necessary to save himself. He'd sell out Jace, disappear, or both. Jace would find himself on an island with Hurricane Molina headed right at him.

Until now, she had stayed one step ahead of everyone. Getting Jace and Cal to move in the necessary directions hadn't been easy and only worked because of what she said and how she said it. Words were her best tool and maybe her only tool. Once the police found Carlos's body, things would spiral out of control. Arturo Molina was the key. He needed to suspect, then conclude, that Jace killed Carlos.

Influencing the Molinas had to be done in person. They had to hear, and most importantly, see the words come from her, which couldn't happen locked in Jace's house. Time to get out.

Cheyenne's escape plan was the best option. Work on Jace and somehow talk him into letting her call Cheyenne and go to mass on Sunday. Threaten, beg, and reason, while nagging and whining. A time-tested method.

If Cal was smart, he'd already picked up Ynez and wasn't looking back. Still, how smart could he be, running off with a nineteen-year-old? That wouldn't last long. He'd spend his energy taking care of Ynez instead of building a life with her. If left to his own devices, Cal would go back to driving a cab. He needed a smart, strong woman to guide, push, and love him. That wasn't Ynez, but if nothing else, he'd make sure she was safe and felt safe. What Cal did best.

A wide, cheek-stretching smile sprang forth. Ohh, that nap, falling asleep with Cal had felt so good. Maybe it was fatigue and the anemia, but curled up against him, feeling out of harm's way. Hadn't felt like that since Bernardo was her pillow.

The tapping on her door transitioned into a hard knock. "Come on out here. Fowler brought something by that you need to see. And we need to discuss."

She cracked the door. "Is Fowler out there?"

Jace planted his foot between the door and frame. "No. He's keeping an eye on Cal."

She nodded and followed Jace into the living room.

He grinned and pointed at the couch. "Have a seat, get comfortable."

That sounded smug. "What's going on, Jace?"

"Dadeland Mall has state-of-the-art security equipment, and I managed to secure a video from

Thursday."

She sank into a corner of the couch, hugging her legs against her chest and resting her chin on her knees. Jace sat at the bar, pointing the remote control at the TV.

"It's a compilation and easy to put together. Just had them follow my credit card charges." His grin widened into a smile as he clicked on the video showing Cheyenne handing over a credit card at Saks. "See anything suspicious?"

Her arms tightened around her legs. Her chin lifted from her knees. "No."

He fast forwarded through Cheyenne at Nordstrom's, then Camuto's, and Victoria's Secret. "What do you see?"

Did he see it wasn't her? Stick with the story. See where he's going. "I'm shopping at the mall Thursday."

"And that's what I'm supposed to see. I watched it a few times before I realized." His smile rose, showing teeth. "It's not what you see, but what you don't see."

Don't volunteer anything. Let him explain. "I don't know what you mean."

"Keep watching, smart girl. What don't you see?"

Cheyenne stopped at another store, again handing over the credit card. Jace was leading up to something. Don't let him see even a hint of uneasiness. She yawned. "I give up, Jace. What don't I see?"

Jace fast forwarded to Cheyenne walking through the mall, then paused the video and walked to the screen. He pointed at Cheyenne signing a receipt.

"I see you maxing out my credit card." Jace returned to his seat, crossed his arms, and hit play.

Thank God the video was a little grainy. He didn't

know it was Cheyenne. If he studied carefully, he'd see an identical purse but a slightly different billfold. Identical clothes but a slightly different face. Cheyenne had done a good job with her lipstick, making fuller lips with a wider mouth. Keeping her head tilted downward so hair hid the sides of her face. But the sunglasses rested on a slightly longer and thinner nose. Jace was so pleased with what he didn't see, he didn't see what was there. But what was he getting at?

Jace paused the video, then walked to the couch and loomed over her.

"There's no Cal, anywhere, in any of the security videos. Not even smoking in the parking garage. He was supposed to stay with you the whole time. Where was he?"

She shrugged, giving her best chagrined smile. Jace thought he was so clever, but he had outsmarted himself. "I guess it doesn't matter now. He was with Ynez."

Jace nodded. "Yeah, I kinda thought so, and that fits. But I can never be sure, because you lie so well."

Turn this around right now. Make Jace think and answer questions. "Which will come in real handy when the police come knocking on our door, and they will soon. You should worry less about Cal and me, and pay more attention to the Molinas. Don't you think they're already looking for Carlos?"

"Yes, I do."

"They'll look for unusual behavior. I've been going to church every last Sunday of the month for six years. It'll look strange if I don't go. Cheyenne will expect me. She'll wonder."

Jace walked to the bar and poured a scotch.

"What's your sister capable of?"

Jace didn't drink this early in the afternoon. Something was up. "She's religious and takes church very seriously. She worries about my soul. She might come looking for me, or even call the police."

Jace took a long drink. "She keeps calling your phone. Five calls today. She's reading bible verses—long ones."

"She isn't reading. She knows them by heart. Let me call. Let her know I'll be there tomorrow. Just to church and back. I don't want the police or the Molinas noticing us. If one of us is caught, both of us are caught. I won't do anything stupid."

Jace drained his glass and poured another. "I'll think on it. But if I let you go, Fowler will drive you and accompany you inside."

She cringed, pressed her hand to her stomach, and pretended to vomit. "He's the most disgusting man on earth. A fat cockroach. I won't use the guest bathroom anymore, because he has. When this is over, I'll fumigate the house, but I still won't use that bathroom."

"Stop being a drama queen. It's either Fowler or you don't go."

"He can't touch me or talk to me."

"That'll depend on you."

She let out a huff. "If that's the only way, I guess I have no choice."

Jace rubbed his forehead and pulled her phone from his pocket. "Call your sister."

"And tell her what?"

Jace sighed and frowned. "That you'll be at church tomorrow." He held out the phone.

She jumped off the couch and ran to the bar.

"Thank you, thank you."

He pulled her phone back. "You won't talk to or visit with anyone."

"Whatever you say, Jace. I just want to go to mass."

"Just in for the service and out."

She nodded and wrapped her hands around Jace's hand and the phone. "Thank you." She leaned forward and kissed him on the cheek. That caught him by surprise, a nice touch. Stay bubbly and appreciative. Make him feel like the master bestowing a favor.

He released the phone. "Put it on speaker."

"It's the only time I get to see Mama." She pressed the numbers. "Mama doesn't see me, but I see her."

Cheyenne answered on the first ring. "Soledad?"

"Yes, it's me."

"Are you all right?"

"Nothing's wrong. I left my phone in the car, and Jace just found it." She smiled at him. "Thank you, Jace." Please, please, Little Sis, know Jace is listening.

"Thank God. I was so worried. You're coming to mass tomorrow, right?"

"Of course. Noon as usual. I'll sit in the back, and I'll be wearing a new dress I bought a few days ago at the mall, black with a veil. But I won't have time to visit. I'm being escorted, and we might leave through the adoration chapel to avoid the crowd." Please, please, understand what I'm saying, understand Jace is listening. You've wanted the plan. Please know the time is now.

"I understand. Just be there."

"I will. I love you. Goodbye until tomorrow." She handed the phone to Jace. "Satisfied?"

Chapter Ten

Sunday, 10:00 am

Cal clicked the cap shut on the Sharpie, stepped back, and studied his mattress propped against the wall. The Fowler-size outline with circles drawn at the groin, belly, throat, and face sagged forward as though mattress Fowler loomed over him. Even as a drawing he looked big and ominous.

Soledad had called Cheyenne, and Cheyenne called him—often. The situation and his own bad luck said Fowler would be Soledad's escort. The question now, where to hit to get the most bang for the buck? Not Fowler's big, hard head. Probably break a hand on that petrified melon. The throat was good for most people, but Fowler had a short, thick, fireplug neck. Maybe the groin? Kick a man in the balls and he'd go down long enough for Soledad to get away. But unless Fowler faced him with legs apart, that was a risky move. Which left the belly, a big, soft target, and hard to miss, especially one the size of Fowler's.

He opened the nightstand drawer, picked up a roll of quarters, and laid them across his palm. His fingers wrapped around the roll. No fingernails digging into the palm, and the quarters made his fist tighter, heavier, and larger, like a small club. Saw it in a movie once, and it worked there.

Soledad and Fowler would exit through the middle door, so come from behind on Fowler's right, then step, pivot, and swing. He took position at the side of the mattress, back to the wall, shoulder to shoulder with mattress Fowler. Swing low into the belly, driving up to the solar plexus. If Fowler saw him coming, probably wouldn't work. The keys were surprise and a good first punch, or the second would be Fowler's.

He stepped, pivoted, and swung as hard as he could. His fist sank into the mattress almost to the wall. He leaned into the mattress, delivering several short, quick punches like a boxer with his opponent on the ropes. Damn, that felt good.

He flopped the mattress across the bed and inspected the wall. Didn't dent it. Not a good sign. He wrestled the mattress back against the wall. After four more practices of step, pivot, swing, he panted and perspired and needed a cigarette. Soledad was right, he smoked too much, and he'd cut down tomorrow. In a hospital bed with a wired jaw, there'd be no choice.

He walked to the kitchen, patting the side pockets of his sports coat. The roll of quarters in the right, phone and an extra pack of cigarettes in the left, and all easily accessible. The coat fit loose enough to allow unrestricted swings. No tie, a person could grab and yank that during a fight. Saw that in a movie, too.

Cheyenne had gone over her plan last night and this morning with every move timed to the second and any scenario detailed. She was a micromanager, and he had his part ingrained through repetition. Wait outside until near the end of the church service, then enter the lobby, which she promised would be empty. Ten minutes before services ended, Soledad and Fowler would leave and enter the lobby. Then step, pivot, swing, and hope for divine intervention.

He poured a cup of coffee and pulled the vibrating phone from his pocket. Cheyenne again. She didn't trust him.

"Cheyenne, I told you last night, I told you an hour ago, and I'm telling you now, I'll be there. Hold on a second, I'm putting you on speaker." He laid the phone on the corner of the table, opened the sliding glass door, and settled into smoking position. One deep drag, a long exhale, then a slurping sip of hot coffee. All set.

"Cal, *Cal*?"

"I'm here."

"Where?"

"At my apartment."

"Still? You're not getting cold feet, are you?"

He frowned and shook his head. "Don't worry, I'll be there early. Are you sure about the empty lobby?"

"Yes. People are doing things. They don't know why, but they'll do them because Father Brady asked. Everything is set. It all depends on you. You're sure you can handle her escort?"

"I know who he is. No problem." Damn, that sounded confident.

"You don't look like a fighter to me."

"Cheyenne, I know what I'm doing. Get off the phone and let me prepare."

"I'll go over the plan again."

"No, I got it." She needed a bourbon bracer.

"All right, all right. I have to go pee anyway."

"Stop worrying. I'll be there. I'll handle it. Goodbye."

He switched off the call. Handle it, no problem,

knew what he was doing. What a crock of shit. But one good punch, that's all he needed. Just enough to break Fowler's hold, then Soledad could sprint to the chapel door while he yelled for help, if his jaw wasn't broken. After that, if he got away, Fowler and Jace would come looking. There were places to lie low for a while. Or maybe just head for Gainesville, pick up Soledad and— *Damn it*. Did it again. Get it straight. Pick up—*Ynez*— and don't look back. He took another long drag. That unscratchable itch was getting more bothersome.

He pulled out another cigarette and held it to the glowing ash of the one he smoked. Fear was there, in his gut and head. Not so much the fear of getting hurt, a given, but the fear of failure. Should've done this for Shantelle a year ago. She would've left. She wanted to leave with him. Could've left in the middle of the night and been long gone before Jace knew. That's a guilt card Soledad didn't need to play. That one he held close to his vest.

Ten years ago, when Jace made the offer to be a driver, he'd accepted with a smile. Kind of exciting, working with beautiful women, and the money was good. He became the nice guy who took care of the soothing, helping things to keep the girls in the business. Jace and Fowler took care of discipline and punishment to keep the girls in the business. Both were needed. Just opposite sides of the same coin. Soledad said he was a good man in a bad business. Lenny said it better, the least harmful of bad choices. Maybe Fowler beating the shit out of him was what he deserved.

On the positive side of the ledger, Ynez was out, and that felt good. Just don't screw-up, and Soledad would be out, too. Didn't make up for Shantelle, but fail Soledad, and he failed Shantelle—again.

He flipped his cigarette butt into the courtyard, then drained his coffee. Don't think about failure. Just go, and remember—step, pivot, swing.

Leaving early allowed a double check to make sure no one followed. He circled a two-block area surrounding the church, looking for anyone waiting in a car. Nothing looked unusual, but still thirty minutes until services began. He parked, lifted his cigarette pack from his breast pocket, took the last one, and tossed the empty pack over his shoulder. Good thing he had a backup pack, that was good planning.

Every good plan had backup, especially at the most critical, and in his case, the weakest point. This was too important to fail. Soledad said not to call the police, but Lenny wasn't a cop when it came to her. Maybe this was the time to call. Lenny would come. For whatever the secret reason, he'd come and make sure Fowler didn't take Soledad. Maybe not the scenario Soledad wanted, but she'd be safe and out.

He pulled Lenny's card from his wallet.

His phone vibrated against his hip. Cheyenne, of course. He dropped the card into his coat pocket.

"Hello, Cheyenne."

"Where are you? Why didn't you call me?"

"Because you're driving me nuts. I'm here, parked so I have a good view of the entrance."

"Thank God. I was worried you got cold feet."

"Stop worrying about the temperature of my feet. Where're you?"

"Where I can see what's going on inside the church. Now remember, I couldn't communicate to Soledad that you're helping. She thinks she's on her own in the lobby, so act quickly before she gets hurt trying to get away."

"Like I said before, no problem." He sat up straight and flipped his cigarette out the window. "I see them."

"Where?"

"Walking on the sidewalk toward the church. Fowler's beside Soledad, holding her upper arm. She's wearing a black dress and a veil. They're walking up the steps." Soledad seemed taller. Hard to tell a half block away, but she looked to be wearing high, narrow heels.

"Cal, I see them. They're entering, and now they're crossing the lobby and entering the nave."

"The what?"

"The sanctuary. The preaching praying area. He's awfully big."

"Don't worry. I know a little quan-doe, chai-tea, fusion fighting. The step, pivot, quarter roll swing to the solar plexus move. Renders your opponent helpless in a paralytic state for at least five minutes."

"Really?"

"Yeah."

"I don't believe you. Sounds made-up to me. Just jump on his back and choke him."

Never considered that, might work. "I'll use that as a backup plan."

"They're taking their seats. I have to check a few things. Don't hang up, keep this call going, and don't go anywhere."

"I'll be here."

He slid his phone into his breast pocket. Distant voices and echoing footsteps came through his phone. Nothings to do but wait and watch.

Chapter Eleven

Sunday, 12:40 pm

"Cal, Cal!"

"I'm here."

"Time to go into the lobby. It's empty and will stay that way for at least the next fifteen minutes. In ten minutes, Soledad will say she wants to leave early. They'll come through the middle door."

"I know that."

"Just reminding. All you have to do is get her loose. I'll take it from there."

"I'm on my way." He slid the phone into his inside coat pocket and exited the car. All he had to do. Cheyenne made it sound so simple. He patted the roll of quarters in his side pocket. Remember, step, pivot, swing. Pray for divine intervention.

Perspiration seeped from his hairline and rolled across his temples as he jogged down and across the street and up the steps. His hand hesitated on the door handle. His jaw tightened as he swallowed hard. His feet weren't getting cold, but this was too important to fail. *Get backup.* He put Cheyenne on hold, snatched Lenny's card, and pressed the numbers.

Answer, please answer.

"Detective Lenny Trumbo."

"Lenny, this is Cal. Come to Saint Anthony's

now—right now."

"I'm at a search site. What's going on?"

"I don't have time to explain. Just come now. If you see Fowler leaving with Soledad, stop them. I have to go." He hung up on Lenny and switched to Cheyenne. "The lobby's empty. I'm taking position so when the middle door opens, I'll be behind it."

"Good. I'm in the chapel with Father Brady. It's up to you now."

And it was, so don't fail. Just step, pivot, swing. His fingers fumbled into his pocket and around the roll of quarters. When the door opens, it will block their view. Let them take two steps, rush Fowler from behind, then step, pivot in front of Fowler, and swing.

"Cheyenne, will Soledad be on Fowler's right or left?"

"I don't know. What difference does it make? Just jump on his back and choke him."

She was right. Simple was better. Just jump and hang on. He dropped his phone into his pocket next to the quarters.

The middle door eased open just enough for one person to slip through. The priest's voice leaked into the vestibule, saying something about the valley of the shadow of death.

He gulped in air. Soledad stepped through first, then Fowler a half-step behind with his right hand gripping her bicep. Another step and the middle door swung shut behind them.

Go. Go now. He rushed, launched, and slammed onto Fowler's brick-hard, hulking back, wrapping his forearm around that fireplug neck.

Soledad snapped her head around. Her wild eyes

met his. "Cal!"

"Run!" His forearm squeezed into Fowler's Adam's apple.

Fowler gasped and stumbled forward, twisting and bucking, grabbing the tightening forearm at his throat with one hand, and yanking on Soledad with the other.

Soledad tried to tear her arm loose, but Fowler's grip held. Her foot shot up, then slammed down, ramming a spiked heel into Fowler's instep. He choked out a gasp and dropped to one knee.

Soledad ripped her arm free and motioned. "Cal! Come."

"I said, *run!*" His hold slipped as Fowler flung him to the floor.

Soledad bolted toward the open chapel door. Fowler pushed up on his good foot.

Do something, you idiot. He gripped the roll of quarters, sprang to his feet, then stepped, pivoted, and swung. His quarter-roll fist rammed deep into Fowler's soft belly, pushing up, forcing a croaking inhale. Another punch in the gut while driving his knee up and forward into Fowler's crotch.

Direct hit. Fowler's croak stuck in his throat. His body clenched.

Just one punch to that fat, yellow-toothed mouth. He drew his fist back and delivered a right cross to the jaw. Quarters flew from his fist as Fowler's head jerked sideways.

Fowler fell backward, banging his head on the tile floor as quarters clattered and bounced. Blue veins bulged on his purple face. He gasped for air and rolled from shoulder to shoulder with one hand on his crotch and the other stretching for a foot he couldn't reach.

The church doors creaked and voices buzzed as the congregation streamed out.

Ahh, shit. *Think!* "This man is having a heart attack. Someone call nine-one-one."

He snapped his head around. Soledad stood at the chapel entrance. He backed away as people circled Fowler and kids scrambled to pick up quarters.

"Cal, this way." Soledad lifted her veil and reached out a motioning hand. "Come, come!"

Go with her. See this through. He took two backward steps and spun. Soledad disappeared into the chapel. He followed. Father Brady stood by the chapel entrance, pointing. Soledad cut into the usher's room, her hand trailing, motioning for him to follow.

He raced across the usher's room as the black dress reached the parking lot. Again her hand motioned to follow. He sprinted across the pavement, twenty feet behind the gliding black dress. His strides lengthened on legs of tired jelly. His lungs burned and gasped for air.

By the time he grabbed the door handle, she was behind the wheel and had the car started. He sucked in a large breath, then climbed into the passenger seat. The car shot forward, made a sharp right, and raced down the street.

He punched his fist into his open hand. "God, that was great. Did you see him go down? I think you broke his foot. Fowler wanted to scream, but when I punched him in the gut, he had no air. He just gasped and turned purple. I thought his head was gonna explode. I loved it!"

He flopped back in the seat, panting, laughing, shaking his head. "When you motioned, I had to come.

I don't where we're going, but I had to come with you."

"Cal." She lifted the veil. "It's me, Cheyenne." Her foot slammed on the break. They skidded to a stop at an intersection.

He glanced at her feet. Flat shoes, no wonder she ran so well. "Where the hell is Soledad?"

"Still at the chapel. After that, I don't know." She stepped on the gas, and the car shot forward. "She had something she had to do. She'll be home in a few hours. That's where we're going."

"You should have told me about this in advance."

"I didn't know you were coming. Soledad changed the plan at the last minute, motioned to you, and told me quite emphatically, 'There's something I have to do. Go to the house and take Cal with you.' I don't argue. I just do what she says."

The car screeched to a stop at a red light. She glanced over, grinning wide. "I guess she wanted you out with her. Are you sorry?"

"No." That answer came fast and easy. But what the hell was she up to? "What exactly *is* her plan?"

The light turned green, and Cheyenne accelerated through the intersection. "I don't know. You'll have to ask her. But before we get home, there's a few things I need to explain. Mama went to morning mass, so she's at home cooking. She doesn't know what's going on. Only that Soledad is finally coming home, and you're the boyfriend that's helping. Lately, she's been more spiritual and nostalgic than usual, and thinks you're some kind of a savior for her little Sho Sho."

"Sho Sho?"

"Mama's pet name for Soledad when she was little. It's from her middle name, so don't get confused.

123

Father Brady will arrive soon, and Cousin Jimmy will pop in and out." She took a deep breath. "Then hopefully, Soledad will be home in a few hours."

Hopefully, that didn't sound definite. But *never* underestimate Soledad. She got people to do what she wanted. For some, she got them to *want* to do what she wanted.

Cheyenne squirmed and squeezed the steering wheel. She turned into a driveway and slammed on the brakes with both feet while pressing her knees together. He lurched forward, bracing both hands on the dash as she swung her door open. "Come on, come on." By the time he closed his door, she was around the car, grabbing his wrist. "Hurry up. I have to pee."

They ran around the side of the house. A back door opened, and Cheyenne yanked him through.

He breathed hard to catch his breath. A thick, delicious aroma brought on a swallow and a stomach growl. He blinked rapidly, adjusting from the midday sun to the dim interior.

A small woman with long black hair wrapped on top of her head peeked outside. A faded print dress hung loosely on her skinny frame. A tied apron scrunched the dress around a narrow waist. She closed the door and turned. "Where is Soledad?"

Cheyenne wiggled and pressed her knees together. "Mama, this is Cal. I'll be right back to explain." She ran down a hall, cut right, then slammed a door.

"Ahh, nice to meet you, Missus Montoya."

She leaned forward and snapped her chin up. "Where is Soledad?"

"I'm not exactly sure. Cheyenne will explain." He tried giving a reassuring smile, but this little woman wasn't buying it.

Her small hands went to her waist. "Cheyenne said you are Soledad's boyfriend. If that is true, you should be with her."

He nodded. "Yes, yes, I should, but she had something she wanted to do by herself. And she can be very stubborn."

She bowed her head and nodded. "She inherited that from me." Her jaw tightened as she looked up and stared. "But I have twenty more years of stubborn in me. When will she be here?"

"In a few hours. Cheyenne will explain."

"Will she explain why secrets are kept from me? Why the curtains are drawn, and why I am kept in the dark? I have patience, so I will wait, but not for long."

"I know what you mean." Please Cheyenne, empty that nervous little bladder and get the hell out here. And what was that heavenly aroma?

Mrs. Montoya's wide mouth sighed a weak smile between full lips just like Soledad's. "But I am forgetting my manners. You are a guest, and I welcome you to our home."

"Thank you, Missus Montoya."

"Isabelle, please. Are you hungry?"

"Yes, ma'am." Liked this little woman already.

"The food will be ready soon, but first I want to show you something." She led him into a dimly lit living room with drawn curtains. The only bright spot was a small altar with two lighted candles. She stopped next to the altar at a small table filled with framed family photographs. "I want you to know my little Sho Sho before she left home."

Cheyenne rushed in and joined them. "Mama, I'll

take care of Cal."

Isabelle turned with crossed arms. "Caridad Cheyenne, when you have to pee that bad, you are nervous. What have you not told me? And did you wash your hands?"

"*Mama.* Of course."

"Then go to the kitchen and check on the food, then change your clothes. I want to talk to Cal. Maybe I will get some truth from him."

They stared at each other, then Cheyenne spun and marched away.

Isabelle separated the front window curtains enough to allow sunlight to shine on the table of photos. Her small, strong hand squeezed his as she pointed at a photo. "This is my little Sho Sho on her first birthday."

She went from picture to picture, telling a small story about each one. Soledad with her father, a short man, probably no more than five-five, but he looked tall next to her. Soledad and Cheyenne in their Sunday best. Soledad on the floor with Christmas toys. He leaned forward and studied a photo of Soledad with Isabelle. As a young woman, Isabelle very much resembled Soledad now. Although, it looked like Isabelle had lost weight in twenty years. Her light brown skin stretched over cheekbones, making her large dark eyes look recessed and her cheeks shallow. But the strong resemblance was very much there, right down to the small rounded nose. She must have been a beautiful young woman.

He pointed to the photo she had skipped, Soledad looking up with an ear-to-ear smile, laying across a big, tan and white Saint Bernard. "Is that Bernardo?"

Isabelle's hand squeezed his tighter. She turned,

faced him, and leaned forward. The small swaying candle flames sent slivers of light that reflected from wide, staring eyes, drawing him in. He wanted to step back, but her frozen stare froze him.

Cheyenne rushed in wearing jeans and a T-shirt with her hair pulled back in a ponytail. She stepped quickly next to them and crossed her arms.

Isabelle broke her stare and pointed at the picture of Soledad and Bernardo.

Then the Spanish started, back and forth between Isabelle and Cheyenne. Not arguing but talking faster than he thought lips could move. The name Bernardo came up several times as they glanced from the photo to him. Then silence. Isabelle released his hand, stepped to the altar, knelt, and began praying.

"Come with me, Cal." Cheyenne tugged on his wrist and led him into the kitchen.

The aroma of something wonderful cooking made him swallow, salivate, then swallow again.

"Sit down." She pulled out chairs from the kitchen table, then sat facing him with a view of the entrance. "So Soledad told you about Bernardo?"

"Yeah, so?"

She leaned forward and folded her hands. "What did she say?"

He shrugged. Hard to concentrate with his stomach screaming—*feed me.* "Ahh, that I drooled like Bernardo, but his tongue was longer. Then about her father bringing him home, how she named him, and that he made a good pillow."

"Really? She talked about Daddy and compared you to Bernardo?"

"Well, my tongue and drool."

"Was she yelling at you?"

"No, she was grinning and laughing at me."

"*Wow.*" She shook her head with a blank gaze like she was picturing a memory.

"What?"

She blinked and gave her head a short quick shake. "When Soledad was eight, almost nine, Daddy and Bernardo died within a few months of each other. Soledad hasn't talked about either since, but she talked to you. What were the circumstances?"

He leaned back and crossed his arms. "I'm sure this is all very important to your family, but I'm more concerned with the present. What's the plan after Soledad gets here?"

She frowned. "It *is* important, and we *will* come back to it." She glanced toward the entrance, then leaned forward. "I only know she had something important to do, and she'd be here in a few hours. She knows that when she comes home, it's for good. She won't leave Mama again. She has a plan, trust her."

"I have no choice." But where was she now? She wouldn't go to the police or back to Jace. What the hell did she have to do? "What's cooking? I'm starved."

"Mama's paella, and I can't believe you're thinking of your stomach."

"My stomach is thinking of me. Meals and I have been strangers lately."

"It's not ready." She popped up, rushed to the window above the sink, and peeked between the curtains. "I hate waiting, especially when the end is so near." She scrunched the curtains shut and banged her fists on the counter. "I need to be doing something. Planning and carrying out, I'm fine. But waiting and not knowing really gets to me."

"Maybe we should eat something."

"I can't eat on an empty stomach."

That made no sense. Focused Cheyenne was slipping, and crazy Cheyenne was emerging. "Just try to relax. Food is good for that."

She shook her head. "I'll do what I do at night." She opened a cabinet door and grabbed a glass and a nearly full pint of bourbon. "This will help."

"Like when you visited me on Thursday night?" He grinned. "I smelled it on your breath."

She dropped her head and looked away. "I just had two thimblefuls in a cup of green tea. Do you want some?"

Couldn't hurt, then slip out for a smoke. "Sure, three fingers, one cube."

She snatched another glass. "What's that mean?"

He joined her at the counter. "Let me do this. How do you take yours?"

"Well, when I can't sleep, in a cup of green tea. Mama allows it. Lately she's been reminding me. But no tea today." She pulled a near empty ice cube tray from the freezer. "What's it taste like by itself?"

"You better have lots of ice." He dropped a cube in one glass, then set the other glass in the sink and rattled and shook the tray until one broken cube and a lot of ice slivers filled her glass. He poured her about an inch of bourbon, then three fingers worth in his glass.

She took a sip and grimaced. "Kinda like a root beer Icee gone bad." She picked up the bottle and led him back to the table, then sipped again. "Better, the ice helps."

"Yeah, it gets easier. So when are the priest and the

cousin arriving?"

She glared. "*His name* is Father Brady. He'll be here soon to be with Mama. Cousin Jimmy is patrolling the neighborhood, but he'll check in." She sipped a longer one and grinned. "With Soledad coming home there's gonna be a whole lot of praying going on."

"Anyone else coming?"

"Josepha, of course. She doesn't know why, but she knows our family needs to be together, and she *will* be here."

"That's the sister in Gainesville?"

Cheyenne bobbed her head and smiled. "She's in pre-law. Soledad says we need a lawyer in the family, and Josepha will be a very good one. She's very smart. Soledad thinks she has a future in politics."

"Yeah, I'm sure. Is her roommate coming, too? Someone named Ynez?"

Cheyenne shook her head. "Josepha doesn't have a roommate. And Soledad doesn't know she's coming. It'll be a nice surprise." She poured bourbon into her glass to the top of the ice. "This is a lot better than in green tea. I better check the window again." She popped up, paused with a slight wobble, then plopped back down in her seat. "I shouldn't stand up so fast on an empty stomach."

"Stay put, I'll check." He walked to the sink and peered through the window as far up and down the street as possible. "I don't see anything. This bourbon in the tea thing. How much and how often?"

"Most nights for the past week, just to relax." She wiggled her little finger as she sipped. "Almost a full thimble-full." She paused and grinned. "Full thimble-full, that sounds funny."

"Yeah, the way you say it, you've already had a few thimble-fulls."

"It's okay, I burn it up."

"Ohhh-kay." This was a different Cheyenne than he had ever imagined. "Ahh, shit."

The car slowing to a stop across the street wasn't familiar, but the man stepping out wearing that stupid Popeye Doyle hat was.

Lenny. Forgot all about him.

"What's wrong?" Cheyenne put both hands on the table, stood stiffly, steadied herself, then took measured steps to the window. "Who's that?"

Lenny leaned against an unmarked Charger while talking on his phone. "A cop I know."

"The police?" She stood on tiptoes, leaned across the sink, and gripped the counter to steady herself. "This is bad. What's he want?"

"Soledad for sure, and probably me, too."

She closed the curtains and looked up with wide and slightly glazed eyes. "You have to stop him. He can't know that Soledad isn't here. No one can, except family."

So this was Soledad's alibi for whatever she was up to. "Then I better get out there and stop him." His index finger pointed straight between her eyes. "You stay here. Go pray with your mother or something, but let me handle this. No arguments."

She bobbed several nods. "Yes, that's good. Mama is probably peeking between the curtains right now. No telling what she might do."

"Then go to the living room and stay with her, and no more thimble-fulls."

Chapter Twelve

Sunday, 2:15 pm

Cal pushed the screen door open and let it slam behind. First, taking on Fowler, then a decoy with Cheyenne, and now an alibi—if he could handle Lenny. Soledad was getting good mileage out of him today.

Lenny saw him coming and put his phone away.

"Lenny." He took long, quick strides across the street, holding up open hands at shoulder height, motioning for Lenny to stay put. "It's okay. Soledad's safe. Sorry I pulled you away from work for nothing."

Lenny grinned, crossed his arms, and leaned his back against the Charger. "Didn't think you had it in you."

"Had what?"

"Takin' down Fowler. Wish I could've been there. I arrived with the ambulance and came in with the paramedics." Lenny stifled a laugh. "He was still on the floor holding his nuts and reaching for his foot. Saw an abrasion on his jaw, too. How's the hand?"

He rubbed his knuckles. "Still hurts a little, but I don't think I broke anything."

Lenny pushed his hat back a few inches. "Roll of quarters, huh. Old trick, but they absorb the shock. The roll broke instead of your hand and you made some kids happy. Where'd you learn that?"

"Saw it in a movie. Is Fowler pressing charges?"

"Nah, this is personal. He'll come after you, but no time soon. That foot might be in cast for a while. Was that your work, too?"

"No, that was Soledad. She's a fighter."

"Well, I need to talk to her."

"Can't it wait a little while? She's with her mother." He sighed and gave a pleading look. "This is a big deal. They need time together."

"It's kind of important, and I'm pressed for time."

They snapped their heads to the slam of the screen door. Isabelle marched toward them, carrying a foil covered plate and a bottle of beer.

Ahh shit. She could ruin everything. Where the hell was Cheyenne? He took off fast, back across the street, and intercepted Isabelle at the curb.

"Missus Montoya, please, I'll handle this."

"Call me Isabelle."

"Isabelle, please, I can handle this."

She didn't break stride. Her flat-heeled shoes slapped on the pavement. Her stare fixed on Lenny. "No, I must talk to this man. And he is a man, so he is hungry, and food always helps."

She brushed past him. Oh God, that plate smelled good. He kept pace with her. "Isabelle, please go back. I'll give him the plate."

"No, I must meet the man who is after my little Sho Sho." She stopped directly in front of Lenny.

Lenny inhaled and swallowed.

"This is paella and some empanadas. There is a fork beneath the foil." Isabelle handed Lenny the plate and the beer. "And that is one of Jimmy's beers."

Lenny glanced at him. "Who's Jimmy?"

"A cousin, I think." He tried unsuccessfully to wedge between Mama and Lenny. "You should go back to the house, Missus Montoya, I mean Isabelle. Please." But short of grabbing and pulling her away, there was no stopping her.

She leaned closer to Lenny. "Why do you want to hurt my little Sho Sho?"

Lenny glanced a puzzled look.

"Sho Sho is Soledad."

Lenny nodded, then turned back to Isabelle. "I don't want to hurt your daughter. I don't even want to arrest her. I just want to talk to her."

"If you are a good man, you will help her."

Lenny sighed. "I'll do what I can."

End it now. Nothing had been given away. He poked his head between them. "See, he's gonna help. Let's go back, Missus Montoya."

But she leaned closer to Lenny, staring up, studying his face. The corners of her mouth curled up, and her cheeks rose. "I have met you. *Como te llamas*? What is your name?"

"Detective Lenny Trumbo."

Isabelle clamped her hands on her hips. "Your parents did not name you detective or Lenny. What is your name?"

Lenny took a breath as if about to say something difficult to a person he felt compelled to answer. "Leonardo."

Isabelle smiled as her small hand motioned for the rest of his name.

"Leonardo, Michelangelo, Trumbo."

Isabelle clasped her hands beneath her chin. "Oh, a proud and beautiful name." Her smile burst across her entire face and erased years of worry lines. "Ahh, I remember. You were the *policia* that came when Bernardo died."

Lenny nodded. "I was twenty years younger and in uniform."

"Ohh, but no one cared but you. *Compasion* lived in your heart. I think it lives there still." She nodded. "Yes, you are a good man. You will help my little Sho Sho."

Lenny's eyes avoided Isabelle's by looking down at the plate. "Thank you, Missus Montoya."

"Isabelle, please." She reached out and touched Lenny's hand holding the plate. "You are always welcome in our home." She clasped her hands against her chest, turned slowly, and walked back across the street to the kitchen door.

He side-glanced Lenny watching Isabelle. There was something on Lenny's face he had never seen before. Sympathy? No, more like guilt mixed with regret. That little woman had reached inside Lenny and touched something, and it wasn't new.

Lenny set the paella and beer inside the Charger, then returned to leaning against the car door with his arms crossed. "Did you plan that?"

"You know I didn't. What just happened was real, and honest, and from her heart. And you know that, too. And if you just lied to Isabelle, if you cause her any pain. You'll go straight to hell."

Lenny swiveled and poked him hard in the chest. "Don't. Don't try to play a guilt card on me. I've seen pain in Missus Montoya before. So, okay, I'll give them some time, a half hour, then Soledad and I will talk." He shrugged. "Anyway, it gives me a chance to see if

135

anyone else shows up."

"Thanks, Lenny."

They leaned shoulder to shoulder against the Charger, staring across the street at the drawn curtains.

That Bernardo story took Lenny pretty far back with Soledad, and Isabelle, too. That must have been some encounter to stay with Lenny all those years.

Lenny suddenly pushed away from the car. "Follow me." He walked around the car to the passenger side and sat in the passenger seat with the door open and his feet on the curb. "I got a half hour, and I'm real hungry." He set the plate on his lap and tore off the foil. "This stuff smells really good." Lenny shoveled in a few forkfuls followed by a sip of beer.

"Aren't you on duty?"

"Shut up." Lenny swallowed and nodded. "Isabelle really knows how to cook."

"I think she kind of likes you." He knelt on one knee, eye-to-eye with Lenny. "*Compasion* lives in your heart, Leonardo Mich—"

"*Hey.* If this stuff wasn't so good, I'd kick your ass, right here, right now."

"Yeah, but that's quite a handle."

Lenny glared and took another sip of beer.

"Okay, *Lenny*. It's our secret. Isabelle is an attractive woman, don't you think? About your age, too."

"Shut up."

"Just saying. You're both single. I hear she likes to salsa dance. Do you dance?"

Lenny wagged the fork at him. "Change the subject, *now*."

He lit a cigarette and took a long drag, trying to

deaden stomach growls. "So what's the story behind Bernardo?"

Lenny glanced at his watch, then stopped chewing. "Why do you want to know about that?"

"It seems to mean a lot to the whole family. Might help me understand them. Tell me about Bernardo. I'll owe you."

"You already do, but okay. There's not much to it. I was a patrolman, only been on the force a few years. We got a call about a kid named Bernardo getting hit by a car. When I got there, an ambulance had just arrived. Soledad was lying across this huge Saint Bernard, just wailing, tears streaming. A smaller girl was latched to her back, wailing, too. Isabelle just stood there, silent and sad, with a crying baby on her hip." He took a slow sip of beer.

"So what happened next?"

"When the paramedics found out Bernardo was a dog and not a kid, they left. I stayed until Animal Control showed up, and helped Isabelle pull Soledad off the dog. Couldn't unlatch the other little girl off Soledad's back though. I tried, but she bit me. She clamped down hard and brought blood. That's about it." He took another sip of beer. "So what do you know about Wednesday night at Jace Richards's house? And where were you?"

"I don't know anything about Wednesday. I was with a girl all night."

"Soledad?" Lenny's eyes froze, then glanced away.

"No. A girl named Ynez. She'll vouch for me if needed."

Lenny frowned and nodded like he wished the girl had been Soledad. Like he wanted her to have an alibi away from Jace's house. Lenny must suspect something or had new information.

A telephone-sounding ringtone came from Lenny's coat pocket. He pulled out his phone. "Micah?" He nodded several times. "Keep the site secure. I want the first walkthrough. Any press there?" His jaw tightened. "Keep them way back, and don't let anyone talk to them. I'm on my way." He snatched the plate and fork and half-empty bottle of beer. "Take these back."

"What's up, Lenny?"

"The shit's gonna hit the fan, so keep Soledad here. I'll send a patrol car to stay in the area. And I'll be back." He slammed the passenger door, rushed around the car, and slid into the driver's seat. He stuck a flashing light on the roof and sped off.

They found a body. That had to be it. Soledad thought Jace and Carlos had dumped a girl's body on Wednesday night, but the shit wouldn't hit the fan for a dead prostitute. When they talked at his place, Lenny had said Carlos was missing. Maybe they found him. Lenny wouldn't send a patrol car unless he thought Soledad was in danger. *Soledad, get your ass back here.*

Cheyenne opened the kitchen door, motioned him in, and closed the door behind them. She looked up with wide and slightly more glazed eyes. "What did Mama do?"

"Whatever she wanted." He set Lenny's empty plate and half bottle of beer on the counter next to the pint of bourbon, which now approached half empty. She'd been sipping. "I think everything is okay, no thanks to you. Where's your mother?"

"In the living room with Father Brady. He arrived at the back door while you were outside."

"Where the hell were you?"

She screwed up her face and bit on her lower lip. "I had to pee again. I was only in the bathroom a few minutes, but Mama can fix a plate real fast."

He shook his head and smirked. "Did you wash your hands?"

Cheyenne pressed her lips together. A fire burned through the glaze in her eyes. A sly grin slowly formed. "You must be hungry." Her grin grew into a wide smile. "Sit down. I'll fix you a plate."

He pulled out a chair at the kitchen table. Cheyenne walked with measured steps to the stove. She concentrated on spooning a mound of paella on a plate, then plopped it on the table under his chin. A mixture of rice, yellow with saffron, shrimp, and pieces of chicken mixed in. Didn't care about the peas, but those slices of sausage smelled great.

Cheyenne's smile stretched to its limit. She plunged two fingers into the paella on his plate and lifted a small pile to her mouth. "Mmm, Mama's paella is so good. I can't resist." She took a small bite, then flicked the remainder back on his plate. She sat down across the table and handed him a fork. "Did I wash my hands? Gee, I forget. *Bueno apitito*."

He stared at the mound and inhaled. Chorizo, definitely chorizo, and garlic. Didn't matter if a cat pissed on it, this stuff was going down. He plunged his fork into the paella and shoveled it in. Flavor filled his mouth. It was delicious, absolutely fantastic, with or without Cheyenne's special sauce.

After several large hurried bites, he looked across the table. Cheyenne's usual tense face and eyes had calmed. She sat back, arms crossed, with her right hand holding the bourbon-filled glass. She took a sip, then held the glass inches from her mouth ready for the next sip, which came pretty quick, only requiring a turn of her wrist and a slight parting of her lips.

He slowed his bites and watched between forkfuls. With each sip her facial muscles slackened, and her eyelids edged down, which looked out of place for Cheyenne. Maybe not a good idea letting her drink, but hopefully she'd get tired, shuffle off to bed, and pass out. But as she sipped and stared, her eyes narrowed, and her mouth drooped into a brooding frown.

There was some real dislike in that look, and it had nothing to do with his crack about her hygiene. Emotional highs and lows could come quick, and from left field, to a person not used to alcohol. She must have been sipping and brooding the whole time he was with Lenny. But no matter, she wasn't going to spoil his appetite.

She sipped again. "What makes you so special?" There was anger in her voice.

"What?" Where did that come from? He looked up from his plate to a hurt face. "I'm not special. What'd I do?"

She pressed her lips together, but they trembled. She was about to cry.

"It's not fair. Soledad doesn't talk about Daddy or Bernardo for years, then is happy telling—*you*." Her voice cracked. "It should have been me she told." She looked down, shaking her head, and the tears flowed. "Bernardo got killed saving me. It was my fault. It should have been me."

Oh no. Nothing worse than a drunk girl on a crying jag. Usually about a man, and kind of was in roundabout way. Why couldn't she wait until after the paella? He dropped his fork on the plate and stood. "I'll get your mother."

"*No.*" She shook her head violently. "Mama mustn't see me like this. I'm the strong one. I've held our family together since Soledad left." She stood quickly and wobbled. He stepped around the table, grabbed her shoulders, and steadied her. She collapsed against his chest with her forehead plunking him in the same spot Lenny had poked. She was crying, and it seemed so out of place for Cheyenne. His hands hovered over her shoulders, then he gently patted with his fingertips.

"She was Daddy's favorite." Her words choked out between sobs. "And Bernardo's favorite. But that's okay, she's my favorite, too." She forced out squeaky words between swallows. "Now *you're* her favorite."

Didn't see this coming, and he wasn't Soledad's favorite. That was just an act.

The sobs and sniffles finally slowed, then stopped. "Are you okay now?"

She nodded but wouldn't look up.

"Maybe you should eat something."

She put her hands on his chest and pushed, then stumbled backward. He grabbed her shoulders. "Are you sure you're okay?"

She looked up and nodded. "I'm just tired and a little dizzy. I better lie down for a little while. Better help me to my room."

He wrapped an arm around her waist. She hung on his shoulder with both hands. He pulled her to the hall entrance. The coast was clear. Cheyenne pointed to the last door on the left. "In there."

He half dragged her, then scooped, lifted, and carried her into the room.

He laid her on the bed, and she clutched his arm. "Cal, don't tell anyone about this."

"It's our secret."

"And I'm sorry. You must be special, or Soledad wouldn't have shared with you. Anyway, you're her boyfriend. She should share with you."

"Get some sleep."

"Wake me when Soledad gets here."

"I will." He stopped at the entrance. She sighed deeply, curled into a ball, and closed her eyes. She looked like a tired little girl who needed a nap.

He closed the door. The appetite was gone, and he needed a cigarette.

As he passed the kitchen, Isabelle stepped from the living room.

"Where is Cheyenne?"

"She's really tired. She's lying down for a little while."

Isabelle smiled and nodded. "That is good. She has not had much sleep for two days. Did she eat?"

"Ahh, well, she had a bite or two of mine."

Isabelle shook her head and frowned. "Nothing but tea and crackers for two days." She clasped her hands and shook them in short quick vibrations. "When Soledad comes home, everything will be all right. Has she called?"

"No, but I'm sure she'll be here soon." He pointed to the back door. "Is it okay if I smoke on the back step?"

"Certainly." She smiled. "My husband, Sergio, used to smoke there after a meal. I will make you coffee."

"That's not—" But she was gone to the kitchen.

He sat on the back step, looking over a backyard of spiny Saint Augustine grass and large patches of brown sand. In the middle sat a rusted and faded blue and white swing set with only one seat and dangling chains for two others. Nearby stood a dilapidated, homemade doghouse. That must have been Bernardo's house. Hard to believe that a dog, dead for almost twenty years, still affected lives so much. Helped to better understand Soledad, though.

Her father and Bernardo were probably the only males she ever loved. For a little girl, to have them die so close together, well, that must be a hurt she still dealt with. And so did Cheyenne in more and maybe deeper ways. She needed Soledad home more than anyone. A lot of guilt eating inside that one.

He inhaled deeply and exhaled long. Same with Isabelle. She probably tried to absorb and shoulder any hurt or guilt her daughters felt. And according to Cheyenne, Father Brady did, too. He certainly had his hands full trying to understand and comfort this family. And then there was Lenny. Whatever was going on inside him had a past and a purpose. Maybe he had a guilt card close to his vest, too. If push came to shove, Lenny could be trusted.

He tapped out his cigarette, stuck the butt in his pack, and pulled out another.

Cheyenne had asked what made him so special?

Easy to answer. He wasn't.

Just another planet revolving around Soledad.

And where the hell was she?

Chapter Thirteen

Sunday, 3:15 pm

Soledad's taxi entered an exclusive waterfront area where houses became larger, farther apart, and separated by high stucco walls, ornate black iron fences, or thick, neatly trimmed hedges. The drive in Father Brady's car from Saint Anthony's to Saint Theresa's and the taxi to the Molina home provided time for a change of mind or plan, to back out of this final step as too dangerous, but too many good people had stuck their necks out not to take it. God bless Father Brady. He had come through and thought the escape from Saint Anthony's was the end with a new beginning. Cheyenne knew there was more but thought the worst was over. Cal knew there was more, with the worst still hanging over their heads. This meeting could lead to ending it for them all.

She gripped her phone and stepped out of the taxi next to a high, thick hedge about twenty yards from the gated driveway. She pressed the number.

"Cal, this is Soledad. Where are you?"

"On your back step. Where the hell are you?"

He was probably smoking and sounded like he wanted to yell but was afraid someone might overhear. "Don't go anywhere. If everything goes well, I should be home in two hours, maybe less."

"You need to get back home *now*. Lenny came here looking for you. I put him off, but he'll be back. He thinks you're here, and I'm pretty sure the police found a body. Probably Carlos."

"How do you know?" If the police found Carlos, Arturo Molina either already knew or would soon.

"I don't for sure, but Lenny got a call and rushed off. Said the shit would hit the fan. Tell me where you are. I'll come get you."

She shook her head as she neared the gate. "No, I have to do this."

"Do what? You have the police and probably Jace and the Molinas looking for you."

"I'm making my family safe from them all." She took a deep breath and let it out. "But if I don't come back, watch out for my family, especially Cheyenne."

"What are you up to?"

"*Cal*, will you watch out for my family or not?"

"I already am."

"You're a good man, Cal. Better than—"

"Don't say that. You could be wrong."

"Better than any man since, well, for a long, long time. Trust me, goodbye."

She turned off the phone and slipped it into her small, black evening bag. So they found Carlos. Tricky timing, a few hours later would've been better. She smoothed and straightened her dress. A good choice, conservative, even old fashioned, with long sleeves, a lot of lace, and a high button collar. This morning the bruises seemed imperceptible, but no sense taking a chance. They needed to be kept secret. But the veil might oversell. She flipped the veil on top of her head, letting it hang down across the sides of her face, kind of like a Spanish senorita. No makeup, this had to be a pure look. When the tears came, the only streaks would be clear, glistening liquid.

For the Molinas to allow her to come to their home on a Sunday said they needed to know things now and were very interested in what she had to say. They wanted to find Carlos and probably already suspected he was dead. The information they gleaned from her would shape their actions after Carlos's body turned up. They'd use everything they knew or suspected to find the killer, then go after the killer much faster than the police.

They would look closely at enemies and associates. Arturo Molina had the resources to find out about Jace's and Carlos's big deal. Allude to the deal without knowing about it. Let Arturo Molina reach his own conclusions. Assume he has the same information as the police and Fowler, and assume Fowler knows her client last Friday was Carlos. A connection the Molinas would be very interested in.

Arturo Molina would test with questions he already knew the answers to. So tell the truth whenever possible. He probably knows about Cal and Ynez. A good misdirection with Jace, but the Molinas would see it for what it was, a side story, only useful for putting people in place and time. For them, everything was important as a connection to Carlos and their family. Connect Jace wherever and whenever possible.

She stopped in front of the gate. The three-story, white stucco house had reddish brown roof tiles and balconies extending from the second and third floor rooms. The redbrick driveway continued past the house to a garage large enough to hold at least six cars. There was no sign of heightened security. The house seemed like others in this exclusive area, owned by someone very rich who liked privacy.

"Miss Montoya?" A man's voice came from an intercom box.

"Yes, sir."

"We are expecting you." The gate swung open. A tall man in sunglasses, wearing a dark suit with a solid red tie, stepped from the front door and motioned to her.

She swallowed. Her heels clicked on the red bricks, and her dress rustled. She passed from early afternoon sunlight into the shadows of palm trees that lined the driveway. The tall man removed his sunglasses and smiled as they met. In his mid-thirties, a handsome face with calm confidence and bright, friendly eyes. He looked familiar, not from seeing him in person, but from studying the Molina Family online. This was the oldest son, Manuel, a widower, and the family's Harvard lawyer. He resembled his father. Carlos took after his mother.

"Welcome, Miss Montoya. My name is Manuel." He held out a hand toward the front door. "Please, come in. My father is expecting you."

"I apologize for intruding on your Sunday."

He nodded. "Usually Sunday is for church and family, but your call was about family."

He motioned her into a large foyer with a tile floor, an oriental carpet in the middle, and a large potted plant on each side. Arched doorways to the family rooms let in a mixture of voices and the clinking of glasses and plates like the setting of a table.

"Please come this way." He led her past a spiral

staircase that curled to the second and third floors. They continued down a wide hallway to a set of double doors that opened into a large, well-lighted room. On opposite sides sat matching cream-colored couches and chairs with thin, dark green pinstripes and intricately carved arms and legs. End tables with the same ornate legs sat between them. Renaissance style paintings hung on three walls. All furniture was pushed against the walls except for a large wooden desk near the middle of the room with two straight-backed chairs. A chandelier hung from a high ceiling, spotlighting the desk.

Manuel motioned her to the chair in front of the desk. "My father will be with you shortly. May I get you something?"

She nodded and sat. "Water, please."

"I'll see to it." He left and closed the doors behind him.

When lying to Jace, there was time to work on him before and after. With Arturo Molina, there would be one shot. Tell the truth about everything he knows or might know. Weave in the lies. Let him come to his own conclusions, because what Arturo Molina figured out for himself meant more than what others figured for him.

When the double doors opened, she turned in her chair. Manuel entered first, carrying a silver tray with an empty glass and a pitcher of ice water with lemon slices. An older, shorter man wearing a dark gray suit with a solid blue tie followed and walked to the opposite side of the desk. His thin face had squint lines between eyebrows of dark, deep-set eyes. Isolated silver streaks contrasted his thick black hair. He studied her with a calm, unreadable expression. Manuel set the tray on the desk, filled her glass, then moved to one of the cream-colored chairs against the wall.

This was it, the performance of her life.

"I am Arturo Molina. Welcome to our home, Miss Montoya." He smiled politely and sat opposite her.

She hunched her shoulders, pressed her knees together, and folded her hands in her lap. Everything depended on perception. Tell him everything possible no matter how degrading. Be reluctant when appropriate. Be harmless. "Thank you for seeing me on your Sunday and on such short notice."

He leaned forward with his elbows on the desk. "Miss Montoya, why are you here?"

"I know your son is missing, and I believe I have information about that."

He shook his head. "No, that is what you bring." His squint lines became deeper and closer together. "Why are you here?"

She picked up the glass with both hands and sipped. "If something bad has happened to your son, no one is safe, including my family."

"We do not harm the innocent."

She looked up and let a smile spread from her mouth to her cheeks and into her eyes, like God Himself had given His word that her family was safe, because they were innocent.

His squint lines relaxed as he sat back. "What makes you think my son is missing?"

Let the smile fade. "I called Cal Lee. He told me that Detective Trumbo is investigating Carlos's disappearance, and that he hasn't been seen for a week." Take a deep breath. "Wednesday night, I saw Carlos at Jace Richards's house."

Manuel shifted in his chair. Arturo Molina sat still, but his eyelids moved slightly and made his eyes deeper set. This was new information.

He blinked and nodded. "Tell me everything you know. Start at the beginning."

She sat up and sipped some water. Start with the truth, then weave in the bare minimum of needed lies that only Jace could contradict. In the end, make it her word against his. But most important, sell herself, make them *want* to believe. A successful lie started before the words and continued after.

"I live at Jason Richards's house. Wednesday evening, Carlos came to the house, and Jace immediately sent me to my room. I heard loud voices that sounded like an argument, then Carlos and Jace left in separate cars. Jace didn't return until early the next morning."

She paused to sip and let him ask a question, but he waited for her to continue. Manuel sat back, propped his left ankle on his right knee, and folded his arms.

They let her talk without interruption about everything that happened, starting with Thursday morning with every true detail about Cheyenne shopping, Cal helping Ynez, the flat tire and Fowler, Jace grabbing her ponytail and bending her arm behind her back, and finally the escape at Saint Anthony's.

Arturo Molina nodded. "Where is Ynez Pascal?"

She looked down at her folded hands. He already knew. Be reluctant, show a willingness to protect and sacrifice for family, something they understood and respected. She closed her eyes and slowly shook her head. "I can't."

Arturo Molina leaned forward with his elbows on

the desk. "Miss Montoya, look at me."

She looked up and bit on her lower lip.

A slight smile eased into his eyes. "I repeat." His voice softened. "I have never harmed an innocent."

She swallowed and nodded. "She's with my youngest sister in Gainesville. But Josepha is just trying to help. She's completely innocent, and so is Ynez."

"And where is Cal Lee?"

He must know this, too. Fowler probably called from the emergency room. "At my family's house. Waiting for me." She leaned forward. "Please, Cal is a good man in a bad business. He helped Ynez, he helped me, and now he'll have to deal with Jace and probably John Fowler, too."

He nodded. "Yes, more than likely. Was my son ever a client of yours?"

She tensed. Arturo Molina's squint lines narrowed. Manuel uncrossed his legs and leaned forward with his forearms on his knees and his hands clasped. They might or might not know. She looked down and nodded. "Once."

"When?"

"Last Friday. Sometimes when Jace has business dealings that aren't connected to his escort service, he assigns me to a client as a..." *Show shame.* It was real and it was there. She closed her eyes, hunched her shoulders, and look down.

"Miss Montoya. I'm not judging you, only the merit of your words. Please continue."

She held the glass with shaking hands and sipped. "As a thank you. His sweetener for big deals."

"And that was your role with my son?"

She nodded without looking up, then raised her

chin to sip again. Arturo Molina leaned back and stared with his head slightly cocked. Manuel watched while slowly nodding. Suddenly, but smoothly, Manuel pulled out his phone, studied the screen, took a deep breath, and put it away. He walked to his father and whispered in his ear.

Arturo Molina's visage didn't change except for the tightening of his jaw. His eyes stared through her, and his torso froze as if fighting to control his breathing. He stood slowly. "Excuse us, Miss Montoya. Is there anything we can get you?"

"No, sir."

They left her alone.

Word had come. They knew. They would discuss and judge every word and every impression she had given, and possibly watched right now. She bowed her head, folded her hands beneath her chin, and prayed. Silently moving her lips, seeing Mama suffering and crying and hoping. Feeling Cheyenne's need and guilt and sacrifice. Only coming home would ease their pain. Only coming home would ease hers. It was there, and very real, welling in her chest. *Use it.*

The entrance doors opened, then closed. Manuel stood with his back against them. Arturo Molina walked quickly to the front of the desk. She hunched her shoulders and looked down at her folded hands.

"Look at me, Miss Montoya."

She looked up. The welling in her chest rose to her throat.

"You came here for something. What is it?"

As planned, the black veil contrasted and framed her face. The light from the chandelier filled shadows and would illuminate every emotion and every glistening tear. She swallowed. Everything she was, everything she caused, and everything she wanted pushed past her throat, making her lower lip tremble.

"Miss Montoya, *what do you want*?"

She looked up into a cold, calculating face. This would decide the Molinas' course. Say it barely audible with the voice cracking at the end, like a truth just discovered coming from the heart. It was real and it was there. "I...I want to go home." Tears leaked. She stared up and made her eyes as big as possible, and they probably glistened.

He nodded. "Go home, Miss Montoya. And stay there."

She squeezed out a small smile between trembling lips. "Thank you."

He walked to the doors, then stopped. "My son will drive you home."

Manuel walked to her and held out his hand. "Please, come with me." He helped her up. They walked without talking as she wiped tears and sniffled through the foyer. No voices or sounds of clinking plates and glasses. The family had withdrawn to a more private area.

A black Lincoln Town Car waited. Manuel opened the front passenger door and motioned her in. He drove slowly down the driveway, turned onto the street, and waited until her sniffling stopped.

"If you're okay now, I have a few follow-up questions."

"Just a minute, please." She took a tissue from her evening bag. Now, the second part of the interrogation. She wiped her eyes and nose. He would look for details that supported or contradicted what she had said and what they knew. She put the tissue back into her evening bag.

"Better now?"

"Yes, sir."

"Don't bother with directions. I know the way. Now Wednesday evening you said Carlos arrived and Jace Richards sent you *immediately* to your room. Did you see Carlos?"

"Only on the monitor in the kitchen, driving up and then walking from his car. I was in my room by the time he came into the house."

For the next thirty minutes, Manuel asked short, specific questions. He let her talk and go off on tangents, interrupting to get the day and time of everything that happened as though he had other things with days and times he compared them to. He remembered every word she had said to his father, sometimes quoting her verbatim, then asking for details and explanations. Always having her clarify who they or he or she was.

About halfway home she finished the entire story again, complete with all the background of Cal and Shantelle and Ynez, and every detail of Cheyenne's plan and the escape at Saint Anthony's. With the description of her heel to Fowler's foot and the quarters flying from Cal's fist, Manuel grinned and shook his head.

"The entire episode with Ynez Pascal and Cal Lee has nothing to do with Carlos, does it?"

He had eliminated that misdirection. She shook her head. "No, nothing at all. Bad timing, but I don't care. Ynez is out." She looked up and smiled, and it must have been a good one, because Manuel smiled back.

"But maybe good timing, because I think Jace is so occupied he won't bother with Ynez or me."

They drove in silence for the next several minutes. Manuel exited the freeway and slowed down. "You indicated that you served as a thank you to my brother for a business deal with Mister Richards."

This part of her story interested them the most. She hunched her shoulders, nodded, and squeaked out, "Yes."

"How do you know this?"

"It's the main reason I live at Jace's house." She shrugged. "I'm for special clients when the money involved is significant. I never know what is happening, only that it is."

"How well did you know Shantelle Williams?"

She froze. This was unexpected. He wouldn't ask unless he knew Shantelle had a connection to Carlos. Don't lie now, he knew something. "She was my best friend. I loved her like a sister. I still call Detective Trumbo for updates, but he just says it's an open investigation and there's nothing new."

Two blocks from home he pulled over and parked. He turned. "Look at me, Miss Montoya."

She rotated at the waist and looked up to a closed-mouth smile and set, dark eyes.

"Show me your neck, please."

She leaned back and put her hand to her chest. "I don't understand."

"Just unbutton your collar, fold, and separate it." His smile widened slightly. "You'll do that for me, won't you?"

She nodded. "Yes, sir." He must know something about his brother's sexual practices. Neck bruises were his calling card, and Manuel probably saw the police photos of Shantelle's body. Her fingers felt like trembling but didn't. Her right hand unbuttoned the collar, then both hands separated it.

"Look up and turn your head to the left." He leaned forward with his index and middle fingers together and slowly stroked the side of her neck twice. "Now to the right." He stroked the other side of her neck. "Thank you, Miss Montoya." His lips parted slightly, and his gaze softened.

Manuel seemed glad he hadn't found any makeup-covered bruises. Maybe because it eliminated a motive for her killing Carlos. Or maybe he didn't want to picture his brother squeezing her neck. Maybe both. He watched as she buttoned and straightened her collar. He leaned back with a small shake of his head.

"Tell me, Miss Montoya, and you don't have to answer if you don't want to. Why did you decide to work for Mister Richards?"

This had nothing to do with Carlos. This was for himself, and all about her. She looked down and closed her eyes. "Because the money was needed very much." She looked up, straight into his eyes. "And I put it to very good use. Better than most who make money from things they aren't proud of." She clenched her jaw and held a stare.

He nodded. "I apologize if I've offended you. It was unintended, and I took no pleasure from it." He turned and drove the last two blocks in silence. He pulled over in front of her house on the opposite side of the street. "Enjoy your homecoming. I may want to talk to you again."

She opened the door, stepped onto the curb, and

looked over the roof of the Lincoln.

Mama came running from the front door. Cheyenne ran from the side, kitchen door. She sprinted around the front of the Lincoln, running with arms wide apart. They collided in the street. First, Mama, crying and hugging and kissing, then Cheyenne latching onto her back, crying and squeezing them all together.

Their six little feet moved the huddle in small uncoordinated steps toward the house. Father Brady came through the front door and stood to the side, hands folded, praying, watching the huddle slowly move up the sidewalk. Cal sat on the front step, grinning, holding up his phone, recording the reunion. Manuel watched from the Lincoln, then drove away.

The scene couldn't have been choreographed any better. *Thank you, God, that had to help.* Maybe Manuel had doubted everything she'd said, but after what he'd seen, maybe he wanted to believe. If everything else was equal, that could tip the scales.

Chapter Fourteen

Sunday, 6:30 pm

Soledad ended her call to Josepha and hung her black dress in the closet. Some of her high school clothes still hung there, dust on the shoulders and misshapen by hangers and gravity. Cheyenne had probably taken what she could wear as she grew into them. Never much there anyway, and Mama had far less. Mama had done her best to make sure her daughters didn't dress like the poor kids, but schoolmates noticed when the same clothes were worn too often. A knot tightened in her stomach. Probably a big reason she'd left, and maybe why she loved shopping so much.

Beneath the clothes sat several pairs of neatly arranged shoes. On the shelf above lay a few scattered belts and hats, including her cap from the high school swim team. She turned and surveyed a room that hadn't changed since she left. Same twin bed and floral print bedspread, which raised a smile. Not the bed, but underneath, her favorite hiding place with Bernardo when they played hide-and-seek with Daddy.

Cheyenne always wanted to hide with them. Bernardo would drop to his belly and shimmy under, then turn sideways, which only took a few seconds, but always seemed like several long minutes as Daddy covered his eyes and counted to ten. She and Cheyenne would snuggle up behind Bernardo. Daddy would come in, look behind the door and in the closet, then kneel and look under the bed. Cheyenne had to cover her mouth to muffle her giggles and got so nervous and excited she usually peed her pants. Daddy always asked Bernardo if anyone was under there with him. Bernardo never gave them away.

Same cracked mirror and nicked-up dresser, but everything was dusted and polished. The same light pink walls with her high school academic and swimming awards hanging above her bed in their skinny, black frames from the Dollar Store. Except for Mama's rocker sitting by the nightstand, her old room looked the same, but neater and cleaner.

She leaned close to her favorite award, a framed newspaper article and picture of her receiving the first-place medal for the district one-hundred-meter freestyle. She was small and almost shapeless, but she could cut through the water with little resistance, then tuck, turn, kick-off, and glide underwater, surfacing with arms and legs moving with little wasted motion. Teammates called her the minnow. Mama was so proud. Probably the only year in her school career when she was special. The academic awards never counted for much, except to Mama.

She sat slumped on the edge of the bed next to the rocker. Mama's open Bible lay on the nightstand. Cheyenne said Mama came to her room every night for an hour or two to read her Bible. She'd start with Genesis, eventually get through Revelations, then start all over again, looking for answers Mama said were there for both of them.

She slipped into a pair of jeans, a University of Miami sweatshirt, and a pair of multi-colored, slip-on tennis shoes that Cheyenne had left for her. Better get used to sharing Cheyenne's clothes for a while, because her own wardrobe at Jace's house wasn't an option. She closed her eyes and sighed. Maybe that was a good thing. Let them go. Didn't want a reminder of a life best left in the past. Better get used to discount shopping and mixing and matching.

She leaned over the nightstand to see where Mama had read last. Each chapter began with a bolded summary sentence, making it easy for Mama to look up a particular story or verse.

Genesis 18, Sarah was promised a son, and Abraham interceded with God to help Lot and save Sodom. In that one, Abraham actually bargained with God. If he could find ten righteous souls in Sodom, God would spare the city. Genesis 19, Sodom and Gomorrah are destroyed. Sodom must have been rotten to the core.

Cal had some decisions coming. Josepha was nearing North Miami Beach and should arrive home in less than an hour, and Ynez was with her.

What *were* his plans? Since the homecoming, Cal had stayed in the background, leaving the Montoya women to their reunion, keeping quiet at dinner and very embarrassed when Mama made a fuss over him. He made frequent visits to the back step to smoke. He had questions but was willing to wait.

Cal wasn't the only one with questions. He could have left Friday or Saturday, gone to Gainesville, picked up Ynez, and not looked back. But he didn't, and he'd fought Fowler for her. Why? Going in he knew his chances were slim to none, but he did it anyway. That said more than words. He didn't love Ynez, and he wasn't getting out of here without something said. But he was so damn reluctant to share his fries.

A tap on the door began lightly, then grew louder. "Sho Sho, are you all right?"

"Yes, Mama. I'm changing my clothes. I'll be out in a few minutes." Mama waited to clutch her wrist, just like when she was a little girl, keeping her little Sho Sho from running into traffic. But no one had gained more peace and happiness in the last few hours than Mama. A close second was Cheyenne. Little Sis had latched onto her back with a bear hug and the sour breath of vomit and whiskey. Cal probably had something to do with that, but Cheyenne had eaten an unheard of two helpings at dinner. The healing had begun for Mama and Cheyenne. Everything was worth it just for that. Father Brady, too. He left after dinner with a face that was still tired and gaunt but at peace.

She sat up, took a deep breath, pumped up a smile, and opened the door.

Mama clutched her wrist.

"Mama, I'm home, and I won't leave you. But right now, I must go thank Cal for everything he's done."

Mama nodded and released her wrist. "He is on the back step." She smiled wide. "He is a good man."

"I know he is."

"I think he loves you."

"*Mama*!"

"And you love him."

"*Mama*!" She shook her head, then nodded in a confused bobble. Leave it to Mama to jump the gun.

161

"We haven't talked about that."

Mama eyed her with a small, tight smile. "Love is not something you discuss. Love is like the spark of life. Science cannot explain it, because it comes from God. It is something you feel. The words will come." Her smile transitioned into a knowing grin as her eyebrows raised. "And a man will show love long before he can say the words."

"Well, Cal hasn't done either." She took a step, but Mama blocked her.

"Has he not? I do not know what all is going on, but I think he has risked much, maybe everything, with nothing to gain but you. I see from the outside. Sometimes that is much clearer. I see the way you two look at each other when the other is not looking." She sighed. "Men in love are like frightened little boys with a secret. They act up, because they want to tell, but are afraid, so it has to be drawn out of them."

"I'll keep that in mind, and I'll think about what you said."

Mama took hold of her hands and squeezed. "What is in your heart, and his, cannot be thought away. You love each other."

"*Mama*! Stop that."

"I hear no denial."

"I'm going now." She walked to the end of the hall, paused, and looked over her shoulder. Mama kept poking a finger in the direction of the back step, and her smile grew with each poke.

Cal sat on the back step smoking a cigarette. She stopped at the screen door and clenched her jaw. Mama thought from the heart, something she couldn't allow herself to do. The plan was what mattered, and a clear head was needed for that.

She took another deep breath, pushed through the screen door, and sat beside him. She took his hand. "We need to talk."

Cal took a long drag, then crushed his cigarette. "Yes, we do. I let you have your reunion, and I haven't asked any questions, but you have some explaining to do."

"In a minute." She stood, pulled him across the yard to the swing, then turned so Mama, and probably Cheyenne, would have a profile view. She squeezed his hand. "Mama and Cheyenne are watching, and they think you're my boyfriend. Let them have it for a little while, please."

"The truth is gonna come out sooner or later."

"I'm counting on it, but first this." She looped her arms around his neck. "Hold me and smile like you're happy to be with me."

"I am." He put his hands on her waist. "But where were you, and who was that in the Lincoln?"

She touched a fingertip to his lips. "That can wait until after this." She raised on her tiptoes, placed a hand on the back of his head, and guided him down. His lips parted as his eyes widened, then closed. He seemed unsure, but the more she kissed, the more he kissed back, and the faster his heart beat. He probably felt hers doing the same.

His hands slid up her back and held her shoulders.

She slowly ended the kiss, then planted the side of her face against his chest, facing the house so Mama and Cheyenne could see her closed eyes and wide smile. That was no pretend kiss—he couldn't act that well. *All right,* Caleb Dean Lee, *think about that for a while.*

He took a big breath, then swallowed and sighed.

She took her own deep breath. "You did just fine. Now push me on the swing while we talk."

She sat on the one remaining swing and held the rusty chains. Cal's fingertips gently pushed her shoulders. This was a scene Mama had wanted for years. She was getting it now and was either crying or nodding an I-told-you-so or both.

"All right, what the hell's going on?"

That didn't sound like a man in love. "Cal, no matter what I say, keep smiling." She took a deep breath. "I went to see Arturo Molina, and that was his son, Manuel, who drove me home. I told the Molinas everything I know. And I think you're right about the police finding Carlos's body. Are you still smiling?"

"Yeah, but it ain't easy."

"Keep smiling. There's more. I called Josepha. Manuel Molina visited her and Ynez in Gainesville on Saturday night. She tried to call me, but Jace had my phone, and I had already told her not to call Cheyenne. She had enough on her mind. The point is the Molinas know you were with Ynez the night Carlos was killed. The police have evidence. There's always evidence. So very soon they'll find out it was Jace who killed Carlos." She slipped off the swing and took his hand. "Let's take a short walk, away from Mama's and Cheyenne's eyes, so you don't have to pretend."

They walked in silence around the side of the house and down the sidewalk. The sun had set, and streetlights blinked on. Cousin Jimmy drove by in his ten-year-old Honda Civic. He beeped, and she waved in return. "That's Cousin Jimmy."

"*Who* is Cousin Jimmy? And why haven't I seen him except to slip into the kitchen or bathroom, then slip out again? He wasn't even at dinner."

"He's a third, no, fourth cousin by marriage, down from school in Jacksonville. He's cruising the neighborhood, keeping an eye on things. Josepha is on her way, and he's waiting to have dinner with her. He's in love with Josepha, and like any good Puerto Rican young man, he wants to help the family of the woman he loves."

Cal had to see that obvious parallel. Why else was he still here? But he made no comment, just clenched his jaw and lit a cigarette. Maybe he didn't like what he felt, but he felt it. "Ynez is on her way here with Josepha."

"*What*?" He spun and faced her. "Tonight?"

"Yes. She and Josepha should arrive soon. Ynez is frightened, wouldn't stay alone in Gainesville, and wants to be with you. The Molinas aren't after you or Ynez, and Jace has bigger things to worry about. You're free to go. What're you going to do?"

He grimaced and rubbed his forehead. "I don't know. For the past few days the plan each morning has been to make it through the day."

"Each morning has been someone else's plan for you. It's your plan now. Have you thought about going away with Ynez? She has."

"Kind of."

"Kind of? You either did or you didn't. Which is it?"

He shrugged and took two quick puffs. "Kind of."

"Well, you can *kind of* go get your car, and you two can leave and not look back."

"I guess I thought she'd start a new life with the money we gave her."

Oughtta slap him upside the head. Money didn't buy, or buy off, love. "She doesn't want money. She wants you. Or are Jace's girls somehow not deserving of the same things as girls outside the business?"

"You know me better than that. They deserve more. You deserve more."

"I'm not sure what I deserve, but I know what I want." She raised her hands and placed them on his cheeks. "Look at me, Cal. What do you want?"

He shrugged a weak smile. "I want you and your family to be safe."

Mama said it had to be drawn out. She frowned and dropped her hands to her hips. "Yes, I know how that works. That's why Cousin Jimmy is here. For the family of the woman he loves. Why are you here?" Couldn't make it any clearer than that.

He looked over the top of her head, took a long drag, and flicked his cigarette into the street. "Ahh, shit. Lenny's Charger just pulled up across the street. This can't be good."

She clenched her teeth. "He can wait."

"No, I need to handle this." He pointed toward the house. "Who's that pulling up in front?"

She snapped her gaze over her shoulder. "Josepha and Ynez. Cousin Jimmy is pulling up behind them."

He grabbed her shoulders. "Go, keep your family inside, and stay with them. I'll see what Lenny wants." He turned her around and gave her a push. "Go."

Chapter Fifteen

Sunday, 8:00 pm

Cal took long strides across and down the street, glancing back and forth between Lenny stepping out of his Charger, and Soledad running toward the arriving cars. Isabelle and Cheyenne burst through the front door as Soledad reached the sidewalk in front of the house.

A tall young woman stepped from the driver's seat of the first car. That had to be Josepha, because all the Montoya women converged beneath the streetlight hugging and laughing and crying. Cousin Jimmy stood in the background, smiling nervously at Josepha. Poor Cousin Jimmy, he had no idea what he was in for getting involved with a Montoya sister. Good luck with that.

Lenny's Charger sat parked across the street, equidistant between two streetlights but in the glow of neither. Lenny leaned his back against the car door and crossed his arms. He didn't look happy. Soledad said they'd found a body, so it had to be about that. Maybe a good thing to have Lenny here. If anyone else was watching, they'd know the police were, too.

He approached Lenny with a tired smile and a sigh. "I guess you need to talk to me."

Lenny opened his collar and loosened his tie. He

surveyed the scene across the street. "What's going on?"

"The youngest sister just arrived from college." The hugging was still happening, but Soledad and Cheyenne stared at him and Lenny, and they weren't happy either. "They're having a reunion."

Lenny shook his head. "Doesn't matter this time. I need you and Soledad to come downtown."

"Can't it—?"

"No, it can't wait."

"Okay, I'm ready, but please, think about this. If you take Soledad in now, the whole family will follow, including Isabelle. And she's been running on God and adrenaline for two days now." He gave Lenny a shrug and frown. "She might have a heart attack."

"Shut up." Lenny rubbed his forehead. "Isabelle is not going to have a heart attack."

"Maybe not, but she's close to passing out. Look at her." They both glanced across the street at a wobbly Isabelle draped on Soledad. "She could pass out, hit her head on the curb. *Bam*, hematoma." He snapped his fingers. "Gone like that."

"Shut up, just shut up. You oughta sell used cars with that shtick." Lenny's thumb pushed his hat back a few inches. "Get Soledad over here—right now—by herself."

That might work. Soledad had a way of talking people into or out of things. "Sure, whatever you say, but consider this. Soledad can make an excuse and slip away from her mother later. You two can talk. Think of Isabelle."

Lenny added a clenched jaw to his glare. "Get Soledad."

"All right, all right, I'm going." He swiveled from Lenny. Everyone on the sidewalk watched. He walked toward Soledad and motioned her to the middle of the street. She nodded and shifted Isabelle into Josepha's hold.

"Cal?" The voice came from the passenger side of Josepha's Honda. Oh yeah, Ynez. Forgot about her. No question about it, this was bad timing. She stepped out of the passenger side. "Cal." She took two tentative steps, then ran and wrapped her arms around him. "What's going on? I'm scared."

He held her shoulders and pushed space between them. "It's gonna be all right." He glanced at Lenny. "But I have to go with the detective."

"Now?" She squeezed his arms and gazed up with big, brown, tear-leaking eyes and a trembling lower lip. "Are you coming back?"

Oh God, she looked so much like Shantelle. This wasn't fair. "I promise I'll be back. You stay with Josepha's family. You'll be safe here."

Soledad stepped beside them with crossed arms and a wry smile. "So what are *you* going to do?"

"I'll be leaving with Lenny, but right now, he wants to talk to you, alone."

She narrowed her eyes. "You know what I mean."

"Yes, I do. And I'm working on it." He shrugged. "Can Ynez stay here?"

"Of course, we planned on it." Soledad motioned to Cheyenne, who came running. Soledad put an arm around Ynez's shoulders and handed her off to Cheyenne. "Take care of Ynez. She's staying with us as long as she wants." Soledad gave him a stare and a frown. "I better go see Lenny, and you better do some thinking." She spun and marched toward Lenny.

Cheyenne put an arm around Ynez as they pivoted toward the sidewalk. "You'll have to share a room with Josepha—or me. Is that okay? I'd really like to get to know you." Ynez nodded with her head down. Cheyenne glared over her shoulder. "*Cal.* Stay right here. I'm not through with you." She guided Ynez back to the sidewalk.

Stay right here? Where the hell would he go? Maybe takeoff running down the street, but after having seen Cheyenne run from the church to the car in a dress, she'd run him down in half a block, no problem.

Walking in a small circle didn't change things. And neither did giving Ynez a reassuring smile. She just stared like a deer in the headlights. Every detail spotlighted and every inside feeling coming through clearly on her face. And none of it was a lie.

He switched his gaze to Soledad half in shadow and half in dim light at the streetlight's edge. Lenny talked and poked his finger in front of her face. Soledad hunched her shoulders, bowed her head, and bobbled nods like a little girl receiving a scolding. That was a good sign. Lenny was laying down the law but giving her time. Probably wouldn't take her in right now. He couldn't bring himself to drag Soledad away in front of Isabelle.

"*Cal.*"

He flinched and snapped his head around. Ah hell, not Cheyenne again.

She took a wide stance with her hands on her hips and a narrowed-eyed stare. "Soledad said you were helping a friend. Just how good of a friend *is* Ynez?"

He fumbled for a cigarette. This was the middle of

the damn street. Where was the damn traffic when he needed it? "We don't have time for this now."

Cheyenne pursed her lips, seethed out a few breaths, then dropped her stare and shook her head. "Cal...I was just starting to like you."

He lit his cigarette and pointed at Lenny. "You see him? That's Detective Trumbo, and I have to go with him. There's things going on you don't know about. Let Soledad and me handle them. Now please, take care of Ynez. And please, be nice to her."

"Of course I will. She's not the bad one here. She'll have our hospitality and protection, as much as we can give. But what about Soledad?"

"She's gonna have to go downtown and talk to Detective Trumbo, but I don't think he'll take her now. So you'll have to help her slip out later. She'll be all right, trust me." He took a long drag. "No one means more to me right now."

"Oh, really." Cheyenne cocked her head. "What about later?"

He took two quick drags. "Let's just leave it at that for now. I have to go."

She grabbed his arm. "I don't know what to think of you. You were very brave today. I saw you fight like David against Goliath. But you're a coward, too. I think you want to go off with the police." She poked her chin up and out. "But we'll all be waiting here when you get back." She spun and marched back to her family.

She had a point. Tough questions ahead and behind, but at least Lenny wouldn't cry over the answers. And there was less chance of physical harm from Lenny than from Cheyenne.

"*Cal.*"

He flinched and almost jumped. Soledad grabbed his arm. "Lenny's waiting for you." She looked up with a puzzled smile. "He called me 'young lady.' And lectured me like...I don't know, but not like a policeman. A little strange, but I liked it. He gave me an hour." She put her arms around his neck and whispered, "Tell Lenny everything. And I mean everything, except about my bruises. Not the bruises." She kissed him and ran to Isabelle.

Tell everything, but don't mention the bruises? Jace must have seen them, but okay, she was always a step or two ahead. Four days ago, simple assignment. Pick up Soledad for an afternoon of shopping. Shouldn't have gone to the apartment, and never should have started that nap with her. And now, she *did* mean more than anyone else. How did all this happen? Never make shopping plans with a woman. Nothing good could come of it.

"*Cal!*"

Goddamn it, if one more person called his name...

"Get your ass over here." Lenny pointed to the front passenger seat of his Charger, then slid behind the wheel.

"Coming, Lenny." He dropped his cigarette, stepped on it, then looked at the stars looking back. They weren't aligned.

He closed the passenger door and glanced over his left shoulder. The whole family, plus Ynez, watched them drive away, and soon they'd talk. If Cousin Jimmy was smart, he'd make himself scarce. When women got together, they usually agreed to blame the man, then all men, and Jimmy would get it by proxy.

Lenny glanced over. "Looks like I came at a bad

time. There were a few people there I didn't recognize. The tall one that got out of the Honda. Is that the sister from college?"

"Yeah, Josepha, she's the youngest."

"And the short one that looked like she wanted to bite your head off."

"That would be Cheyenne, the middle sister."

"So that's Cheyenne. Looks a lot like Soledad. And who was the lost-looking guy?"

"Cousin Jimmy. You had one of his beers when Isabelle brought you the paella."

Lenny smacked his lips and swallowed. "Yeah, that stuff was really good. And who was the frightened one that glommed on to you? She looked familiar."

"Ahhh, that's Ynez Pascal. One of Jace's new girls, or I guess she used to be. The one I spent Wednesday night with. She's kind of been my girlfriend."

"Oh, that sounds real permanent."

"It's a confusing situation."

Lenny cocked his head. "I know I've seen that girl someplace."

"Well, she looks something like Shantelle."

Lenny slowed to a stop at a red light, leaned back, and stared blankly. "Yeah, I can see it, after I block out the bruises on Shantelle's neck. But I gotta tell ya, Cal, it didn't take a trained detective to see that something was going on back there. How many girlfriends you got anyway?"

"Lenny, I'm working on that. And thanks for giving Soledad some time and not cuffing me and throwing me into the back seat."

"You're not under arrest. You're voluntarily coming in for questioning. If you unvolunteer, then I'll

173

arrest you. As for Soledad, she has an hour. There're two units in the area, one to bring her in and another to keep an eye on the house."

"What's gonna happen when she comes in?"

"Same as you. Cooperate, answer the questions, and we'll probably send her home."

"Probably, but not definitely."

"Well, things are out of my hands and moving fast, and both of you are real popular right now. I'm taking you to the North Precinct. There's an ADA waiting for us."

Yeah, the shit was hitting the fan all right. The police would talk to Jace for sure and probably the Molinas. "Maybe Soledad and I should get a lawyer."

"You disappoint me." Lenny shrugged as he turned left. "But why not play it this way? Start the interview, then at any time you can stop and request a lawyer. Of course then"—Lenny glanced and glared—"both your asses will end up in jail."

"*Jesus Christ*, Lenny. I kinda thought—"

"You kinda thought *what*? Listen up, asshole. I gave Soledad an hour, which I'll have to explain to that little prick of an ADA." Oncoming headlights flashed across Lenny's face. His jaw clenched, and he shook his head. "Donald Dillard, I've dealt with him. He's politically ambitious, likes high-profile cases, and when Carlos Molina's body turned up, that case went to the top of his list. He comes prepared with judges and warrants in his pocket. Everything will be scrutinized. And he's a real asshole."

They rode in silence for several blocks. Lenny kept shaking his head, then clenching his jaw like scenarios were running through his head that didn't work.

"What're you thinking about, Lenny?"

"How to keep Dillard from screwing up the interviews."

"You ever arrest Soledad before?"

Lenny shook his head. "No, but about eight years ago, when Fowler and I were still partners, she was a witness to an accidental discharge of a firearm. We interviewed her at the scene, and that was it."

"Did you recognize her?"

"Whatta-ya mean?"

"Well, she was the little girl hugging the dog when it died. You were there, remember. Isabelle recognized you. When you questioned Soledad at that weapon discharge eight years ago, did you recognize her as that same little girl grown up?"

Lenny glanced right then left, then settled on looking straight ahead. "Almost twelve years between the two times." He shook his head. "I don't remember."

Bullshit. There was more to that story than Lenny was letting on. Something happened. Go with the gut feeling on this one. Lenny had an agenda when it came to Soledad and probably Isabelle, too. "Will Fowler come after her later?"

Lenny shrugged and turned onto Biscayne Boulevard. "That depends. I was his partner for five years. He'll take calculated risks for money, but he won't risk his life for anyone or anything, including revenge. Anyway, he knows he'd have to tangle with me. But he'll sure as hell come after you. And he likes to inflict pain. He's not stupid, so he won't kill ya. Well, not on purpose anyway."

That was reassuring as hell. "Got any advice?"

"Go for that foot. It's a weak point and fresh in his

mind. He'll move to protect it."

"I'll keep that in mind. Can you take him?"

Lenny shrugged again. "Maybe. Fowler thinks he can take me but not with enough certainty to risk it. Like I said, he ain't stupid, he just looks that way."

The Charger slowed as they approached the police station. Lenny stared straight ahead. "One more thing. I'm lead, so you're my interview, but Dillard has decided to assist. Any inconsistencies in your story, and he'll jump on them. So think hard. Think real hard about how you answer the questions." Lenny swung the car into police parking at the back of the station.

Think hard. What the hell did that mean? What was Lenny saying? Think hard and tell the truth? Think hard and lie? Think hard and tell the truth except when it came to Soledad, then lie like hell? Whatever Lenny was saying, he was playing his cards close to the vest. But it didn't matter. Tell everything, but not about the bruises.

Chapter Sixteen

Sunday, 11:00 pm

Cal slouched in his chair at a scarred three-by-six table in the middle of a brightly lit twelve-by-twelve interrogation room. Just like Soledad instructed, he told them everything from the shopping to the escape, with details, but not about the bruises. Detective Trumbo said that after they questioned Soledad, they might have some follow-up questions, then he could go home. When he asked—what about Soledad? Dillard said it depended on the interview.

Overall, the questioning seemed to go well, except when he reached across the table, grabbed ADA Dillard by the knot of his tie, and jerked him nose to nose. The little prick called Soledad a whore, and something snapped. Luckily, Lenny stepped between them and calmed things down. They could have locked him up right then. Assault was a legitimate charge, and Dillard didn't seem like the forgiving type. Could only be one reason. Jace and Fowler were smart enough to lie low until things became clearer. Dillard needed bait to draw them out or some other player.

He leaned back and for the fourth time checked the last two cigarettes in his pack. Nearly three hours since his last smoke and no telling how long until the next.

The door opened. Lenny walked in, leaned his back

against the wall, and crossed his arms. "We're keeping Soledad, but she wants a few words with you before we send you home."

"Lenny, please. Let her go. Keep me."

He shook his head. "It's already been decided."

Dillard strutted in, followed by a female officer holding Soledad's upper arm. She looked small and tired with her head bowed, letting hair flow forward hiding the sides of her face.

He stood and stepped around the table.

"Stop." Dillard pointed. "You can hear her just fine from there."

Soledad's eyes glanced from side to side, then focused straight ahead. Her irises shifted to the top of their sockets, staring straight at him. She gave one small nod, then jerked her arm free from the officer's hold, and sprinted. Dillard froze for a moment. Soledad raced across the room and launched herself.

He opened his arms and caught her, taking a step back to keep his balance. Her arms wrapped around his neck. Her lips grazed his ear. "I want out. Go to my home. Have Josepha call Manuel Molina to be my lawyer." Her lips slid from his ear to his mouth and kissed him firm and deep.

The officer grabbed Soledad's shoulders and pulled her back.

Her eyes popped big. "Please, before Mama wakes up. I'm counting on you."

He nodded while swallowing her Diet Coke flavored kiss. What the hell was she thinking? Manuel Molina as her lawyer? And why have Josepha make the call?

The officer returned Soledad to where her run

started. Dillard rushed around the table to the middle of the room. Lenny hadn't moved a muscle except to swivel his eyes to follow the action.

Dillard glared at Soledad. "*What*, before your mother wakes up?"

"I want Cal to go to my home. When Mama wakes up, I want him to be there to tell her not to worry about me."

Dillard shook his head. "We can't let Mister Lee go to your house." He poked a finger at each of them, then pointed at opposite sides of the table. "Sit down, both of you." They slid into chairs as Dillard moved to the end of the table. He delivered a short, sharp nod at Soledad. "Say what you have to say to Mister Lee."

She reached across the table and gently held his hands. "As soon as the police allow it, go to my home. Jimmy is a boy. They need a man at the house. And call Father Brady. Mama will need him."

He nodded. "I will as soon as I can."

"Thank you." She dropped her gaze, took a deep breath, then looked up with her lips pressed together. "What are you going to do about Ynez?" She frowned at him, then swiveled her attention to Lenny. "Ya know, his girlfriend arrived from Gainesville tonight."

Lenny hadn't moved from his stoic stance. "Yeah, I picked up on that."

"She's very pretty, like a young Shantelle." She returned her gaze to him, sighed, and squeezed his hands. "Do you love her?"

"This isn't the time or place."

"Oh, I think it's perfect. You won't lie to the police." She swiveled back to Lenny. "We were getting to that when you pulled up and took him away."

Lenny shrugged. "Timing is everything."

She snapped her stare across the table. "Do you love her? Don't think, just answer."

First, he looked at stone-faced Lenny, then at Dillard, who seemed curious and a little amused.

"Cal! Don't look at them. They don't know. Look at me."

No makeup and very tired, but she was beautiful. Yeah, at that point where she was beautiful all the time. "No. I don't love Ynez." That came out easy and true.

The corners of her mouth lifted slightly. She softened her tone. "But she loves you."

"I guess so, kinda."

She shook her head. "There's no kinda. A woman is either in love or she isn't. That's something you'll have to deal with, in person, and soon."

"I know, and I will."

"She saw me kiss you in the middle of the street. She knows something's up, and so do you."

She looked up at Dillard. "That's all I have to say. The rest is up to him." She scooted her chair back and stood. "I have to go pee now."

The officer led Soledad out. Dillard gave Lenny a little I-told-you-so sneer, then strutted around the table.

"Mister Lee. We have a squad car ready to take you home. Stay there. If you try to leave, you'll be arrested. And don't call anybody at the Montoya residence. We'll know."

Could Dillard do that? Electronic surveillance could, and Lenny said he came prepared and with a judge in his pocket. Could be a bluff. Better not take a chance on calling. Deliver Soledad's message in person.

Two officers were summoned. Without a word they led him to the police parking, then shoved him into the back of a squad car. Traffic was light, and the officers seemed in a hurry and not happy with their assignment. One yawned as he drove. The other turned from staring out the window and faced him with a sour look.

"You just extended our shift, and we're short on relief tonight. When we get you there, stay put. Try anything, and I'll make sure you resist arrest, maybe twice. Do you read me?"

"Officer, I want to go home, get something to eat, drink some beers, and watch some—"

"Shut up. I don't give a shit what you do, as long you do it there." He turned back to his window.

Whoa, don't piss these guys off any more than they already were. But he had to chance it. Soledad was counting on him. She thought quicker than any person he had ever known. But what was she up to? Was everything after that initial whispered message just for show? The attitude sounded real, and so was the kiss, but just like the last time, something came with the kiss. First time was a show for Isabelle and Cheyenne, this time to pass a message.

That message came out of left field. Call Manuel Molina and before Isabelle wakes up. She probably meant that, too. Would Manuel Molina even accept Soledad as a client? She must think so. Not sure about the rules of disclosure, but the prosecution at some time or another had to turn over all their evidence to the defense lawyer. That certainly would give the Molinas a lot of control over things.

Would the Molinas even want a trial? There were

things about Carlos his family would rather keep under the rug. Shantelle might not be the only girl he killed. They had nothing to gain from a trial. The media would swarm all over it. And they sure wouldn't want CNN and FOX airing the family's sordid laundry to the world.

But why have Josepha call? Soledad could have stopped talking, demanded a lawyer, and called Manuel Molina herself. She must want that particular delivery method for a reason. It wasn't just what she did, but how she did it.

No one, not the police, not Jace, not even the Molinas would see this coming. If the Molina family represented her, what message would that send to the police, to Jace? And what would Jace do? Soledad was forcing him into a corner. Jace wouldn't know whether to shit or go blind. He might run, and if he did, he'd look guilty as hell. Jace might not have any other choice. How long did Soledad have this move in her pocket?

What about all that stuff about Ynez? Was that real or misdirection or both? She seemed jealous, especially with those comments to Lenny. She got the truth out of him about Ynez. He wasn't in love with her. With Shantelle, the process had been gradual. But with Soledad, everything seemed accelerated to near light speed. And what was everything? A cigarette was needed to numb that unscratchable itch.

They drove past Marny's Café and made a left onto his street. Officer sour face turned to his partner. "When and if we're relived, wanna stop at Marny's for pecan pie and coffee?"

"You bet."

They had a plan, and he needed one, fast. His car was still parked near Saint Anthony's and might be under surveillance. But that didn't matter, if he could get to the car, he could get to Soledad's house. Better think first about getting out of his apartment. Front door, bedroom window, bathroom window, sliding glass door, those were the options.

The squad car slowed to a stop. Both officers exited. The sour-faced officer opened the rear door and motioned him out. "Remember what I said. After we're relived, do whatever you want. You'll be someone else's paperwork. Get going." He turned to his partner. "Flip you to see who has to cover the back."

He took long strides toward his front door. The officers stood beside their cruiser flipping a coin.

Officer sour face didn't realize it, but he'd just provided a break. Don't hesitate. Go straight through and out the patio door before it was covered. On the way through, make the apartment look like someone was there, and grab the last throwaway cell and backup pack of smokes.

He unlocked his front door, closed it, and flipped the deadbolt. He snatched the remote control, turned on the TV, and raced through the living room, running his hands across the closed blinds as he passed them. He continued to the kitchen, flipped on the light, opened the cabinet drawer, and snatched his last throwaway cell.

Three long strides, and he was out the sliding glass door. Slide it easy, easy, and shut.

Scuffling footsteps on the sidewalk at the side of the building grew louder.

He cut left behind the patio wall of the adjacent

apartment. The footsteps reached his patio and kicked something.

Yeah, never did sweep up that broken cup from when Lenny visited. A scraping sound followed by a plop. The officer that lost the coin flip had just sat in the lawn chair.

"I'm in position. The blinds are swaying a little. Musta just closed them. When're the detectives due?"

Then the familiar metallic click of a Zippo lighter, followed by that wonderful aroma.

Ah shit, and damn it all to hell. Forgot the pack of smokes.

Chapter Seventeen

Monday, 1:05 am

Cal knelt on one knee inside Bernardo's dilapidated doghouse, smoking his next-to-last Camel. He tasted burning filter, then crushed the butt into the sandy soil. Nearly two hours getting here, but so far, so good. Only thirty more feet to deliver Soledad's message, then somehow get back to the apartment and sneak in before dawn.

A police van sat across the street in front of the house, and a patrol car cruised the neighborhood, but after fifteen minutes of watching, no policeman had walked behind the house. He crawled out of the Saint Bernard size opening, stood, and brushed the dirt from his hands and knees.

At the near end of the house, light shined through the kitchen curtains. Probably the easiest place to enter, but Ynez might be there, and this wasn't the time to deal with that situation. She must be frightened and confused, but the Montoya family would take care of her until things got straightened out. Later wouldn't make it easier, but at least it was later.

The back door and his smoking step at the middle of the house were dark, but at the far end a ceiling light shone through an open window. If memory served, that was Cheyenne's bedroom, which might be the best entry point.

He stepped past the swing set and halted. Someone entered the lighted room. Too short for Josepha or Ynez, must be Cheyenne. She'd been pissed off when Lenny took him away, and after time with Ynez, that probably increased. *Don't let her get started.* Just take control and focus her energy on getting Soledad out of jail, and before Isabelle woke up. Not sure why that was important, or why Josepha should make the call, but Soledad must have her reasons. She had a plan and reasons for everything.

He hunched and jogged to beside the bedroom window. No voices, only a plop and the creak of a bed. He edged sideways and peeked between the curtains. Cheyenne lay with closed eyes on a made bed.

"Cheyenne, it's me, Cal."

She popped up, gave her head a shake, then rushed to the window.

"Cal, is—?"

"Open the screen and let me in."

She slid the screen to the side, leaving about a three-foot opening. "Is Soledad with you?" She poked her head out the window. "Soledad, Soledad?"

"Shhh. She's not with me. Just move and let me in."

She held a hard glare while stepping back. He pressed his hands on the chest-high sill, jumped, and threw a knee up and forward. His head and shoulders dived through the opening. His hip and right knee came down on the sill. Cheyenne grabbed his arms and yanked. He twisted and hit the floor on his shoulder and hip.

Her gripped slipped, and she plopped on her butt.

She sat staring and looked a lot like Soledad had at the police station, no makeup, very fatigued, and shadows beneath tired eyes. She wore sweatpants and a baggy University of Miami sweatshirt, which seemed to be the Montoya Sister uniform for the night.

"*Where* is Soledad?"

He rose to his knees. "She's still at the police station, but as far as I know, not under arrest."

"You shouldn't have left her. She wouldn't have left you."

"She sent me, and I don't have time for your bullshit. So just shut up and listen." That felt good, and it shut her up, but she seethed.

She sprang up, rushed to the door, and opened it enough to poke her head through. She ducked back inside.

Her fists went to her hips. "Well, I'm listening."

"Soledad has a message for Josepha. Where is she?"

"In the kitchen with Jimmy." Her eyes narrowed. "What message?"

"Go get Josepha, and you'll find out. And don't tell Jimmy."

She glared but slipped out the door.

He checked the pack in his shirt pocket. Good, the last cigarette hadn't been crushed. Would need it dealing with Cheyenne. She could be a real pain in the ass, but she got things done, and if the instructions came from Soledad, she'd follow them.

The door sprang open. Cheyenne rushed through, pulling Josepha in after her.

Cheyenne closed the door. Josepha stood rigid with a confused look. Tall and slender, at least five-ten, with the Montoya light brown skin and long black hair. Higher cheekbones than her sisters, which accented gorgeous green eyes. Absolutely stunning. Very easy to see why Cousin Jimmy— "*Owww*. Why'd you hit me?"

Cheyenne shook her fist. "You were staring. She's only nineteen and a half, just like Ynez."

"I wasn't staring. I was thinking." He rubbed his shoulder. "And you have pointy little knuckles."

"And we still have things to talk about."

"Not now." He smiled at Josepha. "I'm Cal. I'm helping your sister."

She nodded. "I know who you are. Ynez talked a lot about you. And Cheyenne told me all about you, too."

That couldn't be good. He took a deep breath and pulled out the throwaway cell. "Soledad wants you to call Manuel Molina and ask him to be her lawyer."

Cheyenne stepped between them. "That's crazy. They're after Soledad, too. I think you got the message wrong. Anyway, I've already been looking into lawyers and—"

"*Stop*." He shoved a hand in front her face. "I got the message right, so—"

She slapped his hand away and took a position in front of Josepha. "Then I'll make the call. I'm the one—"

"*Stop*. Just shut up and stop. When I see you coming, it's like the Tasmanian Devil. A tornado spinning around, kicking up dust. And when it stops, it growls and snaps. That's you."

Josepha giggled, then covered her mouth.

Cheyenne snapped her head around. "*Josepha*."

"Sorry, I couldn't help it." She pressed her lips

together and frowned. "But I still don't like him because of what you told me."

Of course. That figured. "I don't care if you think I'm the devil incarnate. Time is important. You need to call Manuel Molina—right now."

Cheyenne bobbed on her toes. "How? We don't have a number. Should we Google mafia lawyers?"

"I have it." Josepha smiled and pulled a card from her hip pocket.

Cheyenne spun back to her sister. "*What*? *How*?"

"Mister Molina talked to Ynez and me in Gainesville on Saturday night. He gave me his card and wrote a number on the back. He said call anytime if anyone in our family needed help."

Cheyenne leaned closer to Josepha. "Why didn't you tell me all that?"

Josepha took a deep breath. "Soledad told me not to."

Cheyenne didn't move for a long few seconds, then slumped and sat on the edge of the bed. She looked down, shaking her head. "Why? I'm the one. She always tells me."

Josepha sat beside Cheyenne and wrapped an arm around her sister's shoulders. "Soledad worries about you. She wanted you to get some sleep and eat something. And you did."

Cheyenne closed her eyes and sighed. "What else did she say?"

"That she would tell me when to call Mister Molina for help. To tell the truth no matter what he asked, just like Ynez and I did in Gainesville." Josepha hugged Cheyenne tighter. "I'm her sister, too. It's time I stepped up."

Cheyenne nodded and slumped smaller.

Couldn't help but feel for Cheyenne. From Tasmanian Devil to realizing again she wasn't always the biggest, fastest, closest planet revolving around Soledad. They'd work it out. He switched on the phone and handed it to Josepha. "She wants that help now. Make the call."

"What should I say?"

"Just tell him that Soledad is at the North Precinct building, that she wants him to be her lawyer and get her out of jail tonight. Oh yeah, and before your mother wakes up." Actually, not a bad move. Showed that with all her problems, Mama came first.

Josepha didn't hesitate. She held the card, touched the numbers, then leaned with the phone between her and Cheyenne.

"Mister Molina? This is Josepha Montoya. Yes, sir, I'm home now. I apologize for calling so late, but my sister, Soledad, needs your help." Josepha looked up. "He said hold on. I think he's talking to someone." She nodded several times. "Yes, before Mama wakes up." She looked up again. "I think he's laughing." She returned to the phone. "Usually she's up by five, and if Soledad isn't here, well, Mama will be very upset, and she hasn't been eating. We're all worried about her." She nodded again. "Yes, Ynez is here, but she's sleeping. I'm with my sister Cheyenne and Cal. He brought the message from Soledad. I don't know. I'll ask him." She looked up. "How did you get here, Cal?" She held out the phone.

He leaned close. This was no time to lie. "Ahh, the police questioned both of us, then drove me to my apartment and told me to stay there. I sneaked out, caught a taxi at Marny's Café, then came here and climbed in through a window."

Josepha pulled the phone back. "It's me again, Mister Molina." She shrugged with a smile. "Soledad says he's a good man but kind of confused. Cheyenne thinks he's very confused." Her eyebrows raised. "Me? Well, I just met him tonight." She furrowed her brow, then nodded. "He has honest eyes. And a sense of humor."

Honest eyes, that sounded good. Have to check them out in a mirror sometime. Their conversation went on for several minutes. Josepha described Lenny's arrival and departure, how Soledad lay down with Isabelle until she fell asleep, then slipped out and let the police take her to the station.

Josepha spoke without hesitation. Her voice had honesty, like lying wasn't a consideration, which was easy to see and plain to hear. Maybe that's why Soledad wanted her to call. She knew Manuel Molina had met Josepha and already saw all of this. She counted on it. How could anyone know this family and still cause them pain?

"Goodbye, Mister Molina, and thank you very, very much." She handed the phone back and smiled. "He already knows where she is and is nearby. He says he'll do his best to get Soledad home before Mama wakes up. How'd I do?"

"You did great." So Manuel was already nearby. Soledad must've made quite an impression at their earlier meeting.

Cheyenne hugged Josepha. "Go check on Mama, then Ynez. Make sure they're still asleep. Then wait for me in the kitchen. Cal and I need to talk."

Josepha nodded and slipped out. Cheyenne turned the lock and leaned her back against the door. "What's going on? What's Soledad's plan?"

"I don't know. It's complicated, but I'm pretty sure she knows what she's doing. Manuel Molina gets things done, so I'm sure she'll be here before dawn. She'll explain." He sidestepped to the window and scanned the yard. "Right now, I need to sneak back to my apartment."

He stuck a leg through the window and straddled the sill. A clear sky and a half moon put the backyard in faint light.

They both turned to a staccato knock and Josepha's excited voice. "Cheyenne, come quick. Detectives are knocking on the front door."

Cheyenne cracked open the door. "Stall until I get there. Use your lawyer stuff." She turned. "What should I tell them?"

"What Soledad has said all along. Tell the truth about everything, except that I was here. Better leave that part out."

She tightened her jaw and nodded. "I'll handle it." She rushed to the door, flipped off the light, and was gone.

Cheyenne would not go gentle into this good night. Whatever disappointment she felt in being left out of the loop didn't matter now. Soledad needed her to take charge and carry out a plan. What she did best. The detectives would have their hands full. He lifted his other leg through the window, sat on the sill, then dropped to the ground. No time to try and find a taxi. Go to Saint Anthony's and get the Chevy.

Chapter Eighteen

Monday, 2:10 am

Soledad sat in the interview room, sipping from her third can of Diet Coke. An officer slouched against the wall between the door and a wall phone. She glanced at the wall clock as its hand jerked and clicked to the next minute. Still no contact from Manuel Molina or anyone representing his family. If Manuel didn't show up soon, call him. Wouldn't have the same innocent, heartfelt effect that Josepha brought, but the Molinas needed to be on her side now, and for everyone to know, especially Jace and the police.

The phone rang. The officer snatched the receiver.

"What's up, Sarge?" He nodded. "Yeah, she's here. The only instructions I received were to stay with her until the detectives returned." He nodded again. "Check, I'll hold." The officer smiled a small sneer. "There's someone here to pick you up."

"Who?" Either Cheyenne had decided it was time to bring her sister home, or it was Manuel Molina.

"A couple of shyster lawyers. The desk sergeant is calling the lead on your case for instructions. Why exactly are you here?"

"I came in voluntarily to answer some questions. Which I did. Then the detectives asked me to stay for a while. Said they might have some more things to ask."

She inhaled with a yawn, then exhaled a sigh. "But that was three hours ago, and I want to go home now." Dillard wanted to question Jace, then her again. Evidentially, they hadn't found Jace, and they wouldn't. He probably went into hiding the minute word came that the police picked her up.

The officer put the receiver to his ear and nodded. "Okay, we're on our way." He stood and motioned. "Come on. Lead detective says you can go home."

She smiled and stood. They must have called Lenny. God bless him. Cal was right. Lenny was looking out for her.

The officer led the way down a hall, then buzzed them through a door and into the near empty public waiting area.

"You're free to go." He shrugged, then walked back down the hall.

Manuel Molina and a man in a three-piece suit talked with the sergeant behind the wall-to-wall information desk. Perfect. The Molinas had decided.

Manuel turned from the desk with a tired smile and motioned her to the empty wooden bench near the entrance. She trudged to the bench, sat with slumped shoulders, and pulled out her phone. Manuel approached, wearing the same dark suit and red tie from their meeting earlier that day. He sat beside her and turned with a sigh. Clean shaven and hair neatly combed, but his eyelids drooped, and his shoulders sagged.

"Miss Montoya, it's been a long day for both of us."

"Yes, sir, and I apologize for taking you from your family, but I had nowhere else to turn."

He nodded and sighed. "My mother is sleeping, and I'll be back before she wakes up, which according to your sister, is what you want to do for your mother. So I'll get to the point. I'm surprised they're releasing you, but your situation may change quickly. If you'll permit me, I'll inform the police and the DA's office that I represent you."

Good. That news would travel fast. She sighed with a smile. "Thank you. And my family thanks you."

Manuel pulled a card from his coat pocket and wrote a number on the back. "If the police want to talk to you again, call this number. Either me or Mister Abrams"—he pointed at the man in the three-piece suit—"will come immediately. Don't say anything without our counsel. Not for any reason, no matter what they promise or threaten. We *will* take care of you." He stared and held out the card. "Do you understand?"

She bobbed her head and took the card. "Yes, sir."

His stern expression softened. "If I sound harsh, I apologize."

"That's okay. I know you're helping me. May I call home? My family needs to know I'm all right."

"Of course."

She pressed the numbers. Cheyenne picked up on the first ring. "Cheyenne, this is Soledad. Yes, I'm on my way. How's Mama?" She closed her eyes, leaned back, and smiled. "Good. Not now, tell me about that later. Send everyone to bed. I'll be home soon." She turned off the phone and held it in her lap. Even at two thirty in the morning, Cheyenne had a Cal story she wanted to tell, but it could wait.

Manuel suppressed a yawn. "Is everything all right at home?"

"Yes. Detectives came to our house and questioned Ynez and my sisters, but Mama slept through it. And I'll be home before she wakes up."

"Your family is very important to you."

She gave a firm nod. "Especially Mama. God has saints the church doesn't know about. Mama is one of them."

His face went blank for a long second, then a blink of realization flashed like something he felt deeply had just been put into words for the first time. That said a lot. His mother was key to how he felt and thought and how he wanted it all to end. *Use it.*

He nodded slowly. "I understand." He stood and motioned to a tall man in a dark suit and black tie. "James will take you home. Expect to hear from me after both of us get some sleep."

James escorted her to a waiting limousine and opened the door. She climbed into a back seat, long and wide enough to lie down and stretch out on. She yawned with closed eyes and inhaled. The interior smelled like cold, clean leather. She wished there was a pillow.

The partition lowered. James glanced over his shoulder. "I know the address. You'll be home in about thirty minutes." The partition raised as the limo pulled away from the precinct building.

One more call to make. She pulled out her phone and pressed the numbers.

"Cal, it's Soledad. Where are you?" Pulling in to Marny's Café. Somehow that wasn't surprising. Then the questions came. When would he realize the police didn't matter? What the Molinas decided would determine the outcome. "Cal, stop. It's out of our hands and in the hands of the Molinas." Her body ached with fatigue, wanting every muscle to go limp and every brain cell to switch off. "I've answered all the questions and done all the thinking I'm going to do tonight. We'll talk tomorrow." She shook her head. "No, I guess I mean later today, but not over the phone. I want to see you."

She frowned and shook her head. "I don't care who's watching. I just want to be with you. Can't you understand that? Cal, stop stammering. We'll talk later. Just think about what we were saying when Lenny drove up and took you away. You remember, *don't you*?" Sounded like selective memory loss. "Well, I remember everything everyone said to me tonight. And I'm anemic. Let's meet at Jake's around six this evening." They had some fries to share. "I'll be home in a few minutes. And don't worry. God is on our side. Goodnight, Cal." She switched off her phone and held it in her lap.

She was safe from Jace. The Molinas had taken a side, and Jace either knew or would know soon. Jace was smart. He'd realized there was no good option if he stayed. He had an escape plan and would put it in motion.

Cal was safe. Manuel had talked to Josepha and Ynez in Gainesville and believed them, because they told the truth. He knew Cal was with Ynez the night Carlos was killed and the morning the body was dumped. What the Molinas believed, the police would, too. Cal was an easy part of the equation to figure. He was in love. Maybe they weren't sure with whom, but everything he did put him at risk and gained nothing for himself. Mama was right about that. Cal didn't want to be brave and avoided situations that might require it, but when he couldn't say no to someone, he came through. And there was only one reason why he couldn't say no.

The limo slowed as it approached home. Cheyenne, Josepha, and Cousin Jimmy sat on the front step, then jumped up and ran to the curb. Another good scene. Hopefully James would give a good description to Manuel. Another little edge, another finger on the scales.

Chapter Nineteen

Monday, 4:00 am

Cal sat at the end of the counter, sipping black coffee and savoring the last taste of his second slice of Marny's signature pecan pie with real whipped cream. From several blocks away, Marny's blinking, rotating, neon pie-wedge, dripping with whipped cream, cut through a dark night and beckoned. Sunday nights were somewhat busy, but Monday mornings brought a larger crowd of those starting the week early or ending the week late.

No matter how tired he was, Marny's Café always had a rejuvenating effect. Their strong coffee helped, but even more reviving was the brightness of the place. Reflected light gleamed off glass, silverware, and every polished, stainless steel appliance behind the counter. Booths with red vinyl seats and white Formica table tops with red speckles lined the picture window walls on two sides. Backless swivel stools with the same red vinyl ran the length of the counter.

Linda reached over the counter and refilled his cup while frowning at his dirty clothes, tangled hair, and overall bedraggled appearance.

"Are you all right? You look like something the cat dragged in."

"It's been a long day. Is Marny here?"

Linda glanced toward the kitchen. "She's supervising the morning pies."

"I need to talk to her."

She cocked her head. "Are you in some kind of trouble?"

"I just need a favor."

She held the coffee pot in one hand and placed the other on her hip, then nodded. "I'll get Marny."

This long day's journey into night, and now morning, was almost over. Message delivered, and Soledad safe at home for the night, and probably for the near future. After a three-block walk he'd be home, too, provided the police didn't pick him up sneaking into his apartment. Soledad said it was in the hands of the Molinas, and that God was on their side, which seemed contradictory, but supposedly God worked in mysterious ways. Soledad definitely did.

Tomorrow, or rather later today, they'd talk. Of all the things going on, his complicated feelings for Soledad came out first and foremost. Even as Lenny waited to take him to the station, with Ynez looking like a deer in headlights, and Cheyenne like a banty rooster itching for a fight, Soledad had told him to do some thinking about what he wanted.

He had evaded police, hid in a doghouse, sneaked through a window, and fought Fowler in a church. All in one day. That wasn't just circumstances getting out of control. Every step of the way he put himself there, and he'd do it again.

Marny approached the counter wearing her tall white baker's hat and chef's coat. She always reminded him of a taller, more muscular, and heavyset Rachael Ray. The café was her life, which she protected by giving police officers special attention. They liked her food and stopped in frequently. Should have thought about that earlier.

Marny glanced at Linda, then nodded at a just-vacated booth. Linda hurried away with a bussing tray and rag.

"Linda says you need a favor." She leaned across the counter. "What kind of favor?"

He yawned with a smile. "Can I leave my car parked here for a while?"

She straightened and crossed her arms. "What's going on, Cal? It's after four in the morning, and you look like—"

"Something the cat dragged in. Yeah, I know. The police might be looking for me. Well, actually they're watching my apartment right now."

Marny glanced right then left. "Come around the counter and follow me. We'll talk in my office."

She led the way, past the entrance to the kitchen, past the employee locker room, and into a long narrow office with a large window overlooking the bakery. She took off her hat and sat behind the desk.

"Well, out with it."

Lying took too much effort. Might as well tell the truth. That's what Soledad said all along to everyone.

"The police are watching my apartment. I sneaked out earlier, and now I'm trying to sneak back in. All I want is a smoke, a shower, and my own bed to sleep in. But if they find my car here, they'll ask you some questions."

"Cal, are you asking me to lie to the police?"

He smiled and shook his head. "No. If they ask, tell the truth, whatever they want to know. When I arrived and left, what I looked like. Tell them what you know or have heard about me. Who I've been here with. Tell them everything. Even this conversation. It doesn't matter. In fact, the truth is the best thing I got going for me."

Marny blinked and stared with wide eyes. "Wow, never heard anything like that before." She leaned forward. "A few of your girls come here regularly, and my girls wait on them. They overhear things and like to gossip. I know who your boss is and what you do."

"Not anymore."

Marny leaned back with a puzzled look, then a small grin rose. "So you're getting out of that business you're in?"

He returned her grin and nodded. "Yeah, but not alone."

Her grin sprang into a smile. "With that girl you've been bringing here recently? Our bright lights show a lot. I see the way she looks at you."

"Ynez?" He shook his head. "No, but I sent her away. She's out."

"I'm glad to hear that. She seems like a real nice girl and has a strong resemblance to Shantelle. She was always one of my favorites. So who's the lucky girl?"

"Do you remember Shantelle's friend?"

She stared and blinked like recovering a memory. "Ohh, the princess. She always came dressed in her Sunday best. You drove her those days. You'd have pie and coffee at the counter while she and Shantelle had the same in the corner booth."

"That's her. Once a month I drove her to church, then brought her here to visit with Shantelle."

"She stopped coming after Shantelle was killed."

Marny leaned back and crossed her arms. "Cal, I don't know what to think of you. You've been coming here for years and always treat my girls with respect. They all like you, and from what I hear, all your girls like you. I don't like the business you're in, but I'll judge you on what you do now. But answer me one question." She uncrossed her arms and leaned forward with a twinkle in her eyes. "Are you in love with her?"

He closed his eyes and shook his head. "I don't know. Maybe. I think so." He opened his eyes and shrugged. "She's occupied a lot of my thoughts lately. And there're some other things going on, too."

Marny scanned his tangled hair and dirty clothes. "Yeah, I'll bet there are." She nodded and grinned. "My pie has assisted more than one romance. Sure, you can leave your car here for as long as you want."

"Thanks, Marny."

She leaned back and studied a wall-mounted monitor. "Two officers just walked in. I know them, officers Ramos and Evans." She pointed to the office door. "Make a left then another left, go through the dishroom, and you can leave through the loading dock."

He walked to the door, stopped, and turned. "I owe you."

"Just let me know how it all works out."

The three-block walk to his apartment complex gave him time to smoke that last hoarded cigarette, which should have been the best tasting smoke ever. But it was gone without the realization of smoking it. Soledad's fault.

He took a deep breath. Just concentrate on getting into the apartment. Waiting within was a shower, a bed, and that backup pack of smokes in his drawer. From now on, tape spare phones and spare packs together, keep them as a set.

He cut between apartment buildings and into the courtyard, backtracking the same way he'd left five hours ago. He eased onto the patio two apartments down from his and stretched his neck past the dividing wall. An officer sat in his lawn chair, watching his sliding glass door. The officer yawned, cleared his throat, and hocked a loogie over his shoulder.

Only a few scattered apartments showed life, but gradually bedroom lights, followed by bathroom and kitchen lights, would pop on. And sooner or later, some of the earliest risers would wander outside for morning coffee on their patio. Noise carried well in the still morning air, and already a few sliding doors had briefly opened to let out a cat. Hopefully the residents of apartment A-103 were late risers and didn't own a cat. Why the hell didn't that officer go around the corner and take a piss? That would be enough time.

The officer's radio crackled. He pulled a cigarette from his breast pocket. "Nothing's changed. Blinds are still closed, his TV's been on all night, and no movement that I can tell. What's the word?" The officer bolted upright, slid the cigarette back into his pocket, and stepped quickly across the grass to the edge of the building. "They're bringing Marny's pie and coffee? Send it back as soon as it gets here and tell Ramos and Evans I owe them big time." He stretched his neck around the corner and stared down the side of the building.

This could be the break and probably the last chance. Soledad had said God was on their side, so ten seconds of divine intervention would help right now.

That officer needed to take just one more step. If he did, he'd be out of sight, but not out of hearing range. Getting to the door could be done quickly and quietly enough. The door was unlocked but opening it and the vertical blinds would make noise.

Shit. Apartment A-103 had an early riser. Light shone from somewhere, probably the bathroom. They'd either go back to bed or come to the kitchen. Still dark enough to creep back. Please, officer, just one more step and you'll be out of sight. Ten seconds. Just ten seconds. Go to the pie. You know you want to. It's delicious and probably still warm.

Hell. No mistaking, A-103's kitchen light, and those blinds might open any second. Got to make a move one way or another.

The officer inhaled deeply, then called, "I think I can smell it from here. Hey, don't fool around. You drop that, and I'll tear you a new asshole."

Then go to it. Just one more step. Follow that pie. Please. Heaven awaits.

The officer stepped out of sight.

Even God must know about Marny's pie.

Four, long, fast strides on soft damp grass. Quiet so far. Onto the patio, step over the broken cup, and slide the door open. Easy does it. Step through. Goddamn it, those rattling blinds. Spin, face outside. Slap on the patio light. Give him a good yawn and stretch.

"Morning, Officer."

The officer wandered around the corner and looked up from his Marny's takeout bag. "What're you up to?"

"Just woke up." He slouched his shoulder against the door jamb with his head poking through the blinds. "About to make some coffee. Want some?"

"Shut up."

Same officer all right. Guess they didn't get relieved.

The officer opened the bag and inhaled. His radio crackled again. He nodded and sighed. "Best news I've heard all night. Send him back." The officer grinned. "You have a visitor. A detective is here."

"Am I getting arrested?"

"That's up to the detective. Hopefully, you're not my problem anymore."

Lenny rounded the corner of the building, carrying a Marny's takeout bag.

Ahh, shit. Lenny had to know. Probably saw his Chevy and knew it didn't get from Saint Anthony's to Marny's by itself.

Lenny pushed his hat back a few inches. "Anything to report, Officer?"

"Yeah, I sat here five hours staring at a closed door. He got sleep, and I got older."

"Well, we're pulling the surveillance. He's not worth the manpower."

"Wish you guys woulda figured that out five hours ago." Officer Newland took two steps into the grass, then stopped and stared over his shoulder. "This is all your fault."

And it was. "Sorry, but you're getting pie."

"Shut up." Officer Newland trudged around the corner, sniffing the open takeout bag.

Lenny held up his bag. "Guess where I've been?"

Early Monday mornings, Marny's must be the nexus of the universe.

Lenny scanned him up and down. "Get inside. I'm hungry, and we need to talk."

Lenny sat at the kitchen table, opened his bag, and carefully lifted out a large coffee and a wedge-shaped container. He took one sip of coffee, then opened the pie box. Warm, sweet aroma hovered over the table. Melting whipped cream dripped over gooey, golden-brown, pecan-studded filling. Lenny picked up the black plastic fork and dug in.

"Mind if I smoke?" He opened the counter drawer and ripped the cellophane off the pack.

Lenny pointed his fork at the patio door. "Over there, and blow the smoke outside."

He opened the blinds, leaned his back against the doorjamb, and flicked his lighter. His eyes closed as he inhaled slowly and deeply. This was the best cigarette ever. He sighed out a long stream of smoke and glanced at Lenny, already halfway through his pie.

"Did you arrange the takeout for Officer Newland?"

Lenny shook his head while swallowing. "Nah. A unit in the area swung by and got it for him and his partner. They knew the situation. Cops take care of each other."

"And you just happened to be in the area and stopped for some pie."

Lenny's fork dipped pie into whipped cream. "Not exactly. Coming to see you, but no one in their right mind passes up Marny's early morning pie." He savored another bite. "I was wondering how your car got from Saint Anthony's to Marny's." He leaned back and pointed with his fork. "There's dirt stains on the elbows of your coat and the knees of your pants. You got a tunnel leading out of this place?"

"Lenny, I—"

Lenny held up a hand for silence while scrapping the last bit of pie in the last smidgen of whipped cream. "I'm in no mood for a creative lie. But it doesn't matter anyway. I'm guessing you already know what transpired tonight and probably had a hand in it." He glanced a wry grin. "First Fowler, now this. There's more inside you than I figured."

He flicked the cigarette butt into the grass. "More than I figured, too."

Lenny pushed up from the table and walked over, holding a hard stare. "Just stay put and don't do anything. Soledad, too. Dillard's on the right track, so leave it in the hands of the police and the lawyers." He leaned forward, almost nose to nose. "Do you understand what I'm saying?"

He nodded. Lenny had thought this through. It was all about Jace and the Molinas now. "I understand. I'm gonna shower, then go to bed."

"Good idea. I'm gonna go home and do the same." He stepped onto the patio. "And don't forget about Fowler. He won't forget you or Soledad." Lenny disappeared around the corner of the building.

Whatever Lenny thought, he aimed for what seemed true. Like there was a chance it wasn't. Soledad had turned him into an ally, and not just recently. He seemed protective of Isabelle, too. There was the Bernardo thing, but there had to be something more, maybe much more. What was it about Soledad that drew loyalty out of people? Everybody seemed to love her at least a little bit. But there were unanswered questions.

Better have another smoke.

Chapter Twenty

Monday, 5:45 pm

Soledad turned onto the cross-street at the side of Jake's Tavern. Mama had given strict instructions to bring Cal home for dinner. Mama seemed in a bit of a hurry with life in general and already had definite ideas that Cal should be part of their family. That was too far in the future to think about now.

She parked on the side street and took a close look into the rearview mirror. Makeup completely hid the faint shadows beneath her eyes, and after another good night's sleep and taking that horrible prescription, they'd be gone. Fatigue was her own worst enemy. Should have realized that at the police station when she pressured Cal into saying he didn't love Ynez. ADA Dillard had to be wondering about that whole exchange. Women will lie for the man they love, so a love connection with Ynez put Cal's alibi in question. But maybe not a bad thing, it created motives and tangents that had nothing to do with Carlos's murder. The more muddled the investigation, the better.

Fatigue wasn't a factor when she'd kissed Cal by the swing. His heart had thumped like a person in love, but so had hers. Maybe they were just caught up in the moment, wanting to give Mama and Cheyenne a scene that would ease some guilt and soothe some pain. Then walking down the sidewalk, pushing him to say why he hadn't left, with or without Ynez. She needed to control things like that, but with some things, some times, fatigue didn't matter.

Maybe it was good that Lenny showed up before Cal answered. If he had said *I love you*, then what? Unspoken, it was incentive. Spoken, it became a complication, an unpredictable X-factor. She needed a clear head, because thinking with her heart led to mistakes. But Cal needed to realize why he hadn't left. If it came from his heart, he could be counted on, because a man in love had incentive to go the extra mile, maybe even take a bullet.

She flipped up the collar of her short-sleeved white blouse and adjusted the fluffy blue scarf. The copy of the outfit she'd worn when she and Cal had napped together. Her arm across his chest, snuggling against his side, knowing he was there and she was safe, was a feeling she wanted every night and every morning. Maybe the most honest and beautiful experience she had with Cal. He had slipped away, probably for a cigarette, and woke up on the couch drooling like Bernardo. Bernardo had loved and protected her, maybe the same with Cal.

She checked her phone as she walked around the corner and down the sidewalk toward the entrance. No messages. It was time, and there would be no interruptions. She turned her phone off, slipped it into her purse, and pulled open the front door. The bartender glanced right, immediately turned from his conversation with two customers, and approached the end of the bar.

She smiled. "Mike, that's right, isn't it?"

He nodded with a wide grin. "Sure is. And I remember you, too." He pointed. "Cal's in the pool room. I think he's waiting for you before he orders his usual bacon cheeseburger and fries. Can I get you anything?"

She propped her elbows on the bar, clasped her hands beneath her chin, and leaned forward. "I need a favor."

"Sure, if I can."

"Cal won't be having a burger, just the fries. Bring them when they're ready, and a Diet Coke, no glass."

Mike shrugged. "Sure. I can do that. Something up?"

"We'll see. And one more thing. Can I put up the closed sign for the pool room? Just while Cal and I talk. It won't be long." She cocked her head. "*Please*."

Mike winked. "No problem. Take it down when you're done." He walked back to his customers with a spring in his step. Even Mike the bartender felt good about this. When the fries arrive, give Cal a knowing nod and cute smile for a cute idea. He'll remember the Cosmo article about sharing fries and feelings. Then draw some true feelings to the surface, just enough for him to realize why he hadn't left.

She hurried down the length of the bar and rounded the corner to the pool room. Cal sat with his elbows on the table, head in hands, staring into a steaming cup of coffee. She slid the closed sign in front of the entrance.

He yawned and smiled, then pushed up from the table. He was clean shaven but didn't look rested.

She ran the last few steps, wrapped her arms around him, and planted the side of her face against his chest. He hugged back but without the same enthusiasm. She squeezed tighter, crunching the pack of cigarettes in his breast pocket. He smelled of soap, clean skin, and of course, cigarette smoke. She glanced up. "Everything is going to be all right."

His chin brushed the top of her head. "I don't know what everything is. In fact, there's a lot I don't know."

She clutched his shoulders and pushed space between them. "Everything is my family, and you and me. Nothing else matters today. That's all I want to talk about or think about this evening. Mama's holding dinner for us, and you're coming home with me."

Cal pulled out a chair. "Sit down." He seated her and returned to his chair on the opposite side. He stared at his coffee and twice started to speak but swallowed his words.

"Are you all right? You look tired. How much sleep did you get?"

"Not enough." A weary sigh escaped. "I did a lot of thinking last night, and we need to talk."

Thinking meant questions. But just like Manuel, Cal wanted to believe her. "Yes, we need to talk, but about us. There's nothing else we can do about the rest. It's out of our hands."

Cal sipped his coffee. "There's some things I have to know."

She nodded and crossed her arms. "There's things we both need to know, but you first."

"Well, I'm pretty sure why you asked Manuel Molina to be your lawyer. Brilliant move by the way. No one saw that coming." He sipped more coffee. "And even why you had Josepha do the asking. I'm skeptical about a lot of things, but not her. Manuel saw that, too, and you knew he would. All along, you've told everyone to tell the truth about everything." He focused on the scarf. "But not the bruises. Why?"

"Because they're the same as the ones on Shantelle. And I think Manuel Molina knows Carlos killed her. Revenge for her murder is a motive to kill Carlos. Jace could use the bruises against me. If the police, and especially the Molinas, know about them, they might see everything differently. Cal, please. Let's talk about all this tomorrow."

He nodded, then sipped more coffee. "Just one more thing. What's going on with Lenny? He's been acting strange from the start. Last night he dropped in and basically said stay out of it, both of us. Like the investigation was headed in Jace's direction. Like the truth doesn't matter, just the outcome, which he has a big part in. He's helping you, and I'm guessing, not just a little bit. Why?"

So Lenny was coming through. That would help tip the scales. She leaned forward. "I didn't know until I talked to Mama yesterday. She recognized Lenny when she took him the plate of paella. He was the policeman that came when Bernardo was hit by the car, the officer that Cheyenne bit."

Cal gave a knowing nod, and a small laugh sneaked out. "Yeah, sounds like Cheyenne all right. Lenny told me about that, but there has to be more. I get the feeling, whatever it is, runs deep."

Cal saw things better than most men. Maybe a week ago she could have told the story, and the business part wouldn't have bothered her. But this was Cal, and now, telling him about servicing a client made her stomach turn. When he'd forced her to tell about her session with Carlos, she'd felt mostly anger. But this time, she just felt sick.

She looked down and bit on her lower lip, then held up a halting hand. "Just give me a few seconds. This isn't easy."

She lowered her hands beneath the table, made fists, and pressed them against her inner thighs. Cal separated business from the person, but the business, the servicing, would always be there. From the start, she'd used the term business instead of prostitution, client not john. And session or servicing instead of... She clenched her eyes and gritted her teeth. Call it what it is—*fucking*—*fucking for money*. Suddenly, the whole sharing fries idea didn't seem so cute.

She took a deep breath but didn't look up. "Not something I like to talk about or even think about. I always wonder—what if? But if you'll stop thinking about the past for one evening, it's worth it." She tightened her stomach muscles to stop the churning. "About eight years ago, my first month with Jace, I was at a client's house. After business concluded." She looked up and swallowed. Cal nodded with blank eyes and a calm face, but if he clenched his coffee cup any harder, it might shatter in his hands. Was he picturing her servicing a client? If he loved her, that had to hurt, but he wouldn't show it. Maybe that was his secret of separating the business from the person. He didn't really, but he knew he should. He'd carry and deal with her past in secret. She couldn't let him do that, but for now, she had no choice.

He dropped his gaze to his coffee. "So what happened next?"

"For some reason the client wanted to show me his new gun, a nine-millimeter something or other, like it was a new toy he wanted to show off. I had a lot of anger in me, and when he placed the gun in my hands, I pointed it at the wall, switched off the safety, and pulled the trigger three times. Someone reported the gunshots, and within a few minutes, Fowler and Lenny showed up to investigate."

"That was back when Lenny worked vice with Fowler?"

She nodded. "Fowler was senior partner, and he and Jace had a working arrangement, so it was no accident they were close by. While Fowler handled the client and called Jace, Lenny checked my ID and took a statement. I didn't recognize him, but he looked at me strangely and offered to take me home. I remember smiling, because I was going home to Mama, and I didn't care about the consequences. But Jace showed up, and he and Fowler hustled me to the door. I remember looking back at Lenny, thinking, help me, please. And I know I was crying. Lenny had this look, like he was still trying to place me. Maybe he remembered the little girl crying over her dog, because his look changed into something like..." She shook her head. "I don't know. Like he was ashamed." She shrugged. "Anyway, Jace pulled me out the door, and Lenny didn't come after me. He could have, and taken me home, but he didn't." She gave her head a sharp shake, but the image wouldn't dislodge. She shrugged and forced a smile. "So here we are."

Cal's blank look transitioned into a sad, what if? He leaned back with a slow nod. "That explains more things than Lenny. I had no idea, and I'm sorry."

"Maybe Lenny can't help wondering, what if, about that night. He's a good man with a personal code, and he's settling a debt he's carried a long time. And what about you, Cal? Are you settling a debt to Shantelle by helping Ynez and me? We're both out, and we're never going back. That debt is settled."

He swallowed hard and glanced at his breast pocket. "I've had thoughts swirling around in my head that have made me do things I thought I never would." He tapped his cigarette pack, then looked up with his mouth slightly open.

He looked like a frightened little boy with a secret he was afraid to tell. Just like Mama said. She reached across the table and gripped his fidgeting fingers.

"Cal, I've had thoughts, too. We're in this together and we'll get out of it together. I'm not sure what the future holds, but when we get there, neither of us will ever wonder, what if?"

His fingers tensed inside hers, then relaxed as if he'd been taken off the hook. Relieved that he didn't have to say the words. But they were there, in his heart and on the tip of his tongue. And when the right time came, they wouldn't come easy, but he would mean them. But for now, best to leave them unspoken.

He pulled his hands away and fumbled at his pocket. "I need a cigarette."

"Of course you do. We have a lot of things to talk about, but not in Jake's Tavern."

Mike arrived carrying a tray. "Here's your order." He set the can of Diet Coke in front of her, then reached for the plate of fries.

She held up a hand. "I've changed my mind about the fries."

Mike shrugged. "No problem." He shuffled away munching on a fry.

Cal cocked his head with a sly grin. "Were those the fries of truth?"

She nodded. "But I don't think we need them now." She reached across the table and clutched his hands. "Let's get out here. Mama has dinner cooking, and I think it's something special."

Cal grinned and raised his eyebrows. "She thinks I'm your boyfriend."

"I don't think that's such a bad thing. Anyway, sometimes people pretend the pretending."

He cocked his head and blinked. "What?"

She popped up and pulled him to his feet. "Let's go."

Mike gave a small wave as they rushed past the bar. "Don't worry. Fries and drinks are on the house, and I'll take down the sign."

She pushed through the front door, tugging Cal up the sidewalk and around the corner.

Cal tugged back. "Slow down. I still need that cigarette."

She slackened her pace, then slid to his side and slipped her arm around his waist.

He smoked like each deep inhale was a doubt, and each exhaled stream of smoke was an answer fading away.

"Cal, I can see you're thinking."

"I'm still trying to wrap my head around that pretending the pretending thing."

"I'm bringing my boyfriend home for dinner. It's that simple, so don't make it complicated."

"Your pretend boyfriend?"

She shrugged. "If you pretend." She squeezed his side. "Cal, there's unselfish pretending that gives joy to

217

those you love and doesn't hurt anyone. Then there's pretending to avoid a painful situation. The longer you string Ynez along, the more painful it's gonna be, for both of you."

He nodded. "You're right."

"And you need to tell her before we all sit down to dinner." She opened the passenger door of Cheyenne's Accord. "Get in."

"What about my car?"

"We'll pick it up later. I'm not letting you out of my sight, and we still have some things to talk about."

Chapter Twenty-One

Monday, 7:00 pm

Soledad sat on the front step with her hands folded in her lap, looking down the sidewalk in the direction Cal and Ynez had walked. When she and Cal had returned from Jake's Tavern, Mama was impatient to start dinner and had no idea what was going on with Ynez. Apparently, Mama thought Ynez was one of Josepha's friends from college, and no one had told her anything different.

The screen door opened. Cheyenne slipped through and sat on the step with her forearms resting on her knees. "How long have they been gone?"

"About twenty-two minutes."

"About, huh." Cheyenne laughed. "So getting rid of the competition?"

"I wouldn't put it that way, but Cal needs to have his priorities straight without distractions."

"And you're the priority and Ynez the distraction? I think Cal already has his priorities." She grinned and raised her eyebrows. "And so do you."

She gave Cheyenne a press-lipped frown. "Have you been talking to Mama?"

"Mama says you two love each other."

"And you believe her?"

"She says Cal has a long-distance heart. He'll be

faithful and never love another."

"And Mama can tell this from knowing Cal for only a few days?"

Cheyenne shrugged and grinned. "Mama is mighty convincing. Especially when she has her mind made up. She's on a mission."

"Well, we'll see." But she couldn't help picturing Cal hitting Fowler and quarters flying everywhere. He must have gone into that knowing his chances were slim to none, but he did it anyway.

Cheyenne flicked her chin in the direction Ynez and Cal had walked. "Did you give Cal any instructions?"

"To tell the truth. And he could kiss Ynez once, if necessary. I think she knows what's coming."

Cheyenne nodded. "You slept most of today, but Mama's been bubbling with excitement. At breakfast she talked about a wedding at Saint Anthony's. I watched Ynez, and it caught her by surprise, but she didn't say anything, just looked lost and confused. She doesn't want to contradict Mama. Then at lunch, Mama said something about finally getting grandchildren."

"Oh my."

"Oh yes. Several times. Mama wants to make up for lost time. I haven't seen her this happy in years."

"I've seen it, too, but I wish it didn't have to come at the cost of Ynez getting hurt."

"According to Josepha, she's in love with Cal."

"I know. When we sent her up to Gainesville, I asked her why. She said he made her feel good about herself, and she felt safe with him. That may not be love, but for a person who hasn't had either, it's real important."

"I've talked to her and talked to Josepha about her. She's a nice girl and doesn't have a good place to go back to."

"Well, that won't do." Ynez needed a place she could feel safe, with people around that cared. Everyone should have that. "Ynez has our hospitality, and protection, for what that's worth. She needs to stay here."

"That's what Josepha and I were thinking. Or go back to Gainesville with Josepha."

"No." Ynez was Cal's alibi for the night Carlos was killed. Still might need that. "She needs to stay here with us. I'll handle it." She looked down the sidewalk again, then down the opposite way. "Where's Cousin Jimmy? I haven't seen him or his car."

"Josepha sent him back to Jacksonville. He can't afford to miss school. Josepha will go back when she knows everything is all right here. And don't worry, nothing will keep her from starting law school. The U for sure, and there's still a slim chance for a late admit to Harvard."

She smiled and nodded. Josepha had finished high school early, then fast-tracked through her undergraduate requirements and would finish law school early. But no corporate law firm for her. Either a public defender or the district attorney's office, both were good stepping stones into politics. That was Josepha's future for the family. "And what about you? How's that masters coming?"

"Ahead of schedule. I'm already getting good job offers."

She smiled wider. The family would be strong.

Cheyenne pointed her chin down the sidewalk. "I

see them. They're walking pretty slow with their heads down. Don't think they're holding hands. And now they're motioning for you."

She clutched Cheyenne's arm. "Come with me."

"No." Cheyenne pulled her arm away. "As curious as I am to see how Cal handled this, they want you, not me. I'll go help Mama in the kitchen." Cheyenne gave her a squeeze. "He loves you."

"We haven't discussed that."

"Mama says it's not discussing that makes it so. Now go see what they want."

She took a deep breath, stood, and crossed her arms. No, that would look angry, confrontational. She interlocked her fingers and let her hands dangle in front as she walked toward them. Ynez could say whatever she wanted. She could be angry and hurt. She could yell and cry. Whatever she wanted to do, when it was over, they'd work it out.

Ynez shuffled forward with her head bowed and her shoulders slumped. Cal stared straight ahead with a chagrined look and raised eyebrows, like he'd just wiggled out from between the devil and the deep blue sea.

Ynez bit on her lower lip, looked up with red eyes and a sad smile, then ran the last three steps with open arms. They hugged, each with their chin atop the other's shoulder.

Ynez sniffled. "I don't know what to do—or where to go."

She squeezed Ynez tighter. "You're not going anywhere. This is your home now, and you have three sisters. We'll work this out."

Ynez hugged even tighter and was crying. "I think

I'd like that very much." She sniffled twice. "Cal's a good man. I know he'll take care of you."

What on earth did Cal say to her? He stood rigid. She mouthed the word *how*?

Cal shrugged with the same guilty look and mouthed the word *later*.

She walked down the sidewalk with one arm around Ynez and the other around Cal. He should write a book on good breakups. What on earth did he say?

Cheyenne waved from the front step. "Mama says to come to dinner, right now."

Chapter Twenty-Two

Monday, 8:15 pm

Soledad sat on the swing seat holding the rusty chains, waiting for Cal. Ten long minutes ago she had him by the hand, pulling him through the screen door, when Mama grabbed him by his other hand and pulled him back into the kitchen.

Throughout dinner Mama had fawned over Cal. Serving him first with the biggest and best of the pernil, slow-roasted pork, which she made only on very special occasions. Having him taste each dish first, getting his approval, which he gave by savoring a big bite with closed eyes and a look of tasting something heaven sent.

With Mama directing the Montoya sisters in turns, Cal never had to get up, refill, or even reach for anything. Mama was definitely in a holiday mood. She liked having a man at her table, especially one she viewed as her future son-in-law. Cal lapped it up.

For dessert, Mama made tembleque, a coconut pudding that went well with her pocillo, also reserved for special occasions. When she directed Cheyenne to serve Cal first, there was some curious eye contact between those two, followed by jaw-clenching grins. Cheyenne plopped the tembleque in front of him, then rubbed her hands together and gave him an I-don't-know kind of shrug followed by a satisfied smile. Cal just nodded, obviously holding back laughter.

She would have to find out what that was all about, but first find out what on earth he said to Ynez.

A few times during dinner when Ynez's eyes met hers, Ynez gave a sad, sweet, sympathetic smile. The truth wouldn't do that. Cal lied. No other explanation. Maybe some sad story like, I can't leave Soledad, she's dying of cancer and only has six months to live. Of course, after six months, he'd have to come up with a miraculous recovery story.

The screen door squeaked open. Cal took a last sip of pocillo and handed the cup to Mama. He strolled to the swing with a satisfied smile.

"Isabelle's coffee is really good. She called it pocillo."

"It's Puerto Rican espresso, made with Yauco Selecto coffee beans. Daddy's favorite, only served on special occasions. Do you feel special?"

He grinned and nodded. "Haven't felt this way since, *ever*. Isabelle is a very, very special woman."

"Why, because she's a good cook and fawns all over you?"

"Well, can't deny I like it, but there's a lot more. You should have seen her when Lenny came to get you while you were still at the Molinas. She was like a she-wolf defending her cub, but at the same time, she charmed and disarmed Lenny without trying. It's easy to see who you take after. You even look alike, especially now that she smiles all the time. Makes her look younger. Isabelle is a very attractive woman."

Cal was right about that. Mama hadn't looked this good in years. "You seem to have a beneficial effect on all the women in the household." She cocked her head and narrowed her eyes. "Including Ynez. What did you tell her during your walk?"

"Oh, that." He shrugged with a sick smile. "Mind if I smoke?"

"Yes, I mind. No crutch. Just out with it." Smoking gave time for pause, time to come up with a lie, which he wasn't good at anyway.

"Well, I know she prays at night, so I told her God sent you and me a sign that we were meant to be together."

Cal should listen to God, not use him for a defense witness. "What kind of sign? And don't beat around the bush."

He looked at the sky as if asking for God's help, so it must be a whopper.

"Just tell me."

He shrugged. "I told her you've been sleeping so much lately because—" Back came the chagrined smile with raised eyebrows like his only defense was his own stupidity. "You're pregnant with my child."

"You told her *what*?"

"That you're—"

"I heard you. I just can't believe it." He had no idea what he'd done. "How could you be so stupid?"

He squeezed his eyes shut and winced. "And…"

"*There's more*?" And from his look, it was worse. "And *what*?"

He opened one eye and rushed his words out on a breath. "And you've been abusing prescription opioids, and I'm helping you get off them."

She snapped her head back like getting hit by a cartoon hammer from nowhere. Staring, then blinking, gripping the chains tighter. "My God! How could you? That has to be the stupidest thing you've *ever* done."

He held his hands in front of his chest like a shield. "The idea just popped into my head, then rolled out my mouth. In hindsight, I could've handled it better."

"*Ya think*?" That was beyond lying. Compared to that, a lie looked like a, a—moral absolute. "What on God's green earth were you thinking?" She popped up and poked her finger in his face. "You're going to tell Ynez the truth." She stared. "And soon." She planted her hands on her hips. "And you made yourself a hero. And me a—"

"A slightly troubled woman." He shrugged. "That's all."

Incredible. Absolutely incredible. She looked down, clenching her eyes and teeth. "I'm too angry to talk about this now." She exhaled hard through her nose. "But we will."

"Honestly, I just wanted Ynez to know that nothing was her fault. She could hate me, hate the circumstances, but not hate you. She's more worried about you and the baby than her own feelings."

"There is no baby."

"I realize that." He fumbled in his shirt pocket for a cigarette.

She glared.

He tapped the pack, then lowered his hand. "Ynez came away hurt but feeling good about herself. She's sacrificing for others. Think of it as the good kind of pretending."

She cocked her head. That was well played. Cal was a quick study. But with an honest motive. He hated seeing girls get hurt. Give him credit for that. Still—a troubled, pill-popping, pregnant, and *unmarried* woman. And him a hero. "I'm not very happy with you right now. This could get out of hand. If Mama…" Oh God. Don't even think about that. This was getting complicated, thanks to Cal. She slumped back down on the swing seat. "Come push me."

He rushed behind the swing, pushed her shoulders. "Don't worry. I told Ynez it was a secret. She won't say anything. Anyway, she won't be around very long."

"So you're hoping she'll leave before you have to tell her the truth?" She shook her head. "Well, it ain't gonna happen. She's staying here."

Cal's long sigh sailed over her head. He stopped pushing. "I didn't plan on that. I thought we were getting her out of Miami for her own protection. It was your idea."

"I know, but didn't you hear what she said to me? She doesn't know where to go, because she has nowhere to go. She needs a family now more than ever."

Cal exhaled again. "Kind of an awkward situation. How long is she gonna stay?"

"For as long as she needs." She slid off the swing and faced him. She gripped the chains and leaned her face between them. "Cal, Ynez is only nineteen and a half. So was I when Lenny let Jace and Fowler take me." She squeezed the chains. "I see Shantelle in her. I see me in her. And I won't abandon her. Can you understand that?"

He nodded and sighed. "What can I do to help?"

This would be resolved. The truth would come out, and none of them would die because of Cal's creative story telling. "Just make sure you tell Ynez the truth."

She let loose of the chains, brushed the rust from her hands, and stepped around the swing. "We'll tell her together. That way I'll be sure. And the Montoya women will take care of her. She'll be all right, and she'll be safe. I won't allow anything less."

He nodded.

She took hold of his hands. "Have you thought about what we'll do after everything else is over?"

He shook his head. "Not really. There hasn't been time. I guess I could go back to driving a cab."

"Yes, there's always that. But think about this. I own a small property with a little house near Jayuya. It's in the interior at the base of a mountain. The hurricanes mostly missed it. I have relatives living there now, and they said power and water have been restored for several hours a day. The roads aren't all repaired, but once we got there, it would be a great place to disappear from the rest of the world. Give you time to figure out your future. You need that as much as I do."

Their heads swiveled to the screen door banging open. Cheyenne burst through and ran toward them. "Cal! Come quick."

Damn it, Cheyenne. Not now. But Little Sis kept coming.

The screen door opened again. Lenny and another detective walked toward them. An uncomfortable-looking Lenny lagged behind with Mama tugging on his sleeve. Two officers appeared from around the sides of the house. The closest officer reached behind his back and pulled handcuffs from his belt.

Cal squeezed her hands tighter. "I don't think they're here to ask questions."

Cheyenne reached them. "Soledad, what should we

do?"

She gave her head a short quick shake. *Don't panic—think.* "Cal, don't say anything. I'll take care of the lawyer."

He nodded. "Tell Isabelle I'm sorry this is happening here."

The first detective stopped in front of Cal as the two officers flanked him.

"Caleb Lee, you are under arrest for the murder of Carlos Molina. Place your hands behind your back." An officer cuffed him. "You have the right to remain silent. Anything you say can be used against you in a court of law. You have the right to an attorney before and during questioning. If you cannot afford an attorney, one will be appointed to represent you."

The detective continued reading Cal's rights as they led him around the side of the house. Lenny separated himself from Mama as Josepha wrapped her arms around Mama's waist, holding her back. Ynez stood in the doorway, looking dazed and confused.

Lenny approached, faced her, then flicked his eyes at Cheyenne.

He wanted to talk alone. She nodded. "Cheyenne, go help Josepha with Mama, and take care of Ynez, too."

Cheyenne glared at Lenny as she marched away.

"Lenny, why is this happening? Cal didn't do anything. You know that."

He pushed his hat back a few inches. "This is Dillard's call. I'm not sure why, but it looks like a calculated maneuver. The lab reports came in. Don't panic, but get Cal a good lawyer." He turned and followed the others around the side of the house.

Chapter Twenty-Three

Monday, 9:15 pm

Soledad sat on the front step, looking down the street in the direction Manuel Molina's car would come from. When she'd made the call, Manuel had said he'd be there in fifteen minutes, which meant he was already on his way and must have things to discuss other than Cal.

Right now, what people knew was as dangerous as what they had done, maybe more. Manuel was still determining how much of a loose end she and Cal were. So when they talk, know little, but suggest a lot. Come more from the heart than the head with a touch of panic. And always put family first. Manuel would understand and respect that.

Manuel's black Lincoln slowed to a stop behind Father Brady's car. She stood and walked toward the Lincoln as James opened the rear door and held a hand toward the dark opening. She took a small breath. *Remember, Manuel's highest priority is to protect his family, especially his mother.* Whatever he asked would serve that purpose.

She stepped into the back seat. James closed the door with a sealing thud.

Manuel turned on a recessed ceiling light and gazed down at her with a slight smile. "I want to apologize. I had hoped to handle Mister Lee's problem without intruding on you and your family, but developments require that we confer."

"I understand, and so does my family."

"First, tell me exactly what happened here."

The ceiling light shined on her but left Manuel in shadow. She folded her hands in her lap, turned at the waist, and faced him.

"It happened fast. Cal and I were talking in the backyard when two detectives came to the front of the house, and two police officers came from around the sides. They handcuffed Cal, charged him with the murder of your brother, then took him away."

He nodded. "That wasn't unexpected."

"But Detective Trumbo said that lab results came in. What results are they talking about?"

Manuel's brow furrowed. "The police searched Mister Richards's house and boat last night and are searching Mister Lee's apartment as we speak. Maybe they found something there, or maybe evidence was obtained from Carlos's body. I don't know yet, but I will."

She had no doubt about that. Maybe the police found Shantelle's gun. A good chance that was it. "But I know Cal wasn't involved. What will happen to him?"

"With a murder charge, he'll be remanded. But don't worry, he'll have the best possible representation. When I talked with your sister and Ynez Pascal, both were forthcoming. And I know truth when I hear it and see it. Cal Lee had nothing to do with my brother's murder. I'm sure of that."

He leaned forward. The light illuminated a smooth, expressionless face except for squint lines converging at the corners of his eyes. "We either know or find out when people lie to us. We always discover the truth."

She studied a stare that searched for any sign of uneasiness or guilt. Manuel still wasn't sure of her, so pause, and let the light reveal relief instead of thought, gratitude instead of apprehension. Smile wide and nod. "What you know is more important than what the police believe." She sighed and let her smile droop. "Is Cal safe? Mama is very worried, and I'm worried about both of them." A good response, and well delivered. Make it about Mama, too.

The corners of his mouth lifted slightly as his squint lines smoothed. "Tell your mother that Mister Lee will be fine. He is under our protection. Mister Abrams will represent him. No harm will come to him, in or out of jail."

She gave a soft sigh and a smile of relief. "Thank you so much." Molina protection lasted longer and reached further than that of the police. Cal would be fine.

Manuel leaned back, crossed his arms, and tapped his chin with his index finger. "To help Mister Lee, it is vital that Jace Richards be found. Insight of his most recent business activities would help."

So that was it. Protect their family from Carlos's sordid past by making his murder about business, about money. Jace and Carlos's deal was the perfect cover. A motive the police would accept. Nothing about brutalizing any girls. Nothing about Shantelle's murder.

"I know Jace owns a small janitorial and maid service, a security service, and I think he leases cars, but Jace kept his real business from me. Which fine, I didn't want to know." They already knew about

Jace's real business. His legitimate enterprises laundered his and other peoples' money. They'd find out about his big deal with Carlos and put two and two together, or already had. "But as I told you last night, Jace and Carlos argued about real business. Other than that, I don't know." Give them Fowler, too. Make him a loose end that needed tying up or cut off. "But John Fowler has worked for Jace longer than anyone."

He nodded. "Yes, Mister Fowler. We're following up on that. Can you give any insight into what Mister Richards would do in his current situation? What kind of man is he? How does he handle problems?"

"Well, whenever possible, he solves a problem with money and lawyers. But if that's not an option, I guess that's what John Fowler is for."

"And if Mister Fowler is not an option?"

That took little thought. Jace would run, and soon. She nodded, then looked up into the light and Manuel's shadowed face. "You asked what kind of man Jace is. But I hate him, so my opinion is tainted."

"Please, I want to hear."

She clenched her jaw and didn't hide the hate in her eyes. "He's a coward and has no honor. He loves nothing but himself, although cash is very dear to him. He would trample his own child to escape a burning building, and never look back. The coward in him dominates his character. He'll run, then hide. And never look back."

Manuel nodded like her evaluation agreed with something he knew. "But Mister Richards owns property and has business interests in Miami. Would he abandon all that?"

She gave a slow nod. "He would hesitate, because

of the money, but the coward in him would take over. In the end, no person or thing, not money or revenge, is important enough for him to risk his life. But he won't panic. He'll be prepared, and he'll run smart."

"Any idea how he would escape?"

She looked down, raised her clasped hands and tapped them to her chin. The Molinas wanted Jace dead, but if they talked to him first, he'd say anything to extend his life, including the truth. But she lied better than Jace told the truth. *Trust your instincts.* Manuel wanted to believe her.

She looked up. "Well, he trusts no one, so he'd leave by himself and wouldn't tell anybody. Once I heard him talk hypothetically about escaping on short notice, but that was a few years ago while he and John Fowler drank and watched a football game."

"That might help. Please continue."

She nodded. "I remember that afternoon very well. Jace knows that Fowler disgusts me, so he thought it would be amusing to put me in a bikini and serve food and drinks during halftime. I refused, but he threatened to take away my next Sunday at Saint Anthony's. So I served while they talked. What he talked about was mostly general preparations, not a solid plan."

"What kind of preparations?"

"Well, Jace said for a quick escape a person should have another identity, maybe more than one, with passports, documentation, and lots of cash ready and waiting. He'd have money and property in a foreign country under an alias. Enough to hide in comfort for as long as he needed."

Manuel nodded. "That's been done before. But none of that would do any good if he couldn't escape."

"That's kind of what Fowler said. Jace said the key at crisis time was to leave from wherever he was, without going home or the need for further plans. I know Jace. He had a few drinks in him, but I saw it on his face and in his eyes. He liked his idea. And he's had a few years to set it up."

Manuel leaned back, looking at the ceiling, tapping his index finger to his chin. "Does he know how to fly a plane?"

She shook her head. "No, and I doubt he'd trust anyone to fly him. That would leave a trail. But he's an excellent sailor, and he speaks Spanish. And Friday, he had me pick up two special-order marine bags from L'Voyage for his boat. He said they could float holding fifty pounds."

Manuel's face froze for an instant, then relaxed. "Maybe it wasn't so hypothetical. According to our sources, when the police searched his boat, they found a fake Venezuelan passport, a hundred thousand dollars in cash, and provisions for a month. I saw the police inventory, and there were no special bags. But the boat was fitted with extra gas tanks. So it appears that was his plan, but it's been taken away." He leaned back and again tapped his finger to his chin. "But perhaps not."

She shook her head again. "Then I don't know what else he would do, but John Fowler might."

Manuel pulled out his phone and studied the screen, then nodded and put it away. "One last thing. Who would have knowledge of my brother's dealings with Mister Richards's escort service?"

That had nothing to do with Jace's escape, and everything to do with her and Shantelle. "For special clients, their anonymity was guaranteed. Jace handled the arrangements himself. Neither the girl nor the driver knew the client. Only Jace. If a problem developed, John Fowler was his problem solver. They've had an arrangement since he was a vice detective."

Manuel smiled. "Thank you, Miss Montoya. Again, I want to apologize for this intrusion." He reached across her and tapped the window. James opened the door. "Please call anytime if you need help or think of anything else."

"Thank you, Mister Molina. I will." She started to turn, then stopped and gazed up at him while biting her lower lip. "Part of me wants Jace to disappear, then all my past is put behind me. Another part would feel happy if Jace was dead." She squeezed her eyes shut and shook her head. "And then I feel guilty for what God sees in my heart."

"Miss Montoya." Manuel touched her folded hands. "Everything is out of your hands. Return to your family and stay there."

She stepped from the car, and James closed the door. She walked slowly toward the front step with crossed arms, clutching her shoulders, feeling her heartbeat. Mama, Josepha, and Ynez peeked between the curtains of the living room window. Manuel's Lincoln pulled away. She looked up and smiled at Cheyenne's wide-eyed face poking out the screen door.

That meeting was well done. Very well done, especially the end. Manuel saw torment in her soul, which was true, but not about Jace. He saw worry, but not about Cal. Cal was safe and had a Molina lawyer. Still, Fowler and Jace could ruin everything she wanted. Fowler must surely be a target now, and Jace must be panicking after his boat, passport, and cash were taken away.

She halted. It didn't fit. Not with Jace. He loved cash. A hundred thousand dollars wasn't enough. She nodded. Manuel was right when he'd said perhaps not. For something his life depended on, Jace would have a decoy and a backup. The boat the police had searched was the decoy. He had a second boat with all the same things, plus the bags from L'Voyage, and a lot more cash.

Chapter Twenty-Four

Tuesday, 2:00 am

Soledad drove slowly in Father Brady's car, looking for the turnoff that should come before the entrance to the marina. God bless Father Brady. Just a simple whispered request and he'd parked his unlocked car behind Saint Anthony's with the key under the mat. No questions asked. Cheyenne would have asked hard questions followed by firm objections. But one glass of crushed ice and bourbon to the brim put her out for the night before she caught a hint of what was going on. Mama was the earliest riser, so get back before dawn, before anyone in the house woke up.

Easy enough to find Norris and Son Marina on the computer and get the whole layout, including satellite photos. The marina's south end was under construction. Farther south, a jetty was also under construction. The security lights at the site had been visible for the last quarter mile, and so had giant tire prints of packed soil and compressed sand. Probably from large dump trucks carrying boulders to the jetty. The turnoff should appear soon on the right.

She slowed to a stop. Couldn't miss the marina sign even in the dark and fog. Two lights fanned out from the ground, and three more hung from the top. She lifted her foot off the brake and pulled ahead twenty yards to an unlighted sign advertising Gibson and Gregg Construction Company. An arrow pointed down a wide, unpaved, sandy road. She switched off her headlights and followed the arrow. Just park here, then sneak through the construction site down to the water's edge. From there, less than a thirty-yard swim to Jace's backup boat.

A few yards ahead stood a locked, chain-link gate to a ten-foot-high fence stretching around the entire site. Inside the fence, parked around the perimeter, sat a crane, trucks, and a few large pieces of earth-moving equipment. Stacks of poles, planks, and seawall sections, plus a trailer sat in the center. A generator hummed, probably used to power the security lights.

Wicked-looking barbwire spiraled along the top of the fence. The satellite photos hadn't shown that. There would be no climbing over the fence. Maybe the best thing now, just turn around and forget about it. Keep what she had, her family, her freedom, and maybe Cal. She put the car in reverse and peered over her shoulder.

No. Jace owed her and her family. Money couldn't pay for past suffering and lost time, but it could prevent future suffering and contribute a lot to making her family strong. If Jace left a hundred thousand as a decoy, he'd take ten times as much with him.

She made a U-turn and parked at the edge of the sandy road and out of sight from the main road. A narrow track bordered the outside of the fence, which probably led around the construction site and down to the water. Wide enough to drive on, but the sand wasn't packed, and there might not be a place to turn around. Don't take a chance getting stuck. Best to walk from here, which meant a longer walk and swim, but worth a look.

She returned to the driver's seat and stripped off her sweatpants and sweatshirt to the outfit beneath. From Cheyenne's high school wardrobe, black spandex pants with matching spaghetti-strap top, which fit kind of tight, but the fabric stretched, allowing easy movement. Running shoes, tied tight and double knotted so they wouldn't slip off in the water. Her old swimming cap from her high school swim team days, and Mama's blue, rubberized work gloves.

Take Mama's screwdriver to pry open the cabin door but leave the phone and the car key. Didn't want to take a chance on losing either. Put the phone under the seat, and the key on top of the driver's side front tire.

Coming here was chance enough. Getting discovered was unacceptable. Take one step at a time. If there's light from the boat, turn around and go back. If anyone is in the area, turn around and go back. Go home, be satisfied with what had been gained, and move forward in life.

The walk around the fence took about ten minutes and ended at the water's edge. Thirty yards away, Jace's boat sat moored at the end slip. A twenty to twenty-five footer with a single mast rising from the cabin roof. The bow and cabin hid in shadow, but fog-filtered dock lights mounted on high poles put a soft glow from the stern to the cabin entrance. A low, double railing ran around the entire deck. The cabin rose only a few feet above the deck with a slanted front and a squared back where steps led down to the cabin door.

A still night with only the sounds of lapping water

and the distant hum of the construction site generator. A slight breeze pushed in fog from the ocean, and a low cloud cover blocked the moon and starlight. The boat had no lights turned on, and no one seemed to be around.

She gripped the screwdriver in her right hand and waded in. She bent her knees, leaned forward, and pushed off with an easy breaststroke. Cool night air and cooler water raised goose bumps on her bare shoulders. Don't splash, keep arms and feet beneath the surface. If a light comes on, if a person shows up, just ease around and go back. Nothing gained, but nothing lost.

Originally, climbing onto the dock and boarding the stern from there seemed like the only plan. But nearing the bow, the thought of walking around on a lighted dock, no matter how dim the light, didn't seem wise.

About ten yards away, she stopped and treaded water. The bowline drooped near the surface. Try that first. Go up the rope, grab the railing, slip over the side, and sneak around on the ocean side of the cabin. Should be in dark shadow the whole way. Then down the steps and into the cabin.

She took two deep breaths, clamped the screwdriver between her teeth, then breast stroked to the rope. It looked like a five- or six-foot climb. The gloves gripped the rope tight, no slipping. The water actually gave a firmer grip like a rubber mat in a bathtub.

Up, hand over hand, wrapping her legs around the rope and crossing her ankles. Some splashing as her body exited the water but barely noticeable. She pulled even with the deck, paused for a breath, then grabbed the rail and crawled over. A little noise there, but the cabin portholes remained dark.

So far, so good. No lights, no movement, no sounds except lapping water and the humming generator. She hunched low and took squishy steps across the bow along the side of the cabin. Everything looked fine.

She eased down four steps and placed her ear against the door. Nothing. She turned the knob and pulled. Not even locked. That didn't make sense, unless there was no money. *Turn around and go back.* No, too close to turn back now. Just one quick look around couldn't hurt.

She ducked through the opening, pulled the door shut, and immediately smelled stale cigarette smoke. The interior was pitch black except for a few slivers of dim light wedging between small, black curtains covering the portholes. Darkness in an unfamiliar place always caused her heartbeat to quicken, but now it raced, accompanied by short quick breaths waiting for her eyes to adjust.

"Don't move, Soledad. I'm pointing a gun at you."

She froze. Jace's calm voice was close, maybe six to eight feet away. Get out right now. Duck, open the door, and run. She reached behind and grasped the doorknob.

"Don't even think about it. I've been waiting here in the dark for over an hour. I can see quite well."

She released the doorknob, straining her eyes, willing her pupils to expand. Talk, beg, reason, agree to anything, say anything to stay alive. "Don't kill me, Jace. It'll only make things worse for you."

"Can't get much worse for me, but it can for you."

The staccato tap of his ring seemed to keep time with her heartbeat.

"What are you going to do with me?"

"I'm not sure. This is unexpected, maybe even serendipitous. I've been thinking a lot about you lately. Move to your right. There's a bench and a table. Have a seat."

"People know I'm here. They'll be looking for me." She stepped sideways, feeling her way, then slid into the seat at the end of the table. From the tapping of his ring, Jace must be at the other end.

"I doubt that. I can think of only one reason why you're here. Somehow you figured it out. You came for the money, and you don't want anyone to know. Feel the wall to your left. There's a switch. Flip it up."

She ran her gloved hand along the wall.

"A little higher."

Her fingers slid up, found the switch, and pushed. A small, dim, ceiling light shone on a rectangular table, which was clear except for an ashtray. Jace sat at the other end, holding an automatic in his right hand, clenching his jaw, and shaking his head with a sardonic grin.

"You look like a little ninja, except for the gloves and shoes. And a screwdriver instead of ninja stars. Slide it over here."

She slid the screwdriver across the table next to the ashtray.

"I heard you in the water and climbing up the prow line, so I took a look. At first, I thought you were someone sent by the Molinas. Then slithering over the rail came that beautiful bubble butt of yours, always my favorite part. And I knew."

"What are you going to do with me, Jace?" He couldn't let her go. That left killing her. Stay calm. Stretch this out, keep him talking. Maybe he would slip up and give an opening.

"Haven't decided." He rubbed his chin with his thumb and forefinger. "But first things first." He held the gun on her as he stepped to the opposite side of the cramped cabin to a sink and counter with drawers and storage cabinets beneath. He reached into a small drawer and pulled out two zip-ties.

"Swing your legs from beneath the table." He dropped a tie in her lap. "Put it around your ankles."

She bent forward, looped the tie around her ankles, pushed the end through the slot, and pulled. "If I don't call Cheyenne real soon, she'll go to the police."

Jace eyed her up and down. "I can see the outline of everything, and I mean everything, beneath that wet outfit. And you don't have a phone on you."

"It's in the car. Father Brady's car, and he knows, too."

He shook his head and grinned. "I don't think so, but it doesn't matter. We'll be gone soon. There's a tropical storm forming, and I want to get out well ahead of it. Would've been gone already, but there's a Coast Guard boat in the area on its regular drug smuggler run. They'll move down the coast soon."

He knelt, kept the automatic trained on her chest, then stood as he yanked the tie tighter. "What bothers me, if you figured it out, then others will, too. Not as quickly, because you had more to go on. But soon." He held out the second tie. "Now your wrists, but take off the gloves, the cap, too. Always loved your hair."

She removed the gloves and cap and let her hair

fall over her shoulders. She extended her arms with crossed wrists.

"No, no. Put your wrists together. Ya know, like when you pray. That's all you have now."

She uncrossed her wrists and held the undersides together. Without mobility there would be no mad dash, only words.

Jace tucked the automatic beneath his belt, looped the tie around her wrists, and pulled.

"Stop, you're cutting off the circulation." But there was a little play in the tie.

"That should hold you for as long as I need." He returned to his seat, lit a cigarette, and leaned forward. "Now, how did you figure it out?"

Keep him talking. As long as they talked, she stayed alive. "It was the money the police found on your other boat. It wasn't enough. Had to be a decoy. But I knew you'd go by boat, and alone, because you don't trust anybody."

He nodded. "You know me well. But how did you find this boat?"

"Your credit card bill. More than once you shoved the Nordstrom's bill in my face. Norris and Son, slip fee, was right below. It was easy to look up, and others will, too."

"Eventually, but not soon enough for you. What else did you figure out?"

"That you'd have lots of money in foreign accounts, a passport, and a new identity."

Jace cocked his head with a puzzled stare, like somewhere in the past she'd read his mind.

"A few years ago you talked about it while watching a football game with Fowler. Remember, I was serving drinks in a bikini."

He nodded with a small laugh. "Yeah, I remember. Truth is, it was just an idea then, that is until Carlos killed Shantelle. That's when I started setting everything up." Jace clenched his jaw. "I knew that little prick would fuck up everything. He was stupid, but sooner or later he'd figure out he had to get rid of the person who got rid of Shantelle's body. I lose my property and businesses, but most of my money is safe. I can start over."

Keep him talking. Jace always liked to show how clever he was. "How much money? Has it been here the whole time?"

"Nah, most of the time at the house. Over two million." He took a long drag and exhaled. "I always keep cash close so I have it when I need it. That is, until you killed Carlos. After that, I had to be ready. It's been here since Saturday, which made me nervous, but it all worked out."

"Jace, you have to believe me. I want you to get away. If anyone gets hold of you, it only makes things worse for me. If you disappear, nothing happens to me." She shrugged. "Everyone will think you ran because you killed Carlos."

"I'm sure that's what you told the police, and more importantly, the Molinas. Do they believe you?"

She nodded. "I think so. They know I couldn't have killed Carlos and gotten rid of his body and car by myself. So either you were involved, or you did it all by yourself. But I can help you. Manuel Molina is my lawyer. He'll listen to me. I'll convince him that the best thing is to let you disappear. They don't want a trial or any more bodies."

Jace grinned and shook his head. "Oh, you are desperate." He exhaled an exaggerated sigh. "When Manuel became your lawyer, that was the final straw. I must admit, it caught me by surprise. And I have to give you credit. That was a ballsy move. How'd you figure it?"

"The Molinas don't want an investigation or especially a trial. Too much would come out about Carlos. They don't want their mother to know. Simple as that. Family comes first to them. They care more about that than killing you."

Jace leaned back with a blank look, took a drag, crushed his cigarette in the ashtray, and shook his head. "So Manuel doesn't want his mommy to know. Simple as that. I never figured it that way. You might be right, but they still want me dead. What makes you think you're safe from them?"

"I convinced Manuel that I don't know anything about Carlos's dark side. All I want is to go home to my family. He understands that."

"And you want the money."

"For my family."

He shook his head with a wry grin. "Yeah, I've heard that bullshit story before. But I never gave you enough credit for how smart you are, or how well you can lie and convince people. But Manuel is not an easy man to fool. Did you have to fuck him?"

She glared. "*No.*"

"But if you needed to, you would. Normally I'd say it wouldn't do you any good with Manuel, but there's something about you. Maybe it's your size or that young, innocent face. It sure worked on Cal."

"I'm not sleeping with him either. He's, he's…"

"In love with you? Yeah, I should have seen that coming. Men fall in love with you real easy. The harder a man's dick, the more he thinks with it."

"What're you going to do with me, Jace?"

"Back to that again." He shook his head with a faraway look. "Ya know, a year ago I had a passport and new ID made for you, too. Got them right here with the money." He patted the storage area beneath his seat. "Entertained the idea that we'd escape together, set up in Colombia. You'd run the girls. Wouldn't even have to fuck anyone, except me."

"Gee, Jace, I never knew you cared."

"Didn't you ever wonder why I stopped sampling you after I broke you in?"

She wanted to cross her legs, but the zip tie hobbled her, so she buried her fists in her lap. "I figured I didn't please you. Wasn't your type."

"On the contrary. It was that first audition. Not that you were good at what you did, in fact, you were kind of clumsy. But that had its charm, kind of like a first time. And that silky fine pussy hair of yours." He smiled and smacked his lips. "When a man gets his rocks off, he's sexually drained and it's over, but what you put in his mind stays and grows."

He frowned and shook his head. "You started affecting the way I thought about you. You had a power you didn't realize. When you did, you'd use it on me. Never mix business with anything else. Besides, better to use you to get power over others, which I did. With you as a sweetener, deals became more profitable and happened faster. With Carlos, it got out of hand." He stared, and his jaw tightened. "And then I broke my rule. I sent Cal to get you from Carlos instead of completing the deal."

He leaned forward, wagging the gun like an extension of his finger, then spoke through gritted teeth. "I saved your ass, and it cost me."

"You sent me to him in the first place. You knew what might happen."

He shrugged, leaned back, and patted the storage cabinet. "It was a lot of money, and I needed cash fast. Carlos wouldn't take any other payment. In his heart, I think he was a pedophile, and you were the smallest, most innocent-looking girl I had. The smaller the girl, the smaller the pussy, and the bigger his dick seemed to him. Carlos had problems." He shrugged. "And a tiny dick. Anyway, back to my story, you'll find it enlightening."

He lit another cigarette. "It was a straight enough deal. My electronic money for more in dirty cash. Carlos middle-manned the deal, and his cut was twenty-five thousand from each party. But from me, he only wanted you. I even offered him the money and any other girl, but he wanted you. Can you imagine that?" He shook his head in disbelief. "You instead of twenty-five thousand dollars. For him, you weren't the sweetener, you were the whole fucking deal. So to speak."

"Then why did you send Cal for me? Why didn't you complete the deal?" Soften the voice. Make him think. "It's because you didn't want me dead then, and you don't want me dead now. We can still go to Columbia, together."

He shook his head. "I should've let Carlos kill you. And I won't fix one mistake with another." His sardonic grin returned. "But maybe I can extract some payment. Reacquaint myself with what twenty-five thousand buys." He glanced at his watch. "It's almost time. Just a few things to do before we cast off."

Jace stepped to the right of the door, unfastened a small, red, fire extinguisher secured in a metal mount and clamp. He grabbed her forearms, pulled her to her feet, and lifted. She stood on the balls of her feet, facing the mount. Her elbows bent together in front of her face with her wrists just above her head. He shoved the clamp between her wrists and through the zip tie, then re-clamped the extinguisher in place.

"Like meat on a hook. That'll hold you for the few minutes I need." He snatched two rags from the small sink, then grabbed her hair and jerked her head back. He stuffed one rag in her mouth, then wrapped the other over it and tied a knot at the back of her neck.

"I'm not a man of revenge. There's no profit, and revenge only causes problems. But for you, I'll make an exception." He stood behind her. His hands settled on her shoulders. "Smooth, real smooth. I like a little slender definition on a woman's shoulders."

She tensed. One hand squeezed the back of her neck as the other slid around her waist to her stomach and slipped inside her top. His hand inched upward to her breasts. He fingered her nipples. "Water must be cold, they're poking out hard." She squirmed as his fingers eased down inside her pants and dipped beneath her panties. His lips grazed her ear as his fingertips slid down. "There's that silken pussy hair of yours."

Two fingers shoved between her legs, then wedged up inside her, slowly lifting her onto her toes. She arched her back, twisted, and tried to scream, but only a muffled gasp escaped.

He squeezed the back of her neck harder as his lips hovered at her ear. "Still the smallest pussy I've ever shoved my dick, or tongue, into. Probably not as tight as the first time, but still plenty sweet I'll wager." His fingers slid from between her legs and out of her pants. He sniffed his fingers and sucked on them. "Yes, sir, just as sweet as ever." He rubbed his crotch against her butt. "Always loved your bubble butt. Still a virgin there, and I'll bet plenty tight. That'll be a snug fit. I'm getting hard already."

She snapped her head back and forth, biting on the rag.

His hand clamped tighter on her neck. "You can't scream, but you can pray."

He stepped back and turned to the door. "I want you to think about all the things I'm gonna do to you. And it'll hurt." He ducked, pushed through the door, and shut it behind him.

Get loose now, because once they were out to sea, he would rape her, kill her, then weigh down her body and dump her in the ocean. This might be the only opening.

Jace's footsteps rushed past the cabin toward the prow.

He'd cast off the lines, then they'd leave. Get loose, grab the extinguisher, and when he comes through the door, bash him on the head.

She yanked down. The clamp and mount held firm. She raised her knees and pushed her feet against the wall, but they kept slipping down like running in place. She lifted her feet from the deck, hanging from her wrists. The clamp bent slightly. The tie moved up just past her wrists, digging into the backs of her hands.

Jace's footsteps padded past the cabin, heading for the stern.

She jumped, pulling her knees up, coming down with all her weight. The tie stretched, edging farther up, scraping the backs of her hands. She dangled from the clamp. Her shoulders strained as she pulled and lifted her face even with her wrists. The plastic tie squeezed up to the base of her thumbs, catching on her knuckles. She dropped and bounced.

It moved. Her eyes widened. The tie reached the top of her white knuckles. She bounced. Her hands slipped free. She landed on hobbled feet, wobbled, but kept her balance. Her thumbs hooked the rag covering her mouth and jerked it down. She spit out the other rag, unlatched the clamp, and grabbed the extinguisher. She raised it high with one hand on the nozzle neck and the other on the barrel. When he comes through the door, be ready to swing. Make the first shot count or there wouldn't be a second.

Two distant, almost simultaneous, muffled cracks sounded from outside the cabin. Jace clamored down the steps and thumped against the door. She gritted her teeth and raised the extinguisher higher. Come on Jace, you son of a bitch. You have to duck coming through the door. Her heart thumped faster. She swallowed dry air, wobbled, and steadied herself. One swing, just one good swing.

But nothing. Did he trip and fall down the steps? *Don't wait, go*. If he's unconscious, it might not last long.

She lowered the extinguisher to the deck and hopped to the drawer Jace had pulled the ties from. Lots of zip-ties and tools, including a utility knife and a hammer. She cut the tie holding her ankles, grabbed the hammer, and approached the door.

She took a deep breath, utility knife in one hand, hammer in the other. Push through swinging and running, then go for the water. She turned the knob and pushed with her shoulder.

The door opened several inches, but something blocked it at the bottom. The light was dim, but that was blood pooling on the deck outside the door. She pushed harder and poked her head through the opening.

A gasp caught in her throat. Jace's legs and torso lay sprawled on the steps. His head and shoulders blocked the door. The right side of his head was mostly gone with his brains spilling out.

She pulled the door shut. The two cracks must have been from a rifle or rifles. Had to be someone sent by the Molinas. They hit Jace at the top of the steps and down he came. *Don't panic, think.* Did they know she was here? Did it matter? Would they come to the boat and check their work or pack up and leave? She shook her head. No. If they could see to shoot Jace, they saw he was dead. Professionals used rifles to kill from a distance, and that was as close as they wanted to get. Jace had fallen forward down the steps, so the shots didn't come from the construction site. Maybe they didn't see her.

Stay calm but think fast. First, take care of any evidence that said she was in the cabin, which meant wiping down everything touched. Put everything back and wait, but not too long.

Chapter Twenty-Five

Tuesday, 3:15 am

Soledad stood at the small sink with a rag in each gloved hand, surveying the cabin. Everything she touched or might have touched had been wiped down. The fire extinguisher was back in place, the utility knife and hammer were back in the drawer. The screwdriver, swimming cap, rags from her mouth, and cut ties lay on the table.

Not going to the money first had taken great discipline. The anticipation was there, like saving the best present under the Christmas tree for last. As she stepped to the storage space that Jace had patted, an excited nervousness rose from the pit of her stomach to the middle of her chest.

A heavy-duty padlock hung open on a hasp. Jace must have checked on his money first thing, then left it unlocked. She tossed the cushion aside and lifted the hinged seat. Jace's two special-order marine bags sat side by side. Her heart beat as fast as when Jace hung her from the fire extinguisher. She grabbed the first bag's zipper, yanked it open, then separated the sides.

Oh, my God. There they were, stacks of used hundred-dollar bills wrapped with rubber bands. Jace said over two million dollars, and this must be half. She opened the second bag. The same thing. *Don't go crazy, stay calm, but oh, my God.*

Think calm, think smart, but her eyes stayed on the money. All her plans to take care of Mama, Josepha's law school, and a new start in Puerto Rico sat wrapped in rubber bands. So close, just a thirty-yard swim, ten-minute walk, and a sixty-minute drive, and money would never be a worry again.

She took two deep breaths to ease her stomach and slow her heart. *Be practical, be smart, and not too greedy.* Her shoulders strained lifting the first bag to the table. Her brain said at least twenty-five pounds, but adrenaline made it lighter.

She shook her head. Don't even consider taking both bags or making two trips. One could be handled safely, so leave the other. No one knew about the bags. They'd think one bag was all of it. What better way to say no one came inside than to leave a million dollars?

Think. Jace also said he had a passport for her. She plunged her hands down the sides of the bag. On the left side, wedged next to the stacks of bills, was a Ziploc bag. She slid it out and dumped the contents on the table.

Jace had it covered. American, Colombian, and Venezuelan passports for himself. He hadn't lied about her. American and Colombian passports with her picture above the name Dona Maria Cordova. Take those and destroy them later. He also had two sets of boat papers, and on the second set, the name of the boat was the *Soledad*. Why, Jace, you sentimental fool.

She returned Jace's passports and boat papers to the Ziploc bag, laid it on top of the money in the second bag, then closed the zipper. When the police investigated, they'd find one bag with a lot of money and Jace's documents, just like on the other boat. She shut the seat lid, put the cushions back in place, and locked the padlock. A thief would ransack the cabin, break into the storage space, and empty it. This would look like a hit, not a robbery. Next, into her one bag went the ties, rags, screwdriver, and her passports.

She wound her hair on top of her head and put on the swimming cap. Everything was set. She looped the strap over her shoulder and let the bag ride on her opposite hip as she walked to the door.

That first sight of pooling blood and Jace's brains spilling out had made her stomach turn. *Be prepared for a lot more.* She pushed the door open, sliding Jace's head and shoulders to the side. A thick, warm smell of blood and excrement mixed with diesel and stagnant sea air made her stomach churn. Blood was everywhere with dark bits of splattered brain sticking to surfaces. Don't step in the blood, and don't puke.

For that first step past Jace's body, there was no place without blood, except on his body. Blood had seeped from a bullet hole between his shoulder blades and had run down to the bottom step. His lower back looked unstained, and beyond that, the other steps looked clear. She shifted the bag behind, so it rested on her butt, held her breath, and took one giant step.

Oh God. Jace squished and gurgled. More blood flowed from his mouth and wounds. Her stomach palpitated. Her hands shot out, pushing against the sides of the stairwell, steadying herself. She locked her throat and took another giant step to the deck.

Around the cabin and across the bow. She dropped the loose end of the prow line over the side, then climbed over the rail. The bag shifted, dragging her down, pulling her grip from the rope. She fell feet first, splashing into the water, submerging for a few seconds as the strap slipped off her shoulder and over her head.

She surfaced. Her stomach heaved, her throat unlocked, and curdled liquid sprayed into the water. She coughed and spit and snapped her head away from the floating vomit.

Where was the bag? It had been riding on her butt. Probably no more than ten to twelve feet deep here. She rotated, sucked in air and prepared to dive. She blinked water from her eyes, then froze. A smile rose. There it was, riding on gentle undulating swells. The bag floated as advertised. Thank you, Jace, for being as prepared as a boy scout.

Fatigue replaced the adrenaline that had energized her run. Her tired legs and shoulders ached as she side-stroked parallel to shore, dragging the bag along.

A storm was moving in. The wind picked up, and the water rose and dipped. Large, isolated raindrops plunked into the water. Soon they'd become a downpour with the wind slanting them shoreward.

The return swim took twice as long, but finally her feet found sand. She dragged the bag to shore, collapsed, and gazed skyward as the rain became a downpour. She closed her eyes, opened her mouth, and let the cool rain rinse out the last of the sour taste. Her body felt tired but clean and refreshed as though Jace's touch had been washed away with the vomit.

A heaven-sent rain. Any footprints or glove prints on the outside of the boat would wash away. The same with any footprints in the sand around the construction site. The finish line was within sight. She had the money, and the only witness against her was dead.

Chapter Twenty-Six

Tuesday, 5:15 pm

Soledad's body shook. She groaned from dull aches throbbing through her back and shoulders. What was happening?

"Soledad, wake up. Wake up!"

Cheyenne's voice. Must be at home. "Don't shake me anymore. I hurt all over." She pressed her palms to her forehead and blinked rapidly, clearing cobwebs from her brain. Concentrate. The last things she recalled was putting her clothes in the washer, taking a shower, then lying down on top of the covers, for just a few minutes. What time was it?

"Come on, Sis. Wake up." Cheyenne grabbed her shoulders and lifted her into a sitting position. "The police just drove up in cars and vans. I don't know what they want, but there's a lot of them."

She shook her head. The blinking slowed and stopped, finally focusing on a wide-eyed Cheyenne. *The bag.* They found something on the boat. "Are they coming in the house?"

"Looks that way." Cheyenne clenched her jaw and held a hard stare. "Listen up. I don't know where you were, but as far as anyone knows, you went to bed last night after dinner. You were exhausted from anemia and everything that's been going on. You got up for some breakfast, went back to bed, and slept until now." Cheyenne spun to the dresser, snatched some folded sweat clothes, and dropped them on the bed. "I finished all your laundry." She pointed to the floor. "Your shoes, too."

"What time is it? How long have I been sleeping?"

"It's a little after five in the afternoon. I got you under the covers about ten hours ago. You never opened your eyes. You just groaned."

She took a deep breath. Didn't remember any of that. "I'm awake now. Stay with Mama. I'll be out in a few minutes."

Cheyenne nodded, then rushed out the door and pulled it shut.

Focus. Get the details straight. She threw the covers aside, swung her legs around, and dropped to the floor on her hands and knees. That made every muscle hurt. By the time she got home, that bag had felt like a hundred pounds.

She peeked under the bed. There it was, directly down from her pillow and barely visible in the darkness. How infantile and stupid was that decision? Should have left the bag in Father Brady's trunk. But the thought of having the money out of reach, where anyone could get to it. Just couldn't do that. Not when a new beginning was so close. But even worse was falling asleep. She shook her head. Don't think about that now.

She climbed to the bed and slipped into her sweat clothes and tennis shoes. Cheyenne said vans, which probably meant CSU techs. They came to search. The bag would be found. If it only contained money, a lie might work. Jace gave it to her to hold, along with her passports, so she could join him later. But for the cut zip-ties, gloves, rags and screwdriver, there was no believable explanation. Get those things now and throw them into the backyard or the closet. If the items were found separately, the police might not put it together.

She rushed to the window. An officer patrolled the backyard. She spun and ran to the door. Voices and footsteps approached from down the hall. Too late. Stay calm. Think. She closed her eyes and shook her head. There was nothing. Only a miracle. The bag would be found. The police would reexamine the entire case. Even worse, explaining the money to Manuel Molina. She had put money over family. Everything she'd said to him would look like a lie. All the work of sneaking inside him and making him want to believe her would be for nothing.

The door pushed open. A detective in a crew cut with gray sprinkles flashed his badge. He wore a Lenny-type suit and narrow tie but looked a few years younger and few inches taller. She wished it was Lenny.

"I'm Detective Zimski. We have a search warrant. Please step aside and don't interfere."

She stepped back. This man sounded businesslike. He wouldn't forget to look under the bed. "What are you looking for, Detective?"

"It's in the warrant. This shouldn't take too long." A CSU tech carrying a shoulder bag and wearing gloves followed him in. The detective motioned to the tech. "Start with the dresser."

The tech opened the bottom drawer as Detective Zimski inspected the top of the dresser and desk. He stepped to the head of the bed, ripped off the bedspread, shook it, then dropped it on the mattress. He did the same with the top and bottom sheets.

He was working his way down. It was only a matter of time. When they find it, don't say anything. Let them do all the talking.

Detective Zimski leaned over the headboard, pressed his temple against the wall, and peered down through the narrow gap between the wall and headboard.

Was it against the wall? Don't remember, and it didn't matter. They'd look.

"Find anything, Detective?"

Everyone turned their heads to Lenny leaning his shoulder against the doorjamb. He glanced at Detective Zimski, then looked at her.

She clenched her jaw, tensing every facial muscle, pleading with unblinking eyes. Please Lenny. Cal said you were on our side. If you ever wanted to help me, now is the time. Please, tell them to stop, that it's a mistake.

Detective Zimski turned from the bed and extended his hand toward Lenny. "Detective Trumbo, I was told you were still on the boat."

"Just got back."

They shook hands.

"I'm Al Zimski, your new partner. Just got assigned today. We've met before. Do you remember?"

Lenny nodded. "Yeah, about five years ago. You were with Internal Affairs, investigating John Fowler on that negligent homicide charge."

Detective Zimski nodded with a slight frown. "He has friends on the force. I'm not too popular in some circles."

"He was a bad cop, and there's nothing worse. I'd have done the same. Maybe that's why they're putting us together." Lenny scanned the room. "So what we got here?"

"Search warrant says clothing and shoes for gunshot residue and/or blood in connection with Carlos Molina's murder."

Lenny nodded. "Any luck?"

"Not yet." Detective Zimski turned his head. "Miss Montoya, you don't have to be here. Go join your family in the living room."

"No. If people are going to root through my room, I want to be here."

She stepped to the edge of the bed and sat with her hands folded in her lap. They were looking for clothes with gunshot residue or Carlos's blood. Her clothes from that night were long gone and destroyed, carried out in the Nordstrom's bag with Mama's present that Cal had been so curious about. Maybe they wouldn't look under the bed. If they found the bag, a lot of innocent people would suffer.

"Hey, detectives." The tech motioned them to the closet. "Come take a look."

Detective Zimski walked to the tech. Lenny stopped halfway between the bed and the closet.

The tech pointed. "There's not much here, especially for a woman's closet. See those clothes on the hangers. Dust on the shoulders. Nothing's been worn for quite a while, except for one black dress, and it comes up clean. Same with the clothes in the dresser, all clean and clear, and nothing's been worn in some time. Shoes, too."

Detective Zimski nodded. "The rest of the room is

clean, dust free, and organized, like it was prepared for a guest, or us."

"I could have told you that." They all looked at her. "I came back home. This is my old room. Mama cleaned it yesterday for me. Everything in the closet and drawers is from eight years ago. From before I left home."

Detective Zimski stepped to her. "Where're the clothes you've been wearing?"

"I've been wearing my sister's things for the last two days. I left all my clothes at Jace Richards's house." This was all about shooting Carlos, nothing about the boat. They must have found Shantelle's Beretta at Jace's house and probably already scanned her clothes there. Stay calm. There was no blood or gunshot residue here. They would leave.

Detective Zimski sighed and shook his head. "What do you think, Detective Trumbo? You're lead on this case."

She held her breath. Please, please, Lenny. Tell them nothing is here. Move on.

Lenny scanned the room. "Is the warrant just for this room?"

"Nah, the whole house."

"Then bag the black dress for fibers and go to the sister's room and the laundry room."

Detective Zimski nodded at the tech. "You heard him. Bag the dress, and we move on."

She clenched her jaw to keep from smiling. The tech slid her black dress into a plastic bag, sealed it, and wrote on the outside. He put his equipment in his shoulder bag and stood.

She let slip a slow, silent breath. Thank you,

Lenny. It would be all right.

Detective Zimski stepped toward the door, then stopped. "One last thing, Miss Montoya."

"Yes, sir."

"Please stand and step away from the bed."

She froze. Every aching muscle tensed. Her heart thumped, rising to her throat. Oh, my God. No. Do something, Lenny.

Detective Zimski motioned for the tech.

She looked at Lenny, swallowed, then flicked her eyes at the opening between the bed and the floor. Lenny narrowed his eyes, pushed his hat back with his thumb, and moved next to the bed.

"Miss Montoya." Detective Zimski motioned with his index finger. "Please stand and step this way."

She stood and took two steps forward.

Detective Zimski held out an open hand. "Stop. Please extend your arms to the side and widen your stance."

She obeyed. He wouldn't frisk her. They needed a female officer for that.

Detective Zimski motioned to the tech. "Scan her."

Still about the clothes. She wanted to exhale a deep breath but gave her best indignant frown.

The tech sniffed the air. "Sure, but I can smell recently washed clothes from across a crowded room, especially when there's been bleach in the water."

The tech scanned her cuffs, up and down each arm, all around her torso, then up and down each leg. He repeated the process with the UV light ending between her legs. The light bumped her crotch.

"Sorry, miss." The tech shook his head. "Nothing. No GSR, no blood."

Then this was it. They'd leave.

Detective Zimski nodded and took a look around the room. "Just in case, check under and behind the furniture for any shoes or clothing. Maybe we'll find OJ's bloody glove."

No! Lenny, tell them no. Make an excuse.

The tech pulled out a flashlight and knelt beside the bed.

She glanced at Lenny. He had to see the fear in her eyes.

He knelt beside the tech.

Do something. Her hands went to her hips while poking her chin out at Detective Zimski.

"Just a minute, Detective. I want an apology. You've treated me like a criminal." She glanced at the kneeling tech. He switched on his flashlight and bent lower on his hands and knees.

"And you with the flashlight." The tech stopped and stared up, his head less than a foot from her butt. "Yes, you. I think you liked running those scanners between my legs. And you touched me. Are you sure you don't want to scan my underwear, too?" She hooked her thumbs beneath her sweatpants waistband, pushed down and bent forward, poking her butt toward the frozen tech's face. Her sweatshirt slid up her back as the waistband inched lower, revealing panties to the middle of her butt.

The tech's eyes zoomed in on the several inches of bare skin and blue panties.

"Stop." Detective Zimski glared. "That won't be necessary."

Lenny removed his hat. He took the flashlight from the wide-eyed tech, bent low, and stuck his head, shoulders, and flashlight under the bed.

She straightened and pulled her sweatpants up. How suspicious was that? But panties and adjoining skin can take over a man's thought.

Detective Zimski motioned for the tech to rise, then crossed his arms. "Miss Montoya, I've been courteous and treated you with respect. I thought scanning you would be less intrusive than having you change your clothes. The tech was just doing his job. If you were offended, I apologize. If you wish, you can file a complaint."

She looked down and shook her head. "No, I just want to be left alone."

Lenny backed out from under the bed without a word. He stood, replaced his hat, and handed the tech his flashlight. He turned to Detective Zimski. "Nothing under the bed. I checked the bottom of the mattress, too."

Detective Zimski clenched his jaw and gave her a strained smile. "I appreciate your cooperation. Good day, Miss Montoya." He marched toward the door, motioning for the tech to follow. "You got anything else, Detective Trumbo?"

"Call me Lenny. I'll join you in few minutes. I have a few questions for Miss Montoya."

Lenny waited until the others left, then pointed at the bed. "Sit down and listen."

She nodded and sat. Lenny had seen the bag under the bed, and he was at the boat, so he knew. Not how or when, but he knew.

Lenny pulled the chair from the desk and straddled it with his back to the door. He stared but showed no emotion.

"Lenny, I—"

"Don't talk." He wagged a finger. "Now you listen to me, young lady. Jace Richards was killed early this morning." His voice became low and even. "Dillard's new theory is that Jace killed Carlos over a deal gone wrong. We have the money. Then Jace was killed by hired professionals. The money was left at the scene, so that leaves Molina revenge as the motive. If this search comes up empty, you become a loose end that Dillard will check off his list. Tomorrow, you, your sisters, and Ynez Pascal will be brought down to the station to give statements for the record. Just repeat everything you've already said. Don't do anything and don't go anywhere. It's as good as over. Do you understand me?"

"Yes, sir." She understood. Lenny was on her side. "But what about Cal?"

"Charges will be dropped. Wait a few months, then leave Miami and don't come back."

"I plan on taking my family to Puerto Rico."

"That'll do just fine. And take Cal with you."

"I already planned to."

He stood and motioned for her to rise. "Now come join your family in the living room. The search of this room is complete."

The rest of the search went without incident. Lenny stayed close to Mama, reassuring her this was the last time they'd bother her family. Mama was resentful to every tech, police officer, and detective, but not toward Lenny. She knew he was a good man, the best man in their family's life since Daddy died.

Lenny was right. It was as good as over. Mama had her family home and safe. Cheyenne could finally stop struggling with guilt over something that was never her fault. The same with Father Brady. Thank God he would live to see it through.

Then there was Lenny. A man with a personal code more important than the letter of the law. Lenny knew he should have helped her eight years ago. He saw the consequences on an entire family for his failure. Lenny was paying off a debt. Something he had to do for himself. Nothing felt better than guilt redeemed.

Chapter Twenty-Seven

Thursday, 7:35 pm

Soledad shrugged away a frown, then dropped her phone into her purse as Cheyenne exited the freeway. Cal's cell must be dead. A small inconvenience that didn't matter. If he left the police station when he said, he should be at Jake's in thirty to forty minutes. The way Cheyenne was driving, they'd arrive well before that.

So far, everything had happened the way Lenny predicted. They'd all gone down to the police station, made statements, and answered questions. Her statement was first, longest, and the most detailed. Then came Ynez, followed by Cheyenne, Josepha, and finally Mama, who answered questions only from Lenny.

Ynez told the truth about everything she knew and did. Helping Ynez was a side story, a false lead the police wasted a lot of time on. It had nothing to do with either Carlos's or Jace's murders, except to give Cal an alibi and add credibility to the entire sequence of events. Cheyenne gave her account of Thursday's shopping and going back to Cal's apartment, she and Cal planning the escape from Saint Anthony's on Saturday and carrying it out on Sunday. Finally, Cal sneaking through her bedroom window to deliver the message to call Manuel. Josepha's and Mama's statements confirmed what everyone else said.

The police had already interviewed Father Brady, Marny, and even Mike the bartender. They obtained security videos from Dadeland Mall, the bus station, businesses, and Cal's apartment complex parking lot, which all helped verify every step of her story. Each person's statement corroborated and confirmed everyone else's. Each scene led to the next, telling the story of her and Ynez escaping from Jace. They had to see the obvious love triangle with motives having nothing to do with Jace or Carlos.

The only unverifiable part was her account of what happened at Jace's on Wednesday night. Her lie about that night became the glue that held it all together. With so much truth that followed and fit, the police found a believable and convenient story. Carlos's and Jace's murders had nothing to do with her and Cal but everything to do with a deal gone wrong and Molina revenge. Shantelle's murder wasn't even mentioned. Her case was cold and getting colder. Just what the Molinas wanted.

The elephant in the room was that she and Cal were obviously under the protection of the Molinas. They supported her story. They had the truth they wanted. This case was as good as closed.

Cheyenne squirmed as she steered her Accord into the right lane approaching Jake's Tavern. "You're sure Cal's on the way?"

She nodded. "I'm sure. He called from the station. Charges were dropped. His lawyer is driving him here to pick up his car." She pointed. "Go around the block and drop me off at the back. I want to make sure his car is still there."

Cheyenne drove past the front entrance and turned right. "Maybe I should wait with you just in case he doesn't show up. Anyway, I think I have to pee."

"No. He'll be here. He has to. I've had some thoughts swirling around in my head, and we have to discuss them."

Cheyenne glanced right, turned sharply into the parking lot, and skidded to a stop. She shoved the gearshift into park and turned with a wide grin. "Maybe the same thoughts Mama and I have. Except ours don't swirl."

"Your opinion of Cal has certainly changed a lot in the past few days."

"Like I said before, Mama is mighty convincing. You should discuss less and feel more."

"I'll keep that in mind." She opened the car door, slipped out, and pushed the door shut.

The Accord sprayed gravel as it made a sharp U-turn, slid to a stop at the entrance, then sped away.

She walked across the mixed dirt and gravel lot. No empty parking spaces, and Cal's car still sat in the space closest to the entrance. Two groups of men stood near the back door, smoking and talking football. Jake's must be crowded tonight, which was fine. Didn't want to spend much time here anyway, but Cal had said he wanted a Jake's Burger and a beer before leaving.

She opened the door to the back entrance. A low roar of loud talk and laughter spilled out. As she walked down the hallway the noise grew, adding clinking glass, chair legs scraping, and TV football announcers. Why on earth did they have to play football on Thursday, too? She wrinkled her nose and stepped quickly past the men's room door.

The mixed smell of hamburger grease and deep fryer oil floated in the air where the hall opened to the bar and seating area. On her immediate left, the few, small round tables leading back to the pool room sat empty with reserved signs. Farther on, the large rectangular tables in the main seating area were all taken with only a few vacant chairs. On the right, the bar stretched toward the front door with every stool filled by men eating, drinking, and watching a football game on televisions hanging from the ceiling.

"Soledad." Mike the bartender waved as he rushed around the end of the bar. He stopped and leaned close, pointing with his eyes. "The pool room is reserved for you."

She looked toward the empty pool room. At a small table next to the closed sign, a man in his mid-to-late thirties wearing a dark suit and red tie sipped coffee and talked on his phone. He sat up straight, but with relaxed shoulders and calm eyes watching her and Mike. It was James. He must be more than Manuel's driver.

"The man sitting by himself. What's he doing?"

Mike shrugged. "Making sure the room stays reserved." He glanced down the length of the bar. A dark-suited man sat at each end. Mike shrugged again. "They're all together."

"What's going on, Mike?"

"Well, the Dolphins are on Thursday Night Football, and it's pool league night, but we're delaying the match. Jake himself is here giving out free beer and appetizers to the pool teams and extending happy hour for everyone else."

"You know what I mean. Who made the

273

reservations?"

"All I know is that Jake gave me instructions to take care of you. Your table is waiting. Want anything?"

"A Diet Coke, no glass."

Mike nodded and turned toward the bar.

She grabbed his arm. "Wait, I'm meeting Cal, but we won't be here long. Can you get a takeout order ready?"

"Sure. Whatever you want."

"A Jake's double bacon cheeseburger with everything. And a large order of fries."

"Steak fries or—"

"No, your extra-long Jake's Skinny Fries. Put them in a separate container, and two cans of Diet Coke." She smiled and raised her eyebrows. "Would it be possible to get a few beers, too?"

"Like I said. Whatever you want."

She reached inside her purse. "I'll pay for everything now."

Mike raised his hands in front of his chest. "It's all taken care of. Anything you want. The takeout order will be ready when you are. I'll get that Diet Coke." Mike took a half step back, then stopped and looked down. "I hope what I told the detectives didn't cause you and Cal any problems."

She touched his hand. Mike looked up with sad, hopeful eyes while holding his breath.

"Mike, you told the truth, and that helped us both." She smiled. "And I'll always be grateful." Just like with Marny and Father Brady, Mike only added truth to her story.

He exhaled big and smiled bigger, then turned and

hurried around the end of the bar with a bounce to his step.

She took a look around. The dark-suited men at each end of the bar weren't talking to anyone, just watching. One was positioned near the front door with a view of the main seating area and anyone entering or leaving. The other sat at the near end of the bar, able to see down the hall past the restrooms to the back entrance, and with a line of sight into the pool room. They had to be Manuel's men, and since Cal's lawyer was a Molina lawyer, Manuel knew Cal was on his way to meet her. And now they knew she was here.

As she approached, James smiled pleasantly. "Miss Montoya, a pleasure to see you again." His left hand motioned toward the pool room. "Please have a seat."

She walked past the two pool tables to Cal's corner table about six feet beyond the last low-hanging pool light. The table was visible from only the end barstool and one occupied table in the main seating area. Two couples sat there watching football. They glanced over in unison, whispering in each other's ear. Then one of the men stood, grabbed his Dolphins hat by the bill, and slapped it against his leg. "Turnovers are killing us!" He waved for a waitress, then sat down. Their attention returned to the game.

Manuel must want to talk before Cal arrived. But why now, and why on short notice? Since she'd talked with Manuel in the back of his Lincoln, Jace had been killed. Nothing but good there. Manuel wouldn't want to discuss that. By now, the police must have found Shantelle's gun and knew it killed Carlos. But the murder charge against Cal had been dropped, and she hadn't been arrested, so that was working out just the way Lenny predicted. Manuel must know something he didn't know before. Something he wanted to act on but wanted to talk to her first, and urgent enough to make quick arrangements at a local bar.

Figure on Manuel knowing everything the police knew and more. At this point, what people knew was more important than what they had done. That might be at the bottom of this quickly arranged meeting. What did she know about Carlos? Specifically, what did she know about Shantelle's death and Carlos?

Mike, still smiling big, arrived with a can of Diet Coke, then hurried away.

She sipped the Coke and took a breath. This meeting would be different from the first time at the Molina house. No church dress, no veil, and no first impression. By now, Manuel had investigated her and her family. He knew she wasn't helpless and harmless. Weakness and vulnerability with tears would come across as false. But he also knew her family was good and innocent and had seen that firsthand.

James put his phone away and stood. The dark-suited man at the near end of the bar did the same. Manuel was near. Stay with the original read. His living family was his priority now, especially his mother. Keep the emphasis on both their families. Maybe, just maybe, a concern for the Montoya family had sneaked inside him. If everything else was equal, that might tip the scales.

Manuel emerged from the back hall with one man preceding him and another following. Like his men, he wore a dark suit, but his was perfectly tailored silk. He looked directly at her with a clean shaven, expressionless face. Well-rested, clear, unmoving eyes stayed on hers as if approaching a reckoning.

Her heartbeat quickened, sending tiny vibrations throughout her body. Her stomach muscles tightened, forcing a swallow. Need to control that.

Manuel stopped at the table and pulled out a chair. "Good evening, Miss Montoya. Would you mind switching sides with me?"

"Of course not." She walked around the table. Manuel seated her. He sat opposite her with his shoulder to the side wall, leaning slightly forward with his folded hands resting on the table. Light shone on one side of his face, the other side was in shadow, and probably the same for her.

"First, I apologize for interrupting your evening, but I have pressing business that needs attention. I want to assure you that no charges will be filed against you, but I will continue to represent you for as long as you wish."

A polite businesslike tone, as usual. She smiled. "I can never thank you enough for what you've done for my family."

Manuel lifted a hand a few inches, waving it slightly like he'd heard that before and it held little meaning.

Mike arrived. Manuel kept his eyes on her as Mike set a bottle of water and a glass on the table, then hurried away.

"Yeah, baby! That's how it's done."

Couldn't see the man in the Dolphin's hat, but it was him. Manuel didn't flinch. She closed her eyes and folded her hands on the table. Heartbeats pulsed through her fingers, urging them to twitch. Need to control that, too.

Manuel unscrewed the bottle cap. "The police will close the murder investigation of my brother as well as that of Shantelle Williams." He leaned forward with an expressionless stare. "Jason Richards was responsible for both deaths."

She closed her eyes and nodded. That was his new information. Pinning Carlos's murder on Jace was easy, but somehow the Molinas had manipulated people and evidence to pin Shantelle's murder on Jace, too. The police cleared two murders off their books, and Carlos became a victim only. Everyone got what they wanted.

She opened her eyes and met Manuel's stare. This wasn't the end. He had his own loose ends to tie up.

He sat back, sipped from the bottle, then set it on the table. "I reviewed the autopsy and forensic reports on Carlos." He raised his right hand to his chest, then tapped his solar plexus three times. "He was shot in a tight pattern." He leaned forward and narrowed his eyes. "No downward entry angle. In fact, a slight upward angle."

Her scalp tightened and tingled. Her ears warmed, suddenly aware of clinking glass and shrill laughter coming from the rest of the tavern. He knew. If Jace shot Carlos, the angle would have been downward. He knew, the shooter was short, even shorter than Carlos.

Manuel sat back and relaxed his stare. "The police have concluded that Carlos was standing in a slightly elevated position, possibly on a stair step, or the killer shot from the hip."

She tucked her hair behind her ears, then folded her hands on the table. Shooting a tight pattern from the hip was highly unlikely. Was he giving her an out? Accepting a scenario he didn't believe, but it worked for what mattered most to him, his living family. *See where he's going.*

He cocked his head slightly. "When we first talked, I believe you said you loved Shantelle Williams like a sister. She was family to you. Are you satisfied with the results of the investigation?"

She took a slow, silent breath. *He's evaluating the person as much as the words.* They both knew what they both knew. Carlos killed Shantelle. *Stick with your original read.* Shantelle's death was what he wanted to bury the most. *Don't lie. Don't be weak.*

She leaned forward and let her eyes meet his stare. "The man who killed Shantelle has paid, and he will never hurt anyone again. Healing can begin." She wanted to sip her Diet Coke, but her fingers might fumble it.

He nodded, but his face remained expressionless. He leaned back and sipped his water.

"Penalties are killing us! That's loss of down, too." Again, the man in the Dolphins hat.

Manuel set his water down. "We both have no greater loyalty than to our families. We will do whatever is necessary to protect them." He paused and held a stare. "And maybe avenge them, too."

A bead of perspiration rolled from her armpit, down her side like a tiny running spider, making her skin shiver. She clasped her fingers tighter to keep them from twitching. *He knew she'd killed Carlos. Don't answer, don't comment. See where he's going. The end is near.*

He continued. "But loyalty has different paths. My mother believes Carlos was killed by my father's enemies. She partially blames my father, and he will accept and carry that blame to save her from further pain." He paused and sipped his water. "There is no greater grief than a mother losing her child, and no greater loss than that child losing his soul."

That was from one mother's child to another. Not just a reckoning, Manuel wanted closure for his family, and peace in his mother's heart. That Carlos died a victim in God's grace, not a predator whose soul was lost.

He set his water down. "What will you do now?"

Tell the truth. Make it about the living not the dead, about the future not the past. Please, let her family creep inside him and tip those scales.

She tightened her jaw and swallowed. "I'll marry Cal, and we'll move to Puerto Rico." A small smile forced its way between her lips. "Mama will come to be with me for my first pregnancy." The smile grew. "And she'll never go back to Miami. And we'll raise my children to be good Catholics." It was there and it was real. She had nothing left. Her stomach muscles squeezed tighter, pressing against the bottom of her lungs. Her temples throbbed in time with each heartbeat.

He sighed. Something like envy briefly entered his eyes until he blinked it away. That said more than any words. He wanted to believe.

"Yeah, baby! This is it. Fourth and goal. Do or die."

Please, Dolphins man—*shut up*. She pressed her lips together to keep them from trembling.

Manuel's face relaxed. He nodded. "I think God is on your side." He pointed with his chin. "Mister Lee—Cal—is waiting for you."

She looked over her shoulder. At the end of the bar next to one of Manuel's men, Cal stood holding two takeout bags and looking surprisingly calm and stone-faced. She turned back to Manuel.

Again, he pointed with his chin. "Go, Miss Montoya."

She pushed her chair back. Was he ending everything? She stood and turned toward Cal. Her knees quivered with each heartbeat. Was it over?

"Soledad."

She held her breath and peered back at Manuel.

The corners of his mouth and eyes lifted slightly. "Go with God. And raise that family."

She nodded, almost bobbing her head. Her words came out on a short, quick whisper. "I will."

She took a step. It was over. All over. Her heart pounded, making her body vibrate inside.

She passed James at the closed sign and quickened her pace, weaving between the last few empty tables.

Cal stepped toward her. She must be smiling because he was smiling back. Tears tried to burst through as she wrapped her arms around him and planted the side of her face against his chest.

"Cal, my legs are shaky. Get me out of here *now*."

He shifted both takeout bags into his left hand while holding her up with his right arm. He strode down the hall practically carrying her on his hip. She kept both arms around him as he pushed through the back door and into the parking lot. A roaring cheer erupted in the tavern.

"Help me into your car."

Cal kept his arm clamped around her. He dropped the takeout bags on the roof, then pressed the fob and jerked the door open. He swung an arm behind her knees, lifted, and plopped her into the seat.

He knelt on one knee and leaned forward with a nod and a smile. "I have a pretty good idea what's going on, and how it turned out. Are you all right?"

She nodded, letting tears leak from both corners of both eyes. "*We're* all right." She held a hand in front of her face, trying to swallow back tears. The past was over, nothing but future ahead.

"Should I take you home?"

"No, no. Just close the door and get in. And don't forget—"

"I got it." Cal reached to the roof and shut her door.

She sat back and exhaled. God had seen everything she'd done and knew why, and still was on her side. He meant for her to have her dream, because it wasn't just for her. Maybe, not even mainly for her. Mama was the saint the church didn't know about, but God did.

Cal slid into the driver's seat, plopped the takeout on the back seat, and started the car. "Where to?"

"Your place." She glanced at Jake's back door, but no one followed. "What kind of exit did we make?"

"Fast." Cal pulled into the street. "But mostly unnoticed. Everyone was busy watching the Dolphins on fourth and goal. I think they scored."

"It's over, Cal. It's all over."

"Well, I studied Manuel's face as you walked away. He looked satisfied, pleased, maybe even envious."

She stared straight ahead. "I think God entered his heart."

"If you say so. You're making a believer out of me."

"No, really, I'm serious." She turned. "*Look at me.*"

He pulled the car to the side of the street and shifted into park. He held her by the shoulders. "I'm looking and listening."

She swallowed. "Manuel said God was on our side. And I know he's right. Do you know how I know?" She shook her head. This might sound stupid, something coming from a crying, crazy woman. "No, never mind. We're only ten minutes away from your apartment, and you're hungry and want a beer."

"A cigarette first, but all that can wait. This is important to you. Tell me."

She sniffed, then wiped her eyes. "Do you know who Abraham was?"

"Ahh, he parted the Red Sea." He shook his head. "No, wait. That was Charlton Heston."

She rolled her eyes. "No, that was Moses. They just look alike." Cal needed to read the Bible more and watch movies less. "Forget about Moses for now. Anyway, God came to Abraham and said he would be the father of a great nation. Abraham's nephew, Lot—"

"Wait, I know that name. His wife got turned into a pillar of salt."

"Yes, but that has nothing to do with the point I'm trying to make."

"Sorry, keep going."

"Well, Lot lived in Sodom, a city taken over by evil. And God told Abraham he would destroy the city and all its inhabitants, but—" She sighed with a frown. Cal wore one of those sympathetic smiles that said he'd agree with anything she said without thinking or even listening. "Don't humor me. This is important."

"I'm not humoring. I've heard of Sodom and Gomorrah. I'm following you."

She nodded with narrowed eyes. "Uh huh. Well anyway, Abraham wanted to save Lot and his family, so he asked God if he would destroy the righteous with the wicked. What if there were fifty righteous souls? Would he destroy Sodom then? And God said that for the sake of the fifty, he wouldn't. Then Abraham said what about forty-five, then forty, then thirty, and finally got it down to ten. And God said he wouldn't destroy Sodom for the sake of ten righteous souls. Do you know what that means?"

"That you can bargain with God?"

"Well, I'm hoping that, too. But it means if there's a small part that's good, just a spoonful, that's enough. For a city or for me. God knows there's good in me, and he wants to save me."

Cal nodded. "I think the Big Guy has used quite a few people to save you. So you must be real important to him."

She'd never thought of it that way, but that sounded good.

Cal wrapped his arms around her, tucking her head beneath his chin. "I can feel your heartbeat, and you're a little damp. Are you sure you're all right?"

She nodded, rubbing her cheek against his chest. "It was strange. Always, when I feel threatened, I can act quickly. But sitting there, knowing everything was so close, all my muscles tightened. I was jumpy but could barely move. All my senses were heightened, but mostly, I was oblivious to everything except my thoughts and Manuel's face and words."

He stroked her hair. "The second I walked in, I

knew what was going on. I studied Manuel's face. Whatever his plans are now, they don't include you."

"They don't include *us*." She sat back in her seat. "I'm okay, really. You can drive now. Tell me what happened with you. Are you out of jail for good?"

"Looks that way." Cal pulled into traffic. "My lawyer, Mister Abrams, said they never had much of a case against me. I had an alibi they couldn't break, and even though Shantelle's gun had my prints on the clip, it'd been missing for at least a year and was found under suspicious circumstances. In fact, it was registered to Shantelle's father, and he's been dead for seven years, Plus, Jace was known to confiscate guns from his girls. It's evidence against everyone, and so no one. Although, Mister Abrams said he got the strong impression the DA wanted to use it against Jace." Cal tightened his jaw and gritted his teeth. "But knowing Shantelle's gun killed that little prick makes me smile inside."

She nodded. "Me, too. So why did they arrest you in the first place?"

"Mister Abrams thinks the DA wanted to shake things up. See who ran and who didn't. Then Jace was killed trying to leave, and Fowler disappeared. Everybody's looking for him now. Plus, they found a cigarette butt with Jace's DNA near where Carlos's body was found. Didn't find it in the initial search of the area, so its admissibility is questionable, but no one cares. Bottom line, the DA decided to use all the evidence against Jace and wrap up two murders. Jace has no advocates, so it'll stand. Most important, Carlos *has* advocates, so it'll stand."

"That's pretty much what Lenny and Manuel said."

"I guarantee you, they both had a hand in it." Cal sniffed and glanced toward the takeout on the back seat. "I'm hungry. How about breaking out the fries?"

"They're for us to share later."

Cal grinned and glanced at her as he turned right. "Ohh, are those the fries of truth?"

"Maybe." She crossed her arms and sat back. "Depends on what you say. But that's for kitchen talk."

"I can hardly wait."

Chapter Twenty-Eight

Thursday, 8:15 pm

Soledad frowned at the side of Cal's face and gave her head a little shake. With every passing streetlight and oncoming headlight, a slight curl rose at the corner of his mouth. Probably had a gleam in his eye, too. Fries of truth. He can hardly wait. Cal had a serious smart-ass streak in him. Better get used to that, because it wouldn't change, but he'd better suspend it for tonight.

Telling Manuel what she really wanted somehow gave everything an urgency. As if the future had started at that meeting, and she needed to move forward fast before something from somewhere snatched it all away. Marry Cal, move to Jayuya, and have children. At least two, a boy and a girl. Hopefully the boy first, so Little Isabelle would have a big brother. She rolled her eyes. That was getting pretty specific and too much to spring on Cal all at once. But she wanted it, and wanted it with only him.

Cal turned right and slowed as they approached Marny's Café.

How could he think of pecan pie at a time like this? "Don't even think about it."

"Would make a nice dessert. Too bad they don't have a drive-thru."

She crossed her arms. "Yes, isn't it." No Marny's in Jayuya, so learn to make pecan pie. Mama's paella was something Cal liked, and she already knew how to make that. Cooking for her man, just like Mama had done for Daddy. Suddenly she just couldn't stop those future thoughts.

Cal parked in front of his apartment and sighed with a frown. "Mister Abrams said the police searched my place Monday. Lenny was in charge, so maybe it's not messed up too bad."

"We only need a table and two chairs." She reached into the back seat. "I got the takeout."

"I'm sure you do." He stepped out quickly.

Ohh, he knew what was coming and had a response percolating. Better be the right one. She followed him to the front door. He slid his key into the lock, swung the door open, and flipped the light switch.

The couch, chair, end tables, and coffee table were tipped over. Cushions, the TV remote, a spilled ashtray, an empty bourbon bottle, and anything else that had been on a table lay scattered on the floor. The police had looked under, behind, and into everything. The rest of Cal's apartment was probably the same.

Cal shook his head. "Musta been looking for a weapon or something to tie me to somebody's murder, but there wasn't anything to find. Probably why I'm out of jail."

"That's all in the past." She grabbed his hand and pulled him through the living room mess and into the kitchen mess. Cabinet doors hung open, and drawers lay upside down on the floor with the contents spread out on the counter. Cal's few plates, cups, and glasses were scattered about, except for a couple broken ones on the floor. A kitchen chair was pushed against the counter like someone stood on it to look on top of the cabinets. Some wineglasses in a top cabinet were tipped over and broken. His small kitchen table remained in the middle of the room with old mail strewn on top.

Cal shook his head. "They really tossed the place. I guess Lenny had to make it look good." He grabbed the chair next to the cabinet and pushed it into place at the table. "Two chairs and a table." He grinned and reached into his breast pocket. "But I need a smoke first." He walked to the patio door, opened the blinds, and slid the door open. "Jesus Chri—"

"Cal, don't blaspheme." If he slipped up around Mama, he'd get a hot scolding followed by a cold shoulder. "Tell me what's wrong." She set the takeout on the table and pulled a Diet Coke from the drink bag.

"Those stupid sons-a-bitches broke the lock. The catch just hangs there. My apartment's been open for three days." Cal clenched his jaw and held out his hand. "I need your phone."

She pulled the phone from her purse. "Who're you calling?"

"Lenny."

She scrolled and held out the phone. "That's his cell, but don't make a big deal about this. Lenny's on our side."

"I know, and I'll be nice. I wanna find out if Monday was the only time they were here." He stomped outside to the patio and lit a cigarette.

She sighed and frowned. This was not how their scene was supposed to start. She set the drink bag in the refrigerator, cleared space on the table, and lifted out the food containers. Mike had double packed everything, including a small Jake's burger, no cheese, no bacon. He must have remembered her order from before and put it in just in case. The burgers felt warm and smelled good, but her appetite was for fries only. She slid the cardboard fry container into the oven and set the temperature on warm.

"Damn it." Cal stomped back inside, then flipped his cigarette butt into the darkened courtyard.

"What's wrong now?" This night wasn't getting any better.

"Lenny said he checked the locks himself. He even came back Tuesday for a second look and said he left the place secure. That means someone else was here since, and that worries me."

She took her phone and slid it into her jeans pocket. "There's nothing we can do about that now. Come to the table and eat your burger." After that, the fries. Not a spaghetti noodle like in her favorite childhood movie, but a Jake's long skinny fry would work just fine and be their own.

Cal yanked the blinds cord down. They clattered shut. "No, I'm gonna have a look around. Maybe I can figure out who was here."

He tried to rush by, but she grabbed his arm with both hands. "Wait. What difference does it make?"

"What if the Molinas were here? Or Fowler? You broke his foot. He hates us."

"Doesn't matter. The Molinas and the police want this to end as it stands. And anyone can see we're under the Molinas' protection, including Fowler. He has to know people are looking for him. He's a fat cockroach. When the lights come on, he'll skitter away and hide in a dark, dirty corner."

Cal nodded. "You're right. Whoever broke in had to see the police were here first. There'd be nothing to find. But Fowler still out there bothers me. I wish the police had him."

She stroked his arm, coaxing him to the table. "Cal, what Fowler knows, especially about Shantelle's murder, is dangerous to him. He can only upset what the Molinas want. They'll do anything to protect their family. If he's smart, and Lenny says he is, he's long gone."

Cal nodded. "If he stays, the Molinas will pull a Jimmy Hoffa on him. He has to know that."

She gripped his shoulders and pushed him down into a chair. "Have your burger. I'll get you a beer." He was pissed off, but at least the gleam had left his eyes. The evening was still salvageable.

She sipped her Coke while he ate slowly. He talked about nothing important. Wondering if renter's insurance would cover damage caused by a police search, then said it didn't matter, because he didn't have any. Estimating the length of a stick needed to lay on the track of the patio door until the lock got fixed. Periodically tightening his jaw, suppressing a grin, stretching the time leading to his so-called fries of truth.

He finally finished his burger and beer and leaned back. The gleam in his eyes was back, along with that suppressed, smug smile like the smart-ass in him had resurfaced with confidence.

She leaned forward with her elbows on the table, forearms raised, and her chin resting on folded hands. "I forgot the fries. They're in the oven. Want another beer?"

Cal grinned and nodded. "What? No blindfold?"

She slowly shook her head, stood, and stepped to the oven. Uh huh, a real smart-ass all right.

She retrieved the fries from the oven, transferred them to a plate, and snatched a beer from the refrigerator. She set the beer in front of him and placed the plate of fries in the middle of the table.

Didn't he see that sharing fries was special? That would be how they said they loved each other. Something ordinary could become uniquely meaningful when accompanied with the right words.

He picked up one long fry. "In jail, I had time for long periods of uninterrupted thought." He lifted the fry above the plate, suspending it between them.

Her stomach tensed. Her eyes opened wider. *He's gonna do it.* This was even better. How did he know? Maybe Cheyenne said something. Just put an end in your mouth and lean forward. We'll slide our lips forward. Our eyes will grow larger knowing what's coming. Our lips will touch. We'll have to bite and swallow, but it'll work.

He pulled the fry back.

What's he doing?

He took a large bite and leaned forward with a wide grin. "Marry me."

No. Not that way. What was he thinking? That wasn't even a question. More like an assumption. Even worse—a favor.

He wiggled the remaining two-thirds of the fry like he had just captured her flag.

She couldn't move. That was it? He didn't say I love you, or even use her name.

He slid the plate across the table next to her Coke. "Have a fry of truth." His grin widened.

A punch line. A damn punch line. She loved his grin, a playful handsome grin, but now he just looked stupid and mean. She blinked and looked down. Her jaw clenched. She gripped the table with both hands. How could he be so insensitive, so clueless? She couldn't look at him. If he still wore that smug grin, she'd lose it.

She lifted her hands and signaled stop. Not another word or he'd wear the plate. This was not the story she'd tell Cheyenne and Mama and Josepha. Not the story Mama would share with aunts and cousins and all the family in Jayuya. And definitely not a proposal they'd remember and celebrate every year.

She looked up, trying not to glare, swallowed hard, and took a deep breath. Don't show anger. Keep the voice low and even. "Cal, we're not playing truth or dare. And I never thought I'd ever say this, but go smoke a cigarette and think about what you just said, and how you said it."

He blinked a few times. "What? I'm asking you to marry me. I thought you wanted me to."

Incredible. He looked confused about what he'd just done. She clenched her teeth to keep from screaming.

Stop. Calm down. This night was still salvageable. She took another breath. "A year from now, I want to look back and remember the first time we shared fries, our first kiss, when saying I love you was on the tip of your tongue. I want to remember and celebrate the only proposal I'll ever want, from the only person I'll ever want it from." She pursed her lips and stared. "And you're on the verge of ruining it all."

He opened his mouth, but he must have thought

better because he sat back, fumbling with his cigarette pack.

Maybe this wasn't all his fault. It was probably his first proposal, and he had no idea about her dream. And she wouldn't be this angry unless she loved him. She needed to give him another chance. Wouldn't be the same, but when she told the story, it'd be close.

She pointed at the plate. "The fries are like the plate of spaghetti that Lady and Tramp shared."

He screwed up his face with a puzzled look. "You mean the old cartoon dog movie?"

"It's *not* a cartoon. It's animated. There's a beautiful scene where Lady and Tramp share a spaghetti noodle. As they slurp from opposite ends, their lips meet, then their eyes meet, and they know they're in love and are meant to be together—always."

He nodded. "Ohh, I see. So we'd be on opposite ends of a fry of truth?"

"That's what you call them. But yes." He was *really* pushing it. But if he picked up a fry right now, held it between them, then motioned her forward, the whole bad beginning would become part of the story that made the end that much better. *Please, Cal, try again.*

"But we'd be chewing when our lips meet."

Her eyes stretched to their limit. "*So we'd swallow first!*" She shot up, threw her hands in the air and waved them in time with her shaking head. "Don't make me flail my arms."

He leaned back. "Too late."

Unbelievable, still the smart-ass. "You just don't get it. I give up. Go smoke a—a damn cigarette!" She stomped around the table toward the hall. "I can't talk to you, listen to you, or even look at you."

"Wait. Don't get mad. Let's try that fry thing."

She turned into the hallway, cut into the bathroom, and slammed the door. She pressed her back against the door, closed her eyes, and looked up. "Help me."

She wrinkled her nose. Great, just great, an unflushed toilet with the lid up. Whoever searched Cal's apartment was a gross pig. She stepped to the toilet, raised her foot and flipped the lid closed, then pushed down on the handle with the same foot. She moved to the far end of the bathtub and sat with her elbows on her knees and her face in her hands.

The tank float clicked. The water shut off. She lifted her face from her hands and listened. Nothing. No gentle knock, no profuse apology, no nothing. This night was not salvageable. She stood and jerked her phone from her pocket. Not the call Cheyenne expected, but that was Cal's fault. The next time he saw Little Sis, he'd better run. She scrolled and pressed.

"Cheyenne. Come get me. I'll be waiting in Cal's bathroom. Just come get me and take me home. *Right now*." Cheyenne's deep inhale and sigh came through loud and clear. "Cheyenne? Are you there?"

"Yeah, I'm here. Just calm down and tell me what happened. Did he propose?"

"Yes. No. Kind of. It wasn't even a question. He just said marry me without even saying he loved me. And he had this smug smile on his stupid face, like it was some kind of joke or like he was doing me a favor."

"*Stop*. That's not true, and you know it. And I can't believe I'm defending him this way, but Cal's a smart aleck. He can't help it. But he also loves you and can't help that either. You're locked in the bathroom, so he knows he screwed up. Right?"

"Ohh, he knows all right. In detail."

"That's good, because I've learned this about Cal. No matter the odds, when he knows what's expected of him, he comes through. We both saw that at Saint Anthony's, and that wasn't the only time, and it's always for you. There's nothing in it for him except you. Because he loves you."

She nodded at the phone. Give him a second chance. Their whole future life together was a second chance. "But I had a dream and a scene."

"*Stop.* You always plan and try to control things too much. No one knows that better than me. From hiding under the bed when we played hide-and-seek with Daddy, to the escape plan, you always get people to do what you want, your way. Let someone else lead. He'll come through, maybe not exactly as planned, but he'll come through. Trust him. Let it come from his heart, his way, then you can be sure."

Little Sis was right. She had to trust Cal to love her, despite her past, because if she didn't, there would always be doubt. They had survived it all and were here because he loved her. *Trust that. Trust him.* "Thanks, Sis. I'm going out there."

She cracked the door.

What on earth was he doing? Sounded like someone straightening up the kitchen, but that made no sense, although Mama often cleaned when she was stressed.

She poked her head out the door. "Cal, is there someone else out there?"

"No, just me. Don't come out yet."

"What're you doing?"

"I'm, I'm—don't come out yet."

"Cal, I'm coming out right now."

"No. Wait."

She rounded the hall entrance and into the kitchen as he reached into the top corner cabinet. His hand jerked back. He sucked on a tiny cut on his index finger, then reached into the cabinet and felt around.

"Cal, look at me. What're you doing?"

"Found it." He turned, holding a ring between his thumb and forefinger.

Her mouth and eyes opened wide and froze. Cal stared back, swallowed, and held out the ring.

"There used to be a bottle of wine that went with this." He shrugged. "I bought it for Shantelle, but... Anyway, I kept it in a wineglass, but that's broken now. I was gonna put it in her wine, and as she sipped and then saw it, well, I was gonna propose." He shrugged again. "Kind of corny, I guess. Do you mind that this was for Shantelle first? I can buy another one."

"No, no. It's good, it's right." She swallowed and sniffled. Not as planned, *better*, because it came from him, not something she had sneaked inside him so she could pull it out later.

He knelt on one knee. His eyes widened, and his jaw tensed. He lifted his knee a few inches, plucked out a piece of glass, then knelt again, never taking his eyes off hers.

"I love you, Soledad. I can't explain it. I just feel it. But I'm more certain of this than anything ever in my life." He took a breath. "And that will never change, no matter what." A small, uncertain smile softened his face. "Will you marry me? Please."

If she opened her mouth, she'd cry like a baby. She could only nod and swallow and squeak out, "Yes." They were meant to be together, no matter what.

He smiled and let out a sigh of relief. "Give me your hand."

She lifted her left hand, steadying it with her right. Hurry, Cal, I'm gonna lose it. No, don't hurry. I want this to last.

He held her hand still, but her fingers trembled as the ring slid past her nail and easily over her knuckle. A little big, but that didn't matter. A smear of blood clung to the band, but the diamond sparkled.

He took hold of her hands and began to rise. She pulled, then wrapped her arms around him and squeezed. His cigarette box crunched. She rubbed the side of her face against his chest.

He stroked her hair. "I don't have much to offer."

"Shhh." Wait on that just a little while. She slid her hand up his back into his hair and looked up into a face that would never hurt her, always protect her, always love her. It was there and it was real. "I love you, Cal."

A good kiss. No, a great kiss. His heart picked up its pace, the cigarette box crunched again, and he smelled and tasted of tobacco and beer, and a little burger. Keep all of this, every detail. All one good story now.

He whispered into her ear. "We can still share the fry. I know what and how much it means to you." He leaned back and grinned, a playful, handsome grin. "So you're the lady, and I'm the tramp."

She nodded and smiled. At the end of the movie, Lady and Tramp had puppies, mostly girls. Better not tell him that part, not yet anyway. She slipped her hand between them and spread her fingers. The diamond sparkled even more. She had to tell someone. And not just anyone.

"Cal, I want to tell Mama tonight. I want us to walk in holding hands, your right on top of my left. Then we'll sit Mama down. I'll say Mama, Cal and I love each other. She'll smile knowingly. She already told me that anyway. Then I'll slide my hand on top of yours and she'll see the ring."

"Sure, we can do that. I was kind of lost as to what to do next anyway."

"Mama and I will hug and cry, then she'll call Cheyenne and Josepha in, and we'll all hug and cry all over again. And we'll probably talk about wedding plans. You might be ignored for a lot of this."

"That's fine with me."

"A big wedding, at Saint Anthony's, with Father Brady administering our vows. We can honeymoon in Puerto Rico."

"Won't that take a lot of money? I was thinking the courthouse. We don't have to set a date and—"

She rolled her eyes. Oh, there's gonna be a date set.

"No, I guess not." He smiled and nodded and gripped her shoulders. "A big wedding it is. We'll manage it somehow."

She took a deep breath. Tell him now. He loved her and said it would never change, no matter what. And he meant it. Couldn't ask for more than that. Tell him now. First the money, then later about Carlos. That part had no place in this evening.

"Cal, I have over a million dollars of Jace's money. It's at the house, and it's ours now."

His eyes went wide, then darted sideways at the

sound of clumping, uneven footsteps.

She followed his eyes. Oh God, no.

Cal whispered as he pushed her toward the patio door. "Go, it's open."

"Whoa, hold it right there." Fowler limped into the kitchen pointing an automatic. "Not another step or I'll kill you both—her first."

She grabbed Cal's arms and whispered, "We're in this together. Stay calm."

Fowler edged along the wall, shaking his head. "Had to end your soap opera. My stomach was starting to turn." He motioned toward the table with his gun. "You, Little Princess, have a seat. Keep your hands on the table. And Cal, you stand right behind her."

She slid into her chair and laid her right hand over her left. That pig was here the whole time and probably heard everything, all about the Molinas, and Lenny, even Cal's proposal. Her stomach churned.

Cal stepped behind her chair and gripped her shoulders. "What do you want?"

"Same as her, the money." Fowler leaned his back against the wall, then stooped and scratched inside his boot-cast. "This won't do." He glanced into the living room. "Cal, go set up the couch and chair facing each other, ten to twelve feet apart. Put the couch on the side wall, farthest from the door. And clear all the shit off the floor in between."

He trained his gun on her chest, but looked at Cal. "And know this. Anything happens, your fault, my fault, nobody's fault, either of you do anything stupid, my gun will always be on her. She dies first. Understand?"

"I understand."

"Good. Go do it now."

Cal squeezed her shoulders, then edged along the counter and into the living room.

Fowler grinned wider, exposing his large yellow teeth. He had dark bags beneath his eyes and a day-old stubble.

"I'd almost given up. But somehow I knew you had the money." He scratched inside his boot again. "I owe you for this, but I'll let it slide, if you do exactly what I tell you."

Fowler didn't sound like a man looking primarily for revenge. He wanted the money.

"What are you going to do with us?"

"That's up to you. First, give me your phone, slowly."

She pulled her phone from her pocket and laid it on the table.

He eyed the refrigerator. "Got another beer?"

She nodded. "There's one more."

"Get it, open it, and put it on the table." Fowler glanced into the living room. "Cal, set up an end table with an ashtray on the left side of the chair, then take a seat on the couch." He watched as she set the beer on the table, then motioned to his right. "Let's go. Stay two steps ahead." He scratched inside his cast. "You're less dangerous that way."

Fowler put her phone in his coat pocket, snatched the beer bottle, and followed her in. She sat beside Cal, leaned her shoulder against him, and clutched his hand.

Fowler sat in the chair, stretching out his foot with the boot-cast. His clothes were crumpled and dirty. He'd been hiding out for the last few days and knew people were looking for him. And just like Jace, he wanted to disappear.

He trained the gun on her as he took a long drink, then set the bottle on the end table. He leaned forward. "Killing you would be inconvenient, but I'll hurt him if need be. I'm going to ask some questions. Don't hesitate, don't lie."

She nodded. "I'll tell you what you want." He wanted the money. He needed the money.

"First, where exactly is that second bag?"

"At my house in a crawl space in the roof."

"How did you get it?"

"I took it from Jace's boat after he was killed, before the police arrived."

Fowler eyes widened as he grinned and nodded. "I'm impressed. Does anyone else know you have it?"

She shook her head. "Just the three of us."

"That's good. Now we have to figure a way to get me and the bag together."

Cal leaned forward. "Keep me here as hostage. Soledad can go get it and bring it back."

Fowler flicked his hand at Cal. "Shut up. You're just along for the ride. That might work, except the other way around. But that would leave me alone with her." He grinned, opening his mouth and running his tongue over his upper lip. A line of saliva stretched from his yellow teeth to his fat tongue. "And, Cal, I would truly love to fuck your fiancée, but—"

Cal surged forward.

She swiveled, shoved her shoulder into his chest, and pushed. "Cal! Stay calm." This was Fowler's revenge, and he might inflict some pain, but killing someone now was stupid.

"Better listen to her. She's smarter than both of us.

And you didn't let me finish. I'd like to fuck her, but that would be stupid. Then I might start thinking stupid. She does that to men." He shrugged. "Of course, we could all go to the house for the bag."

She kept one hand pushing against Cal's chest as she snapped her head toward Fowler. "No." She shook her head fast and hard. Anything but that, even giving up the money. "I can call my sister. She can have the bag here in forty-five minutes. She'll do what I say without question and never tell anyone."

"I don't doubt that. They all do what you say."

She swiveled back to Cal. "Smoke a cigarette."

Cal took a deep breath. "I'm all right."

She patted his chest and turned.

Fowler winked. "Cockroach, huh? Fat cockroach I think you said. I'm just a worker roach, but you're the queen, so you'll understand the deal I have for you."

Fowler took another long drink of beer. "I want the money. Then I'll just scurry away. You can't go to the police or the Molinas. And with what I know, you want me to disappear. Don't you?"

She nodded. Better if his body disappeared. Alive, he could come back. He'd always be a threat, just like Carlos and Jace had been.

He reached down and scratched. "I learned something very important from you. Don't be too greedy, just greedy enough. Two bags, and you took just one. Musta took some real self-control. But smart, very smart. No one but us knows it even exists. And Dillard, well, he'll get a hard-on going after Jace's assets that he knows exist."

Fowler's free hand pulled a pack of cigarettes and lighter from his coat pocket. He lit one, took a long drag, then spoke with smoke coming with each word.

"Sometimes you have to make a deal with the devil, or in this case, a she-devil. And the best way to make this work is to give you a stake in it. I have a good idea how much is in that bag. And you'll appreciate this." He took another drag and exhaled. "I want one-point-one million. You can skim the rest." He sat back and grinned. "You heard me right. I doubt it's six figures but enough to pay for a wedding and a honeymoon in Puerto Rico." He winked again. "Yeah, I heard that, too. I heard it all."

She flinched, then squeezed and patted Cal's clenched fist. Stay calm. Didn't see this coming, but in the most practical, survivor sort of way, it made sense. It wasn't a ploy.

Fowler took a drag and narrowed his eyes. "I can see your mind working. You know exactly how much is there and how much you'll keep." He tamped out his cigarette, pulled her phone from his coat pocket, and tossed it to her. "Call your sister. Tell her how many bundles to leave in that crawl space, then bring the rest. Don't tell her why, just have her park right next to Cal's car, then call your phone. I'll give her instructions from there."

Chapter Twenty-Nine

Thursday, 9:45 pm

Soledad ended the call to Cheyenne. Little Sis knew things weren't going as planned but also knew to follow instructions exactly. Fowler with a gun in her family's house was completely unacceptable. Whatever happened would happen here, stay here, and hopefully end here.

Fowler motioned. She tossed her phone to him.

"So you get to keep eleven bundles. Knowing Jace, that's a hundred and ten thousand. More than I thought, and a pretty nice payday." He shrugged. "But that's fine. Gives you a bigger stake and more incentive to keep this between us." He winked. "Silent partners until death do us part. Which reminds me." He held the beer bottle up as if making a toast. "Where're my manners? Congratulations are in order."

Cal slid his right hand over her left.

Fowler set the beer on the table and grinned at Cal. "A little marital advice. Don't piss her off. Carlos and Jace did, and she shot one and set up the other."

She winced. Cal didn't respond, he just stared at Fowler. Didn't want him to find out about Carlos this way.

"Hey, *Princess*. Look at me."

She faced a grinning Fowler as Cal squeezed her

hand.

"So you didn't tell him about Carlos. Well, as Ricky said to Lucy, you got some 'splainin' to do. But don't worry, I can tell you what's on his face. He knows about Carlos, or at least he's pretty sure. But he doesn't care. You're his prize. You're everybody's prize. Carlos, Jace, though he never admitted it. Even Lenny's on your side. Always thought he had a thing for you, starting way back when we questioned you about shooting the wall at that client's house. But that ain't all of it. There's something deeper." He shrugged and shook his head. "Doesn't matter now. Hell, you even have a priest working for you. But the key was Manuel, and you got to him first." He leaned forward with a wry grin. "What you gonna do when Manuel finds out you killed his little brother?"

She clenched her jaw and stared.

Fowler leaned forward, studying. "You're not worried about Manuel. I can see it in your eyes. He knows, doesn't he? And he's letting you live. Why?"

"God is on my side."

Fowler threw his left hand in the air. "Why the hell not. Everyone else is. They all have their own angle, but the reason is you. Everything revolves around you. Hell, I didn't even kill anybody. I just helped dump a dead whore. The Molinas know that and want me dead anyway." He leveled the gun at her chest. "And I owe it all to you."

She swallowed. Her heartbeat quickened but didn't race. This was a bluff. Fowler wanted to slip out quietly and forgotten. Leaving bodies behind would have everybody looking for him. She had felt more threatened and uncertain when meeting with Manuel.

With him, there was nothing to bargain with but family. Money wasn't even a consideration. But with Fowler, it was all about money.

Fowler shook his head and sat back. "But a killing needs a better reason than revenge. There's no profit in it, only unnecessary risks. Anyway, revenge is a dish best served cold. What about you, Princess? Did you have a better reason than revenge?"

She stared back. "Carlos threatened my family and would have carried it out."

Fowler nodded. "Yes, yes, he would have. Shantelle wasn't the first, and you wouldn't have been the last. Carlos was a crazy little motherfucker. He hated to be laughed at, and Shantelle had an active sense of humor. Rumor had it, when Carlos couldn't get it up, he'd snap. Probably why he killed Shantelle. And you'd be dead, too, if Jace hadn't sent Cal to get you that night." Fowler frowned and shook his head. "I knew that was a mistake. Never guessed how big a one."

Headlights shone on the drapes, then slid to the side. Fowler limped to the window, peered out, and glanced at his watch.

"Too early for your sister, but not too early to prepare."

He limped back to the chair and motioned with his gun. "Princess, crawl over here next to me."

She slid off the couch and crawled, looking up at Fowler. His eyes followed her butt until he winced and shifted weight to his good foot.

"Stop. That'll do. Damn, Soledad, watching that bubble butt of yours makes me want to reconsider my plan."

An empty threat. He wouldn't take risks before he had the money. After, he wouldn't do anything to risk losing it. *Please, Cal, realize that,* and don't do anything brave and stupid.

"Okay, on your stomach, and keep your arms snug against your sides."

She lay down about two feet from Fowler's soft cast.

"That's good." He trained his gun on her forehead. "I want you at point blank range. Now you, Cal. Do the same in the middle of the floor."

As Cal crawled, Fowler kept his gun trained between her eyes. The gun was something to be very aware of but didn't elicit the tense uncertainty that came when Manuel had trained his eyes on hers. Then her heart pounded, and her legs went weak. Manuel had power that reached through distance and time. Fowler only had a gun, right here, right now, that he didn't intend to use unless he had to. *Please, Cal, don't do something brave and stupid.*

"That's far enough. Down you go. Now look at me. And remember, Cal, your fault, my fault, nobody's fault. She dies first."

"I understand."

"I know you do. What you care about most is her. Not sure what her first priority is, but it ain't you. Now face the couch, both of you." He sat down with his head half turned toward the front door. He lit another cigarette and relaxed back, resting the gun on his knee with the barrel tilted and aimed at her head.

She faced Cal. He gave a tight-jawed smile and a small nod. Probably meant as a reassurance that they'd get through this. She forced back a smile.

"I said face the couch."

Cal glared up at Fowler and turned his head.

The apartment was silent except for the hum of the refrigerator and Fowler's gross scratching noise. Just wait. If everything went as Fowler planned, he'd take the money, then disappear, and hopefully never resurface. But that cockroach would always be a threat, just like Carlos. If found alive, Fowler would say anything, including the truth, to stay alive. And there was always the possibility that one day he'd creep into Puerto Rico and show up wanting money and revenge.

Cigarette smoke blew into the middle of the room.

"Hey, Cal, ever ask her why she got into the business? And why she stayed?"

Cal clenched his jaw and didn't answer.

"Don't want to know? I'll tell you anyway. Simple and basic. For the money. Spreading her legs is easy and pays better than getting a real job. It's what she does best, and she's real good. Jace could've told you. He sampled his special girls regularly. So every time you kiss those beautiful lips, picture them wrapped around Jace's cock."

She cringed. Cal's back and shoulders rose and fell with seething breaths. Nameless, faceless clients were one thing, but Fowler just gave Cal a familiar face and a particular image. Fowler knew exactly what he was doing. Planting slow poison. *Please, Cal, they're only words.*

"Everything was for her family." Cal's words leaked out on a weak breath.

Don't, Cal. Don't try to justify anything to this cockroach. Moving forward means leaving all that behind. Please, when he leaves, let his words leave with him. You have to.

Fowler laughed. "Her killing someone doesn't bother you, but screwing them does. For her, there's only two kinds of men, those who've fucked her and those who will."

Cal's hand slid from his side toward her. She reached out and took hold. Cal squeezed until her hand hurt.

Fowler laughed again. "Sure, go ahead. Hold hands, lovers." His chair creaked, followed by more scratching sounds.

"Your turn, Princess. Look deep inside. I ain't a shrink, but I know your type. You say you're helping your family, then give them money to buy off *their* guilt for *you* being a slut. You ain't any different from the rest, just smarter, and the best looking."

Cal shook his head. "Jace wasn't gonna let her leave."

Fowler laughed and scratched. "You sound like a man trying to convince himself and failing. Because you know how it works. Girls can leave. They're all replaceable. Jace only goes after the ones who stole from a client or know something they shouldn't. She could've gotten out, that is until she killed Carlos, then it became real difficult. That's where you came in. She uses everybody, including her family."

A barely audible clink, like broken glass, and a slight rattle came from the patio blinds. Probably caused by a breeze. She turned her head toward Fowler. Fowler kept scratching and didn't seem to notice. The blinds were closed, but the door was open. Didn't matter. No way she and Cal could pop up and sprint for the patio. Even if they made it, what then? Fowler figured a hundred and ten thousand bought her cooperation. He was right. The best outcome left was for things to go like he planned.

Her ringtone interrupted the quiet. Still too early for Cheyenne unless she broke multiple traffic laws getting here. Little Sis wouldn't risk that.

Fowler picked up her phone while watching the front door, with his gun pointed in the same direction.

A very audible crunch of broken of glass, immediately followed by blinds clattering.

Fowler froze for an instant. Her phone slid from his hand and dropped to the floor. His eyes widened and darted toward the kitchen. He grimaced and rose, wincing, shifting weight to his good foot. His automatic swung toward the kitchen.

She raised her head.

Two hands holding a revolver extended across the kitchen counter.

"*Don't move. Drop it.*"

Lenny came into view, pointing his gun at Fowler's chest.

Fowler's gun stopped in mid-swing. His elbow bent, pointing his automatic at the wall above and behind the couch. "Lenny." He shook his head. "Why am I not surprised it's you?"

"I said drop it—*now.*"

Fowler's grip on his gun loosened, and his finger backed off the trigger. "Guess I'm gonna need witness protection. I have a lot of information to make a deal with."

No! That can't happen. Everything was so close. Couldn't let him rip it away. She shot her fist up, then slammed down hard into the instep of the soft cast.

"Slut!" Fowler's clenched yellow teeth and red face snapped down at her. His grip tightened on the gun as his arm lowered and straightened.

Cal pulled her arm and sprang to his knees.

Lenny fired two quick shots as Cal pounced on top of her.

Fowler's torso twitched as his finger jerked the trigger. Blood splattered on her face. Cal went limp on top of her.

Lenny fired again. She squirmed her head and shoulders from beneath Cal.

Fowler stumbled back and flopped into the chair, still gripping his automatic as Lenny rushed around the kitchen counter and into the living room.

Fowler's gun tilted. She lurched her head sideways. The barrel followed, and his finger curled around the trigger.

Lenny fired two more shots. Fowler's torso jerked, then slowly sagged. The gun slid from his hand and thudded on the floor next to her phone.

Lenny kept his gun pointed at Fowler's chest as he pulled out his phone and kicked Fowler's gun away from the chair.

"Cal. Cal! Lenny help me! Call an ambulance!" She slithered from beneath his body and knelt over him. His hand covered his ear. Blood ran from under his palm. A narrow cut ran across the edge of his jaw. *Please, God. Punish me, not him.* She brushed his hair from his eyes.

He blinked.

"Lenny, he's alive! Help me!"

Lenny knelt. "Cal, you've been shot. Don't move. An ambulance is on the way."

Cal blinked again, then closed his eyes.

She clasped her hands and pressed them to her forehead. *All my fault. All my fault.*

She opened her eyes. His back rose and fell slowly but evenly.

He groaned with dazed eyes. "Soledad? You're bleeding."

"No, I'm fine, and you'll be fine. But don't talk and don't move."

Cal squeezed the bottom of his ear. "I think he shot my earlobe off."

She stretched her fingers to behind his ear. Holding her breath, easing aside his matted hair. No blood-leaking hole, just a bloody ear.

Lenny blew out a long stream of air. "That was close, but you better stay put." He holstered his gun and pulled out a plastic bag. He picked up Fowler's gun by one finger in the trigger guard and slid it into the bag. He turned to her. "We need to talk."

Cal looked up. His eyes looked clearer. "I'm not staying here. Not with that looking down at me."

She followed his eyes to a slumped, motionless Fowler. His chin drooped on his chest. Still, staring eyes seemed to contemplate the bloody holes in his shirt. He'd never be a threat now. *Thank you, Lenny. I'm sorry I made you do this, but it had to be done.*

Cal rolled on his hip and raised to an elbow. "I think the bullet grazed my jaw. I feel like I just got punched—hard. My ears are ringing, and I'm a little woozy. Come on, help me up."

She and Lenny gripped Cal under his arms, helped him stand, and walked him to a kitchen chair. She grabbed a towel hanging from the refrigerator door and pressed it to his bloody ear and jaw.

Lenny glared and glanced toward the patio. "We need to talk—*now*." He walked through the rattling blinds.

She faced Cal. "You might have a concussion. Just wait for the ambulance, then we'll go to the hospital. I need to talk to Lenny." She turned, but Cal grabbed her wrist.

"Hey. I'm not so woozy. Find out how long Lenny was out there. What he heard. And how he even knew to come."

"Okay." She turned, but Cal held her wrist.

"*Hey*. Remember I love you—no matter what. And don't pay any attention to Fowler's gutter psychobabble bullshit. I didn't."

He did, but he didn't want to. That would have to do. "I know. And I'll handle this." She lifted his hand and pressed it to the towel. "Keep pressure on it." She kissed him, then walked through the blinds and slid the door shut.

Lenny put away his phone, pulled hers from his coat pocket, and held it out. "I picked this up in there. Units are on the way. Call your sister. Tell her to turn around and go home."

She nodded. That answered part of Cal's first question. Lenny was out here long enough to know about the money, but what about shooting Carlos?

She scrolled and pushed. "Cheyenne, where are you?" Good, still twenty blocks away. "Turn around and go home and put everything back. Yes, I'm all right. Everything is all right. Cal proposed, but don't tell Mama. I'll tell you all about it later." That should keep her more excited than worried for a while. "One more thing. Did you call a few minutes ago? Never mind, just do what I said. We'll talk later."

She slid the phone into her pocket and looked up at Lenny.

"That was me who called. Fowler needed a distraction. Had to get his gun off you."

"Thank you so much, Lenny. But how'd you know he was here?"

"I didn't for sure. Cal called and said the apartment was broken into. Intruder might still be inside. And I figured Fowler would be looking for money to get away on. And stolen money is the best kind to steal."

"What happens now?" Lenny knew what she'd made him do in there.

"It's a good shooting. There'll be a short investigation, and Dillard will probably give me a medal." He glared and shook his head. "But you forced me to kill a man. He probably deserved it. Maybe I even wanted to kill him, and I'll have to deal with that. But that wasn't your call or mine to make."

She bowed her head and closed her eyes. Lenny had chosen a side when he saw the bag under her bed and didn't do anything. And now he had to deal with the consequences. Just like with Manuel, offer Lenny more reason than herself, better people than herself.

She looked up. "Fowler would have ruined the lives of people I love more than life."

"Just like with Carlos?"

So Lenny heard that, too. Don't make excuses, don't lie, but make him see a specific face. "Think of Mama."

"Don't lay that on me." Lenny poked a finger in her face. "You're the one who's made Isabelle suffer.

We're all here because of what *you* did. Fowler came here because of what *you* did."

She nodded. "I know." But Lenny had made a choice eight years ago when she'd asked for his help, and he did nothing. He'd chosen to let Fowler take over, chosen to let Jace take her.

She looked past his pointing finger and into his eyes. "Once before I asked you for help. Sometimes it's not what you do, but what you don't do." He had a debt and a code. Don't order, don't beg. Just make a soft request for something she didn't deserve, but they both needed.

"I'm asking for your help, again."

Lenny lowered his finger and looked away.

"You're right, Lenny. This is all my fault. I made a bad choice to work for Jace and more bad ones trying to get out. But sometimes there's only bad choices and worse ones." She placed her hand on his arm. "My life is in your hands. What will you do this time?"

He clenched his jaw into a hopeless frown. "I stood out here knowing, whatever I did, whatever happened, I wasn't gonna like it. Bad choices and worse ones." He shook his head, then pushed his hat back. "Remember our conversation in your room after the search?"

She nodded.

"Do it. Move to Puerto Rico and take Cal with you."

"I will. As soon as possible."

"I'll complete and close the investigation, then I'm out of it."

"Bless you, Lenny." But he wasn't leaving her life. He was too much a part of it, one of the best parts, and always would be. "Lenny?"

He inhaled deeply, then let it out slowly. "What is it? And make it quick, units are on the way."

"Will you come to our wedding?"

Lenny blinked, then nodded slowly. He didn't smile, but his face softened. "Yeah, I suppose I can do that."

"And one more thing."

He crossed his arms. "What?"

She smiled and bit on her lower lip. "Will you give away the bride?"

His hands dropped to his hips. He cocked his head and studied.

She pressed her hands to her chest. "That's from my heart. You're the best man in our lives since Daddy was alive. It's you or no one. And I know Mama feels the same way. She knows how very special you are. Don't disappoint her."

Lenny nodded. "Okay, for Isabelle. She's a better person than the rest of us combined." He sighed as his shoulders slumped. "Ya know, after your dog was killed, I drove by your house every week for a few months. Just couldn't get that image of Isabelle suffering out of my mind. I wanted to stop to see if I could help somehow. But I didn't and wish I had."

"You still can. Some things aren't lost. They're just delayed."

He shook his head. "No, I'm through." He lifted a finger and again pointed between her eyes. "Now it's up to you, young lady. Take care of Isabelle. Give her all those things that got delayed." He lowered his finger and gently shook his head, like dealing with a memory that was a constant companion. "You look so much like Isabelle that first time I saw her." He closed his eyes, took a breath, then opened them. "Anyway, better go inside. I can hear sirens. I'll go around and meet the officers out front. Get your story straight with Cal." He stepped toward the corner of the building, then stopped and turned. "You have everything you started out for, maybe more. And no one's after you. So don't blow it." He turned and disappeared around the corner.

Lenny might think he was out, but Mama would have something to say about that.

The patio door slid open.

Cal stepped out, still holding the towel to his ear and jaw. "Kitchen window was open. I heard it all." His smile started slow, then grew until his eyes smiled, too. "You can go home now and never look back."

She reached up and pulled away the towel. The bleeding had stopped. The wounds would be tender for a while, and there'd be scars, but they'd heal. She tossed the towel over her shoulder, then looped her arms around his neck.

"*We* can go home and never look back. We have a lot of future ahead of us." She nodded with a smile. "And I have a plan."

A word from the author...

I am a graduate of the University of Florida. After teaching in Madagascar and The Sultanate of Oman, I returned to Seattle and my first love, writing.

A student of Film Noir, I find the femme fatale the most intriguing of characters. Smart and strong, she evokes love and hate from men who experience her, drawing them into the darkness of her soul. Men can love her, but only on her terms and at their own risk. Writing in deep point of view, I draw the reader into the minds of these characters, to experience with them as the story progresses.

CPSIA information can be obtained
at www.ICGtesting.com
Printed in the USA
FSHW012007241019
63374FS